A QUAINT AND CURIOUS VOLUME OF GOTHIC TALES

"An immersive experience into a world of magic, mystery, and gloom. The perfect escape from reality that will creep into the recesses of your darkest places and connect with you in ways you least expect."

—MJ Pankey writer, writing consultant, and founder/host of Augusta Writer's Critique Group

"An exemplary blend of macabre minds, bygone houses of grandeur, and chilling terror, each story in *A Quaint and Curious Volume of Gothic Tales* will haunt you long after the last page."

—Katherine Silva, author of The Wild Dark

"In this darkly delightful anthology, Alex Woodroe has pulled from a wide array of tone and subject, while keeping true to the spirit of Gothic horror. The perfect book to accompany a long winter's night—Brigid's Gate is fast becoming one of my favorite anthology publishers."

—Laurel Hightower, author of CROSSROADS and WHISPERS IN THE DARK

"Deliciously creepy and haunting! These tales had me enraptured and gave me chills. Each story has its own distinct voice, but a common thread of eeriness seamlessly weaves them together in a wonderfully curated collection. Don't read it alone in the dark!"

—Kathleen Foxx, founder/host of badasswriters podcast

"A haunting anthology of horror that will leave your heart broken and longing for more."

—Doug Weaver, reviewer

An Anthology Edited By
Alex Woodroe

A QUAINT AND CURIOUS VOLUME OF GOTHIC TALES

A QUAINT AND CURIOUS VOLUME OF GOTHIC TALES

Edited by Alex Woodroe.

Cover illustration and design by Elizabeth Leggett.
www.archwayportico.com

First Edition: January 2022

ISBN (paperback): 978-1-957537-01-6
ISBN (Kindle ebook): 978-1-957537-00-9
Library of Congress Control Number: 2022931060

BRIGIDS GATE PRESS
Bucyrus, Kansas
www.brigidsgatepress.com

Printed in the United States of America

Correction to First Edition

In the first edition paperback, "Down With the Holly, Ivy, All" was incorrectly attributed to Alyson Faye. That story was written by Jessica Lévai. It was correctly listed in the table of contents, but not at the beginning of the story on page 69.

The mistake was on the part of Brigids Gate staff, not the editor, Alex Woodroe.

We have corrected that mistake, and the paperback edition of this anthology will henceforth reflect the correct author.

Brigids Gate offers our sincerest apologies to Jessica Lévai for the error.

Dedicated to all the women who grew up being told, "you can't".
You can.

Content warnings are provided at the end of this book.

Contents

Acknowledgments

None of this would have been possible without community and support. I'm blessed in having a writing group who give me something to show up for every day—You're all more wonderful and terrible than I could ever have dreamed of.

Huge thanks to Matt Blairstone of Tenebrous Press for being the first to trust me with an anthology. I've met so many of the amazing authors in this one because of that original search. It's what set the ball rolling, which now gives me the opportunity to thank other present & future collaborators: Steve & Heather Vassallo of Brigid's Gate Press, for giving us all this book you're holding right now; Joshua Demarest of CatStone Books, for a yearly project we can't wait to reveal; and Rob Carroll of Dark Matter, for what will be my first sci-fi/horror blend project.

I'm also thankful to other friends and colleagues who have found room in their publications for my stories or articles, or who simply find room in their day to help me with advice, encouragement, and cheer: Antonia Rachel Ward of Ghost Orchid Press; Alex Ebenstein of Dread Stone Press; Stuart Buck of the Bear Creek Gazette; Robin Knabel and H. Dair Brown of Unsettling Reads; Thornton Gibson of Chapel Orahamm LLC; the whole team at TL;DR Press; and an extra special thank you to Maura Yzmore for giving me my very first sale what feels like decades ago but in reality is only two years.

I'd also like to take a moment to acknowledge the good work done by the SFWA and HWA; and in particular thank the HWA for their Mary Wollstonecraft Shelley Scholarship. We need more grants for women in publishing, and this is a fantastic start.

Finally, I'd like to thank and acknowledge you for reading this book. Choosing to give your time and money to independent fiction publishers is one of the greatest things you can do right now to ensure that all our voices have a chance at being heard. Thank you.

Foreword

by Alex Woodroe

I want to talk to you about the concept of allowing yourself to be transported.

There's a skill to delivering yourself into the arms of a story; a sort of active participation that goes far beyond what the story could single-handedly do to you. Yes, it has to pull its weight—moods, plot twists, sights and sounds—but there is also an element of basic empathy that we, as readers, bring to the table. A door that we leave open to the most vulnerable parts of us.

There are two ways in which this book, in particular, comes knocking on that door. One is with the immediate body of the stories; their windswept mountaintops and creaky asylums, their deadly secrets and haunted corners. If you open the door, they'll seduce you with dark histories and the promise of a romantic kind of horror where you're a treasured guest, rather than a hapless casualty.

The second, equally important one, is with the soul of these stories. In a world where women are losing hard-earned rights they never should have had to earn in the first place, and being erased from the history of literature they founded, and continue to be treated as second-rate beings and citizens, an anthology of stories by women can't help but be rooted in our grief and anger and hope for a better future.

What we wanted most of all was to give these women space to tell a story. We wanted to pull back and ask them what they have to say, and truly listen to the answer. This anthology is the result of that desire.

It can fold you into the cozy and familiar world of Gothic Horror, and into the also unfortunately familiar world of voices who wanted their turn to speak—some of them, for the very first time.

If only you allow yourself to be transported.

Introduction

by Stephanie Ellis

What is it about the gothic tradition that sees it continue to flourish as a genre in the 24/7 internet world? Why do stories of secrets and lies, ghosts and gloom and ancient buildings snag us from the very first page? The answer, I believe, lies in my question. Today, our lives are increasingly laid bare, we are—theoretically—visible in a manner never before experienced. Even if you avoid the lethal tug of the web and the entrapment of social media, you are monitored in other ways. CCTV records your movements on the road, in the street, in the shop. You can't travel very far without your image being captured in one form or another. And then there's the trail of electronic payments, of mobile messages and GPS. Where is there left to hide?

When all is jaded, when all is shown and told, there is nothing left to an imagination which grows hungry for exercise, demands the obscure and the hidden, the ghosts and the places unknown. This is the gothic and it is into this realm the anthology invites you. In the preceding foreword, reference was made to this being a collection created from the pens of women writers. In my discussion here, I will stick to this aspect, for it is one of the few genres—in my opinion—where a female author is seen as equal to their male counterpart. From the start, women came to the fore, delighting in the genre as both writers and readers, all recognizing this desire to stretch the imagination, to play in the shadowlands and at the same time evoke the thrill—and chill—of darkness.

Ann Radcliffe, author of work such as *The Mysteries of Udolpho* (published by G. G. and J. Robinson of London, 1794), speaks to this need to be intrigued, for '*glimpses through obscuring shades…which excite the imagination to complete the rest*' ('On the

Supernatural in Poetry', Vol.16, *New Monthly Magazine*, 1826). Even earlier, Anna Laetitia Aikin, author, editor and poet, asked what was the appeal in reading '*well-wrought scenes of artificial terror*', and declared those words formed by '*a sublime and magnificent imagination*' delivered the '*excitement of surprise*'. Indeed, '*the more wild, fanciful and extraordinary are the circumstances of a scene of horror, the more pleasure we receive from it*', (*On the Pleasure Derived from Objects of Terror, with Sir Bertrand, a Fragment*, Anna Laetitia Aikin, 1773). Nor can the gothic be discussed without reference to Mary Shelley, when writing about how she came to create *Frankenstein*, declared that she sought a tale '*that would speak to the mysterious fears of our nature, and awaken thrilling horror—one to make the reader dread to look round, to curdle the blood and quicken the beating of the heart*'. (*The Life and Letters of Mary Wollstonecraft Shelley*, Volume 1).

The stories within these pages speak to this tradition and to its pioneers and reasserts the position, indeed the primacy, of the female—in its all-encompassing definition—as arbiters of excellence in the genre. The torch has been passed to a new generation and they all burn so very brightly.

Lyndsey King Miller's 'Penance' is full of unbearable pain, a building manifestation of self-punishment triggered by the keeping of secrets which blind us to the truth and only cause harm. Hurt and suffering leach from the page as the maelstrom whirls and draws you into its vortex.

Jen Meirisch's 'The Painted Man' delights in changing reality, step by step, bringing in hints of murder and betrayal. An ancient house, a beautiful and enigmatic owner, a painting, a mystery. All perfect ingredients for a puzzle demanding to be solved. But at what price?

Miriam H. Harrison's 'She Drips' is a piece of flash which turns a haunting on its head, takes fear and sends it packing. Imbued with atmosphere and utilizing the senses it draws you in to discover the truth of the ghost. There is a wonderful ambiguity in the ending, not in terms of *how* it ends, but its effect on you as the reader in what your response should be.

Kasimma's 'Slave of the Dead' delivers the gothic via a different cultural setting, showing you don't need a draughty manor or windswept moor to tell a gothic tale. A family curse spinning down the generations continues until its cause is discovered. Little touches of humor dance alongside the presentation of the woman as a possession, the ultimate reflection of this being in the horrifying way in which the ghost is appeased. A conspiracy of poverty, secrets and ghosts.

Mary Rajotte's 'What the Dead Whisper to the Living' is truly a tale of the hidden. A hidden room, hidden secrets, hidden voices. In a world of shadow, father and daughter seek to be reconciled. Tragic but oh, so delightful.

Catherine McCarthy's 'Mercy' reads like a classic gothic of the 19th century. In fact, you could imagine it being published alongside a Dickens tale in the monthly magazines popular at the time and read to the family sat in the parlour by a roaring fire, the children wide-eyed as the tale is told. Here is a story of the power over life and death and the consequences of its use.

Patricia Miller's 'Picture Perfect' is another short tale set in a mysterious house with a mysterious owner. Family truth is painted on canvas but so much remains in the shadow adding a chilling ambiguity to the phrase 'blood will out'.

Jessica Lévai's 'Down with the Holly, Ivy, All' is a perfect offering of inheritance, greed, and ancient superstitions set in an old country manor. A traditional gothic setting, it invites in the supernatural which adds to the enjoyment of this particular story. To believe or not to believe? That is *always* the question.

Emily J. Cohen's 'The Lake in the Water' is a heartbreaker, a story of loss and coming to terms with it. Blame, self-recrimination, guilt, all conspire against a wintry backdrop to chill the reader as the tale unfolds. Then when all is done, reality is challenged by a ghostly touch to deliver that little thrill of the imagination, the whisper in the ear.

Kathleen Palm's 'The Door to Other Places' is pure darkness. Loneliness and isolation are painted so vividly, you almost weep at the shadow world of demons and madness which tumbles off the page to create an unbearable existence.

Evelyn Maguire's epistolary tale, 'Hello my Name is Goya Wyeth', brings a mystery of delightful ambiguity. An old woman is haunted by her past, or is it the ghost of something more? There is a calmness in the telling which juxtaposes so effectively with what might-or-might-not have happened which leaves you wondering the whole time as the truth is teased out, drop by drop.

Cindy O'Quinn's 'Like-Minded' is set in that most gothic of places, the asylum. The telling is a classic piece of misdirection delivered by an unreliable narrator who questions her place in the world and where she belongs. The ending delivers the perfect twist.

April Yates' 'A Kindness of Ravens' is a terrific tale, with its raven and an unhappy marriage, betrayal and isolation and the revenge which comes. A clever mix of the supernatural, almost dreamlike, element of the raven with a stark and logical reality. The story ticks every box of a gothic chiller.

Erica Ruppert's 'Something After' is the story of revisiting the past and returning ghosts. Throughout, however, is the ambiguity of the haunting, the never quite sure, until subtle little touches convey the truth.

Alexis Dubon's 'An Endless Kind of Nothing' takes you on a looping journey. Dreamlike to start with, it becomes more tangible, until the ending reveals the nature of the ghost in a truly horrifying manner. There is so much to stretch the imagination in this story!

Mo Moshaty's 'Henry' is a short flash of murder and possession and darkness. What is regarded as the truth by the locals turns out to be anything but. Secrets are yielded in the most brutal of ways.

Helen Glynn Jones' 'A Scent of Cloves' is a haunting by the sea and is a story told in the tradition of Ann Radcliffe's writing method in terms of its ending. If I say anything more, it will spoil the tale which is a truly clever web of suspicion and lies.

Anna Fitzgerald Healy's 'The Half-Moon Casita' has got to be a gothic for our times. The isolated setting, the silence of the surroundings, all chosen for the purposes of Instagram. It provides an analysis of self and relationships and the silence between people which is brought to a head by a ghostly presence.

Victoria Nations' 'Scabrous' is a tale of dread, of waiting for something to happen in a place which trapped so many innocents. Will another be added to the midst? The suspense builds at the thought of what might happen, what the ghosts *want* to happen. Tension oozes out of these dark corners.

Deana Lisenby's 'Arbor Hills' is just beautiful. The setting of the residential home, the reactions of staff and residents combine to keep the uncertainty of the truth flowing throughout its telling. Who is haunting who here?

Jolie Toomajan's 'Old Lady Name' brings not just a haunting, but obsession and possession into the mix. An old friendship is revived but its survival depends on acceptance of a more supernatural kind.

Briana McGuckin's 'Speak Ill of the Dead' offers us ghosts and their voice, or at least their actions, from beyond. There is a difference in this story to others in that the ghosts are accepted, their existence not questioned, and above all else, they are kept firmly in their place. Yet it deserves its place in the gothic, the almost hallowed air of the autopsy room is a chilling setting, secrets are present, written in the bodies and their manner of death.

Nor does the volume finish here. At the end is the 'extra' story, the lagniappe, S.H. Cooper's 'The Sweetlings'. Life sometimes feels beyond our control but to have our future taken out of our hands and dictated by something else, something not human is horrifying.

So there you have it, a volume of tales to 'curdle the blood and quicken the beating heart', a volume to revisit again and again on a dark winter's night when the shadows reach out and the candle flickers. The gothic tradition is thriving in the safe hands of these excellent writers.

Penance

Lindsay King-Miller

You open the door before the psychic knocks. Her curled fist hangs awkwardly in the air for a moment. It's not the shock of being preempted; it's the sight of you that leaves her motionless. You're wearing nothing but a sports bra and sweatpants you've clearly had on for no less than 48 hours, and your hair is a mess, but all of that is secondary to the absolute exhaustion in your eyes, so deep it hurts to look at.

"Hi," she says after a moment, smoothing the surprise from her face. "I'm Thelma. I assume you're Robbie."

"You must be psychic," you say.

She's polite enough to ignore this. You stand back so she can come through the door, and she ignores this, too, your care not to speak words of invitation aloud. Not that it matters. What torments you is already inside the house.

Thelma comes to a stop just inside your foyer, turning slowly, taking in the house. You haven't bothered to tidy. You don't much anyway, but today especially you don't want to hide the evidence; you want her to see the full extent of what you're dealing with. You want her to understand how bad it's gotten.

The index finger on Thelma's right hand ticks while she looks around, as though she's counting the phenomena she observes. One: end table overturned. Two: kitchen cupboards yawning open, glasses and plates smashed on the floor. Three: painting hanging askew, glass gone supernova as if from a fist. Four: smear of blood on the wallpaper, eye level.

"Yours?" Thelma asks, gesturing to the blood.

You shake your head. "It was there when I woke up, uh, yesterday morning." In fact, you discovered the blood three days ago; your sense of time has gone vague over the last few weeks. It's unclear whether Thelma notices.

"Is this the worst of it? Are the occurrences localized in this area?"

"No," you say. "No, definitely not." You lead Thelma deeper into the house—deeper into the damage. She steps carefully, avoiding broken pottery and glass. You don't. You walk in straight lines, despite your bare feet. Some people might mistake this for bravery, but Thelma does not.

Every mirror is broken. Every book and figurine is knocked to the floor. Every photograph is facedown. The bed is stripped of sheets and a deep red stain mars the center of the mattress, so dark it almost looks like a hole, a tunnel to somewhere even worse.

"Is this where…" Thelma asks.

"No," you say. She waits for you to elaborate, but you don't. (Though "can't" might be the more accurate word.) Thelma sits down on the edge of the bed, far away from the bloodstain, and gestures for you to join her.

"Do you want to tell me how it happened?" she says.

Instead of sitting, you pace across the room to the dresser. One of its drawers has been yanked out and dumped on the carpet, leaving a dark space like a mouth with a missing tooth. You put your hand on top of the dresser to steady yourself.

Thelma looks at you carefully. Now that you're standing still, she has an opportunity to study your aura, the haze of energy that startled her when you first answered the door. You're crackling with psychic power, flashing red and gold sparks in a field of bruise-blue grief. It would be naked-eye obvious to anyone who knows you, but Thelma doesn't need to recognize your tells to understand that you're in deep, heavy pain. On a better day—in a better life—you might be successful in her line of work; your raw metaphysical energy is astonishing. But now…

You're like an amplifier, she thinks, blaring a feedback loop of rage and grief. The noise is so distorted, it's impossible to make out who's screaming.

"You don't have to tell me anything you don't want to," she says. "But the more I know, the more I'll be able to help."

You nod. Take a deep, shivery breath.

Gently, Thelma prods: "Did she die here?"

It startles a laugh from you, a sound that falls from your lips like a dropped teacup and shatters. You stand very still, afraid to cut yourself on the fragments.

"No," you say. "No, my mother never set foot in this house at all. Not while she was alive."

"Do you want to tell me why not?"

"The usual reasons," you say with difficulty. "I didn't want her here. I didn't want her to know how I lived."

Thelma's voice gets even softer. "Does someone else live here with you?"

"Not anymore," you say. "She left... a while back." You hope Thelma thinks you're being evasive, instead of realizing the truth, which is that you don't know what day it is, or even, with any degree of confidence, what month. "Mother-in-laws are bad enough when they're not pissed-off ghosts." When Thelma laughs, you wince. You can hear her pity.

"So your mother wasn't accepting?"

"Of me being a dyke?" You stick your thumbnail in your mouth, a nervous habit you've had since childhood—not actually biting, just holding it between your teeth. "I don't even think she knew. I never told her."

Thelma nods, although she doubts the accuracy of your assessment. Your hair is buzzed short on the sides, long and floppy on top. You have a forearm tattoo of a pinup girl on a motorcycle. Your given name is Arabella, but you go by Robbie. Your dead mother had many failings, but she was not entirely an idiot.

"I moved out as soon as I could," you say. "Went to college out of state. Never came home, not really. Barely even visited. I don't know, I guess I thought… one day I'd find a way to tell her, even if she hated me for it. But I never got the courage, and now she's dead."

"And you think that's the reason for the phenomena?"

"Yeah." You chew your thumbnail harder, still holding back from biting through it completely. "She was big on gratitude. Duty. Stuff like that. She's pissed at me for being queer, definitely, but mostly for abandoning her." Your face and voice don't change when you add, "I wasn't even there when she died."

Thelma gives that a moment to settle, understanding that anything she says to comfort will only hurt you. Everything hurts you right now. You're the emotional equivalent of a terrible sunburn, radiating agony and cringing from the slightest touch.

Finally, she says, "Let's try to make contact."

In the living room, you sit on the couch where you've slept for the last week, and Thelma drags up a kitchen chair to sit across from you. She holds her hands out, palms up, and after a second of hesitation, you place your hands in hers.

Thelma doesn't flinch, like you worried she would, but you can't miss the way her face goes still when skin touches skin. She saw it as soon as you opened the door, but seeing is different from feeling. The fear, the exhaustion, the loneliness and shame—everything you've been carrying all these weeks is visible in her deep brown eyes. You look away.

"Okay," is all she says. "What's your mother's name?"

"Magdalena Kovar."

She takes a long breath, closes her eyes, and seems to sink into herself. It's like the actual substance of her soul retreats deep into her body, and all you're holding hands with now is a shell.

"Magdalena Kovar," she says, and her voice sounds like it's echoing from the heart of a labyrinth. "I'm here with your daughter Robbie—"

"Arabella," you interrupt, as though your own mother wouldn't know you, no matter what you name yourself.

"We want to speak with you," Thelma says. "Can you hear us? If you're there, please give us a sign."

The chair Thelma sits in slides six inches to the left, as though someone invisible has kicked it. Thelma sways in her seat but doesn't fall or let go of your hands. Her eyes remain closed.

"Magdalena," she says again. "Am I speaking to Magdalena Kovar? Tap the chair once more—gently, please—if the answer is yes."

There's a long pause. In the silence, you take a long, shaky breath in. "Mom," you say. "I..."

The same invisible force slams into Thelma's chair again, much harder this time. The psychic skids sideways, the chair tilting, balancing precariously on two legs for a long, dreadful moment. You tighten your grip on her hands, but it doesn't matter; she's wrenched from your grip and flung to the floor. Her head lands on the hardwood with a nauseating crack.

Cursing, you jump to your feet. Thelma lies stunned, tears pooling in her eyes.

Impossibly, the still, musty air inside the house moves. A wind springs out of nowhere. Thelma drags herself to a seated position. You should help her, but you're too distracted.

"Mom! Please!" you shout into the rising noise of the wind. With nowhere to go, it roars in a circle, eddying hot and fierce. The hairs on your arms stand on end, and the smell of lightning stings your nose and tongue.

"Robbie, we should leave," Thelma says, trying to keep her voice steady. "This isn't safe."

"She's here," you say. "Talk to her. Tell her I'm sorry."

"I don't—"

"Tell her!"

The wind scoops up a votive candle in a glass jar and flings it against the wall, where the glass shatters. Thelma screams. You don't. You just dig your fingernails into your palms, white-knuckle grip on nothing. You're so strong. You've had to be so strong.

"Magdalena, your daughter loves you," Thelma shouts into the gale. "She's sorry. She asks for your forgiveness."

"I love you, Robbie," I say, but I don't have a mouth and I don't have a voice and you can't hear me over the sound of your own pain. I was never able to say it so you could understand. I still can't.

The air thickens, as if with smoke, although nothing is burning. In the shadowy, swirling wind, a face begins to take shape: sinkhole eyes and a wound of a mouth. It's the face of your nightmare-mother, conjured from your deepest fears and given shape by your own mind, the enormous power you wield without even realizing it. This power, not me, is what's been wrecking everything around you all these weeks. I've tried to make it stop, but I'm weaker than you are, darling. I can't break through.

The nightmare-mother opens its mouth and wails.

As a toddler, you had awful tantrums, so furious I was afraid for you. You'd bite your chubby hands, throw yourself down and slam your little head into the floor. I never knew what to do except hold you tight, no matter how you raged, until the storm passed or you wore yourself out. I hated restraining you. I wept every single time, your cheek against mine sticky with both of our tears, part embrace, part violence.

Now my arms ache to hold you again, but they're only the memory of arms and you can't feel my touch. There's nothing to stop you from beating yourself bloody. I don't even have eyes to weep from.

The sound of the nightmare-mother's cry, the bottomless grief and bitterness, shakes the floorboards of your house. Thelma tries to get to her feet, loses her balance and falls. She lands badly on her knee, but you barely register the wet popping sound. You're still staring into the face of the nightmare-mother, your mind's projection of a distortion of a memory, all warped into a new, better way to hurt yourself.

"I'm sorry," you say into the maelstrom. I finally understand why you'd want to bite into your own flesh. If I still had teeth, I would rend myself to pieces between them rather than listen to your apology.

The smoke is getting thicker. You're starting to cough, but you still don't hide. You don't look away from the punishment you've assigned yourself.

I am not trapped here. I can leave. If I cannot ease your suffering, I could choose not to watch. But I don't look away either. You'd hate it if you understood how alike we really are.

The smoke stings your eyes, scours tender membrane with grit. Tears and blood trickle down your face in thin, grimy trails. "I'm sorry!" you shout again, but the nightmare-mother is louder. Her mouth opens impossibly wide. You stare into it, and whatever you see there breaks your heart.

Thelma is on her feet now, despite her devastated knee. The wind howls in her face, grabs her hair and yanks. She folds her hands over her head for protection and staggers toward you. "Robbie, we need to get out of here," she says. I can tell by your face that you hear her, despite the cacophony; still, you ignore her. You square your shoulders and plant your feet, stubborn as you've ever been. As though there's something to be gained by facing down this cyclone. As though by suffering you can prove yourself worthy of being spared.

"Please stop," I beg, the way I used to when you were small.

"Please, sweetheart, you're hurting yourself." My voice is less than nonexistent in the snarling wind.

Thelma's hand catches your elbow, but you shoulder her aside without a glance. She casts her eyes around the room, looking in vain for help. For a moment, her gaze stops on me. I see her mouth fall open. I know she can't hear me, but I hold out my hands in supplication: help her. Make her stop. Save her, since I can't.

She looks at me and I think she understands. She looks back at you, your spine straight as a pillar, ready to carry the weight you're trying to crush yourself beneath.

I see the decision in her eyes as she reaches it. She gathers all her strength, grits her teeth against the pain in her knee, and limps for the door as fast as she can.

Only you and me now, my love. The nightmare-mother bares her unthinkable teeth.

"I'm so sorry," you say again, and I stand here forgiving you with all my strength, and it doesn't matter at all.

The Painted Man

by Jen Mierisch

The first time Valarie's painting changed, she blamed the ancient house and the thunderstorm that had drenched its gables the night before.

She had set up her easel at the edge of the front hall. It was an ideal spot for painting Hazel House's dramatic marble staircase, which arced up to the second-floor landing like a watchful snake.

Approaching her canvas, Valarie frowned at the gray blob at the foot of her painted stairs. The splotch was lumpy, oblong, and oddly textured, resembling a pile of dirty rags.

A glance at the ceiling revealed that Valarie had positioned the easel directly beneath one of the skylights. The seal must have leaked during last night's downpour and dripped dirty water onto her canvas.

She'd have to tell Merel. Merel would have it fixed. Valarie didn't know her new landlady well, but she was sure of two things: Merel van Rensselaer was loaded, and she took immense pride in maintaining the house that had been in the family for seven generations.

But hadn't Merel replaced the roof last year, when she added the skylights? Yes—she told Valarie so, while showing her around the house three months ago. It was right after they'd toured her newly installed, landscaped patio.

Merel wouldn't be happy about a leak in her new roof. And who knew how long it would take to book a repairman out there in the middle of nowhere?

Valarie sighed, shifted the easel several feet over, and raised her brush to hide the murky gray stain.

#

That first day, Merel had seemed so sweet. "Valarie!" she exclaimed, trotting down the steps of the grand front porch as Valarie stepped out of her old Ford. "How lovely to finally meet you." Merel was all smiles and bohemian clothes, wearing a loose, patterned tunic and pants below her floppy hat and dark blonde curls. She looked to be just a few years older than Valarie, perhaps forty. Her speech had that velvety tone and formal lilt people with money all seemed to have.

To Valarie, Hazel House looked like something out of a fairy tale. She could hardly believe a place like that existed in America. Its exterior bloomed with spires and towers and jutting wings. Iron-railed balconies adorned walls built from natural stone and dark-red brick. The grand front hall, which might once have been an imposing space, glowed with sunshine streaming in from the skylights. Upholstered furniture, potted plants, and etched tables dotted the common areas. Surprisingly modern artwork colored the walls, and sculptures stood everywhere, no two alike. Gazing up at the carved trim, Valarie noticed the gargoyles, and giggled to herself. Who had gargoyles inside a house? It almost seemed like a humorous nod to the home's antique past. It was a magnificent Frankenstein's monster of a house, and just about every room begged to be turned into a painting.

Valarie considered herself introverted—reserved, she thought; it seemed a more fitting term in her grand new home—but during the tour of the house and grounds, she found herself chattering to her new landlady. Out came the tale of how she and Adam had separated, and how an accident had killed him. How she'd come here to take some time away, get her head together, and figure out what was next.

In a single fluid motion, like a dancer, Merel paused in her stride and turned. "I'm a widow myself," she said. "I understand. Sometimes you need to make a change." She had given Valarie a small, inscrutable smile, and her blue eyes had almost seemed to twinkle. For a fleeting moment, Valarie felt strangely attracted to Merel, odd because she'd never been attracted to women, unless you counted that one party in art school.

The moment passed, and Merel showed Valarie to her rooms. "Of course, you'll have the whole wing," she said, sweeping an arm to indicate the two bedrooms, sitting room, and bathroom compete with washer/dryer. "An occasional guest or two is fine, as long as you let me know ahead of time." Valarie squelched the squeal that threatened to erupt; she still couldn't quite believe her luck. To cover it, she made a lame joke about memorizing the path to the rooms so she wouldn't get lost. Merel smiled. "I'll let you settle in. Do text me if you need anything. Might be easier than trying to find me."

Valarie schlepped her suitcase into the bedroom she'd decided to sleep in, then stowed her art supplies in the other bedroom. Sitting back against brocade pillows on her new bed, she sighed with satisfaction. It wasn't every day a person had the chance to rent part of an eccentric old mansion, at a great price and with a month-to-month lease. It was the perfect spot for an artist's retreat.

Even better, it was three thousand miles away from everything she wanted to put behind her.

#

The bedroom looked different at night.

Lying on her back in the double bed, Valarie watched shadows shift across the recesses of the tray ceiling as moonlight streamed through swaying branches. She hadn't bothered closing the curtain; it seemed unnecessary in a home not even within sight of its nearest neighbor. Pale light glinted off the silvery vines of the wallpaper. Wide awake, she pulled the covers up to her chin and listened to the breeze whisper outside.

The next thing she saw was Adam's face. It was never far from her mind, but, somehow, she hadn't expected it to make an appearance here, in these new circumstances, so different from any part of her previous life.

Six months before, after yet another argument that was more sad than angry, she and Adam decided to take a break. Adam moved in with his brother, and Valarie stayed in their old apartment, alone with a menagerie of restless questions. What was she now, exactly? Was she married or single? Wasn't "taking a break" a little too college of a phrase to describe a husband and wife? Could their problems be overcome? He had done some bad things, but so had she. Worse things. Should she leave it all behind, wipe the slate clean, and start over? Was thirty-five too old for that? What about the children they'd never had? Would she even want to have children with anyone else?

Then, one weekend, Adam was riding his bike, as he always did, up in the hills, and a blue Chevy sedan hadn't seen him. Her father-in-law called with the news. The next call was from a lawyer: Valarie stood to inherit all of Adam's assets. He'd never bothered making a will.

When Valarie thought about the day everything changed, she pictured the blue sedan, a car that would have been utterly uninteresting in any other context. She watched it glide around curves in the road like a TV commercial, ignorant of its destiny, of the chain reaction of physics and biology it would trigger. She didn't picture the collision, the gore, the aftermath. She didn't imagine whether Adam screamed. She just saw the car, ever moving, calmly, assuredly, as if on a track, traveling as inexorably as a river to the sea.

"I'm a widow myself," Merel had said. Whatever Valerie might be now, she thought, she was not a widow. Widows mourned their dead husbands, gathered the family, handled funeral arrangements. Widows, for better or worse, had closure.

But here she was, lying in a strange bed and wondering what Adam would have thought of this house, wanting to chuckle with him about its quirks, yearning to hear his laughter echo against the high walls. She felt a surge of familiar rage. How dare he go and die before they could figure things out?

Footsteps echoed against hardwood planks in the hallway outside Valarie's bedroom. She gasped as the floor creaked. It must be Merel, she told her racing heart. Nobody else is here. Yet, for a moment, the steps had sounded like Adam's, treading softly, the early bird rising to make coffee for his night-owl wife. Tears breached their dams and soaked Valarie's face. Damn you, Adam, she whispered. Damn you.

When she finally slept, her dreams were filled with cars.

#

The second time the painting changed, Valarie wondered if Merel might have messed with it. The idea seemed ridiculous, but they were alone in Hazel House, unless you counted the regular visits by gardeners, handymen, and maids.

Merel wasn't a nosy or interfering sort of landlady. She left Valarie to her own devices, for the most part, though she did insist her tenant stop by her frequent soirees. She seemed to know everybody in the local community, from the Jaycees to the police chief to the Daughters of the American Revolution. Nobody ever seemed to turn down a catered event at Hazel House.

She seemed delighted to have an artist as a tenant, coming over to admire Valarie's half-finished sketches. Sure, it was a little weird to be living in the same house as one's landlady, but Merel was hardly ever home anyway, going out every morning to do whatever it was she did in town.

Still, there had been… moments. Valarie sat cross-legged on the lawn one day with her sketch pad, trying to capture the rolling hills and pines, when she felt a gaze. Glancing back at the house, she saw an upstairs window with the curtain pulled back, and Merel standing there, watching. Displaying no bashfulness at being discovered, Merel smiled, lifted her hand, and continued gazing at Valarie, who awkwardly returned the wave. After a few minutes of trying to ignore the eyes on her back, Valarie had gotten up and moved to a spot behind some shrubs.

"Beautiful jewelry," Merel said one morning in the kitchen. "Are those turquoise?" She leaned close to peer at Valarie's earrings. Valarie stopped herself just in time from flinching backward. A bit too cheerfully, she told Merel about buying the earrings in Arizona during her cross-country drive to Hazel House.

One morning, Valarie, her hair still wet after showering, had passed Merel in the hall. The landlady turned to her tenant, closed her eyes, and inhaled luxuriously. "Mmmm," she'd said. "Lilacs." And with another of her indecipherable smiles, she disappeared out of sight. Later that day, when Valarie drove to town for groceries, she found herself adding some unscented Dove shampoo to her cart.

Was she imagining things? Surely Merel was just being friendly. Of course she was interested in her tenant. She had nobody else in the house to talk to. Surely it would be more peculiar if she completely ignored Valarie.

Crossing the spare bedroom where she kept her canvases, Valarie paused as she passed the free-standing, full-length mirror in its heavy oak frame. Her long brown hair, which she'd kept in a ponytail for the past few months, could use a trim. Her T-shirt and jeans seemed to hang off her in a way they never used to. Even her face seemed thinner, her eyes seeming to peer out of shadowed hollows. She shook her head. She hadn't been sleeping well, that was all.

She continued walking, and that was when she saw the half-finished staircase painting, which she had stashed there while she worked on a landscape outdoors.

But no. Merel couldn't have added the new streaky blotch to the canvas, in the same spot as the first stain, right at the foot of the painted stairs. Merel wasn't an artist. "I dearly love art," she had told Valarie, "though I have absolutely no talent myself. Me with a paintbrush would be like a fish trying to play a bugle!"

Valarie squinted at the new blotch and cocked her head. It was gray, like the last one, but longer and more distinct, rounded in places that made it look like a person laying on the floor asleep.

#

The day after the painting changed for the second time, Merel asked Valarie to paint her portrait. With a free month's rent as payment, it was an offer Valarie wasn't about to refuse. Merel was an ideal model, dressed in one of her loose flowing outfits and perched serenely on her favorite plush chair near the living room window.

When the painting was finished, Merel was so delighted with it she had it hung in the library, just above the hearth. When the handyman arrived, Merel called Valarie in to watch, then stood to one side and smiled as he climbed the ladder. "A bit to the left," she told him, waving her hand as if the gesture itself would guide the painting into the correct position.

Valarie hadn't spent much time in that room. She drifted idly, glancing at titles on the books' spines, recognizing nearly none, except one or two that she'd failed to finish in high school English.

"Perfect!" Merel exclaimed, and the man stowed the hammer in his tool belt and began his descent. After the ladder had been cleared away, Merel stepped back and took a picture with her phone. "Beautiful work, Valarie. I'm so pleased." With a smile, she turned and swept out of the room.

It seemed to Valarie, looking up at the painting now, that portrait-Merel's eyes had a certain penetrating gleam above her signature smile. Valarie wasn't quite how she'd achieved that effect. She didn't know whether to feel proud or a little unnerved.

Beneath the portrait, the mantel shelf was crowded with framed photographs. Valarie stepped closer to have a look. A few old sepia-toned photos of toddlers in nightdresses sat nestled among photos of well-dressed men and women from various eras of the twentieth century. It took a minute for Valarie to spot the wedding photo, which was toward the back, behind several others.

A younger, beaming Merel in a splendid white gown stood next to a tall, handsome blond man in a tuxedo. Their backdrop was a tall green hedge Valarie thought she recognized from the formal garden on the grounds of Hazel House.

Next to the wedding picture was a close-up photo of Merel and her husband. Merel gazed off at some distant object to the left of the photographer, and the man was looking at Merel's face. Valarie stared at it for a minute, then abruptly turned and left the library.

Her feet took her back to the spare bedroom, but her mind was trying not to think about how much Merel's dead husband looked like Adam.

She paused in front of the staircase painting. The gray blotch was back, and it seemed darker, more distinct. Valarie gaped at it. Not only did it look like someone laying down asleep, but certain brush strokes resembled clothing. The fabric covering the narrower half of the body, if it was a body, was dark and fairly form-fitting, like workout pants. The rest was covered in a loose blue fabric that had a sheen to it, like an athletic jacket. Like the jacket Adam used to wear when he went biking.

Valarie gasped.

She hadn't sleepwalked since she was a child. But someone was adding to that canvas, conscious or not.

#

Valarie examined her reflection in the bedroom's full-length mirror. She still looked tired, and too thin, but the sundress helped. She had swapped out her usual paint-stained jeans in anticipation of Merel's latest social gathering.

She hoped it wouldn't be awkward. Yesterday, Merel had passed Valarie in the hall and said curtly, "You know, Valarie, I don't mind if you play music in your rooms. But please, not at two in the morning next time."

Valarie had stood there, stunned. "Sorry," she mumbled, steamrolled by Merel's certainty. She did not recall having been awake at two a.m. recently. If anything, she was sleeping so deeply it had been hard to wake up. Maybe her old transistor radio was shorting out.

The sunshine on the bright patio lifted her mood. Merel was hosting the Chamber of Commerce today, and the scene was lively with the cocktail chatter of veteran networkers. Accepting her glass of wine from the bartender, she turned and stopped short of the two eager faces that had appeared before her.

"Barbara Jackson," said the gray-haired Black woman in the red sheath dress, extending a hand. "I own Act Two Remodeling. I understand Merel has you to thank for that lovely portrait in the library."

"Stunning work," added the tall white man with the goatee and the summer suit. "The eyes are particularly arresting."

"Thank you," Valarie mumbled, "Mister.... uh..."

"Emmett Weber," he said. "I run Weber Accounting downtown."

"Come. I'll introduce you around," Barbara said, placing a friendly hand on Valarie's shoulder to guide her across the patio.

Before she knew it, Valarie had met just about everyone, who all seemed to know her already. "Of course," they said. "The portrait artist!" In a swirl of chats, compliments, and requests for additional portraits, she nodded, smiled, and forgot most of their names immediately.

Finally, the mob moved off, leaving only a swarthy middle-aged man tugging at his sweat-stained collar. "Sonny Marocco," he said by way of introduction.

Valarie shook his hand. He held hers a beat too long.

"Watch out for this crowd," he said. "Young pretty thing like you, someone's bound to snap you up."

She forced a smile, pushed away the mental image of a snapping crocodile, and casually stepped to one side to put more space between herself and Sonny. "And what do you do?" she asked, to change the subject.

"Ristorante Primo Piatto, on Tenth, that's my place," he said. "Soon to be expanding to our second location on Arbor Way."

She nodded, contemplating how to make a graceful exit, but Sonny already seemed to have lost interest, looking past her across the patio. Valarie followed his gaze to where Merel stood. Her smiling face lit up with whatever story she was telling the two men standing in front of her. Sonny's eyes traveled down Merel's dress, which draped snugly over her curves. "Excuse me," he said, giving Valarie a nod before walking a confident path toward his hostess.

"Don't mind him," said a voice. "He's harmless."

Valarie turned to see a striking blue-eyed woman, her dark hair swept up into a loose bun above her floral-print dress. The woman extended a hand. "Rhonda Rhodes. Paradise Salon and Day Spa," she said. "Sonny's been after Merel ever since Jakob died. Poor man doesn't have a chance, but I don't have the heart to break it to him. Apparently, neither does Merel." Her laughter was light.

"When did her husband pass away?" Valarie asked, trying to strike the correct balance between curious and solemn. She had never gotten up the courage to ask Merel directly.

"Let's see. It's been about two years now," said Rhonda, her smile dimming. "A terrible day. To pass away in such a freak accident, and at home, too." She clucked her tongue. "Poor Nicky. She was very fond of him. I don't think she's quite adjusted to being the most eligible bachelorette in town."

"Nicky?" asked Valarie, puzzled.

"Oh, that's just my pet name for Merel," said Rhonda. "Nichols was Merel's maiden name. We've known each other since kindergarten. The two of us and Emmett Weber were all in the same class. Oh, and Chief Bronson. He was Billy back then. Her first crush, back in seventh grade." She smiled, casting an affectionate glance at Merel across the patio.

Valarie sipped her wine thoughtfully. "It must have been hard for her, to be suddenly all alone in the big house," she said.

"Certainly," said Rhonda. "Although they always seemed like an odd match to me. She was such a free spirit, and he was a stern, businesslike type of man. But they were so active in the community, great patrons of the arts. And they seemed happy enough. Marriage is a business partnership, after all." She smiled. "Excuse me, there's someone I need to go say hello to."

Valarie had drained her wine. She moved toward a collection tray to set down her glass. A catering employee carrying empty hors d'oeuvre plates arrived at the same time. The woman offered Valarie a clean napkin from her apron. Valarie took it gratefully and dabbed at her forehead.

"Thanks," Valarie said.

"Of course, ma'am." Her hair was long and curly, and she wore black pants, a white button-down shirt and a tag bearing the name LUISA.

"Do you work a lot of parties here?" asked Valarie, still in chit-chat mode.

"All of them," Luisa said with a smile. "I've been with the company for five years, since before her husband died."

"I'm renting some rooms here at the house," said Valarie, "It's quite a place."

"Yes, it is beautiful," Luisa agreed. "Such a shame, though. All those rooms, and no children."

"I suppose they could have had ten children and still not run out of bedrooms," said Valarie.

"It seems they tried," Luisa said matter-of-factly. "I was at several parties where she was pregnant. And then, at the next party, she wasn't."

"Oh," said Valarie. "That's too bad."

Luisa shrugged. "It's up to God," she said, stooping to lift the tray, then disappearing into a pipe-and-drape tent at the patio's edge. Valarie tried to imagine God, sitting on a cloud, doling out babies. Instead, she saw a blue car, driving around curves on a hilly road.

The party guests lingered long after Valarie had gone inside. Later, walking toward the kitchen, Valarie saw one last small knot of guests calling goodbye to Merel as they stepped out the front door. Merel waved, then crossed the hall to the French doors that opened onto the patio, where a lone man sat, clinking ice in his bourbon glass. Valarie thought she remembered him introducing himself as Brad Prestridge, a partner at a local law firm. At Merel's appearance, he stood and followed her back into the house. The two of them disappeared up the curved staircase and walked toward the bedrooms.

That night, when Valarie closed her eyes, Merel was there. They sat on the sofa in the library, and Merel shifted closer to Valarie, leaning in, watching her eyes. Valarie felt electric, her nerves lit up like holiday lights, like she hadn't felt since Adam was alive. Suddenly they kissed, then they were leaning back on the sofa together, and when the ecstasy came, it was so powerful Valarie woke up in a hot sweat.

#

The next time the painting changed, it was in the middle of yet another party. It had occurred to Valarie to wonder if one of the party guests could have interfered with the canvas. She'd become fairly well acquainted with a handful of them, but how well did she really know them? They spent most of their time outdoors on that landscaped patio, but there was always somebody in the house, using the washroom or admiring Merel's sculpture collection.

She didn't linger at the gathering of Merel's friends from the historical society. After putting in her customary appearance, Valarie slipped away from the schmoozers and sippers and stole back to the spare bedroom. As if pulled by a magnet, she moved toward the staircase painting. Her eyes bulged when she saw it.

The gray smudge was no longer a malformed blur. It was distinct, and it was human-shaped. Added to the canvas by an unseen hand was a man, wearing black pants and a blue jacket. He lay sprawled at the foot of the marble stair, legs and arms jutting out at unnatural angles. Between his blond hair and the floor oozed a shiny streak of cadmium red.

At the top of the stairs, a second figure had appeared. Its features were vague, but it wore a loose gown, and its face appeared to be smiling.

Slowly, the prostrate man raised his head and turned it to look directly at Valarie. His eyes, hollow with pain, seemed to implore her for help. One of his arms lifted slowly and extended, as if reaching for her. As she stood frozen, jaw hanging, the man's head abruptly slumped back down. A drop of red seeped from his hair and dripped viscously down the canvas.

He was not Adam. But she had seen his face before.

Her stomach lurched, and she turned and fled the room.

The house had several twists and turns she hadn't explored. Valarie found herself in a short alcove, ending in an iron staircase that spiraled downward. Pursuing her sole desire, to get away from the painted man, she banged down the steps, winding lower and lower, ultimately emerging into a cool basement. When she flipped the switch, dim light illuminated the area weakly, as if wary of what it might show.

She made her way through the crowded space, past dusty furniture, naked dressmakers' dummies, and paintings of people in Victorian clothes. It seemed the van Rensselaers weren't fond of throwing things away. Valarie paused at a wheeled baby crib equipped with mesh bumpers and a fitted sheet, the only item in the room that looked at all modern. She did a double take at what lay just beyond the crib. Standing stock-still on a table were a bobcat, a raccoon, and a falcon, fur and feathers preserved by taxidermy, glass eyes glittering from the shadows. Hurrying past them, Valarie came to another stair, tucked in a corner and spiraling upward into darkness. She started up these stairs, which seemed far preferable to walking back past the animals.

After some time, she wondered where the stair was going. Surely by now she had climbed high enough to return to the ground floor. The light in this stairwell was even dimmer than the basement. Valarie hurried onward, her thighs starting to ache from the exertion. Finally, she emerged at a small landing with a ladder at one side and a trapdoor at the top. She hoisted herself up the ladder, pushed at the door, and surfaced onto a rooftop deck.

The small, square platform was walled by rough-hewn stone on two sides and wooden railings on the others. A fresh breeze lifted Valarie's hair off her shoulders as she caught her breath. She took in the view of the woods and hills, listening to birdcalls mixing with the faint sounds of cocktail-party prattle from three stories below. She shook her head. Only Merel, with her whims and her wealth, would build a widow's walk this far inland.

In the center of the deck sat a portable fire pit. Valarie bent to examine the chunks of ashy wood, blackened debris, and bits of paper. Newspaper? No, it looked like regular paper, a creamy, heavyweight stock. She pulled at a piece tucked underneath an intact chunk of firewood. It looked like a scrap of letterhead; printed on it in blue ink were the words Blossom Fertility Clinic. The rest had been burned away.

A piece of cream-colored stationery was the only other paper that had survived the blaze. Valarie tugged it free and read the words at the top, just above a singed, ragged edge:

My dearest Merel—

#

In town, Valarie collected the information she was after. At the police station, she showed them everything. Yes, they'd examine the evidence. Yes, she had acted appropriately in making a report. And yes, they'd definitely be in touch.

Anxiously, she returned to Hazel House. She felt certain she'd done the right thing, but what now? Valarie began transferring some of her clothes from the closet into her suitcase. If Merel were arrested, she'd have to move out. It was just as well. She had a feeling she had stayed at Hazel House long enough.

"Valarie? Oh, Valarie!"

She jumped, slamming the suitcase shut.

"Are you there, dear? I'd like a word."

As the footsteps in the hall came closer, Merel's heeled boots clicking louder, Valarie suddenly saw, again, the face of the man at the police station, nodding, listening, intently studying her own.

Chief Bronson, Rhonda Rhodes had said. He was Billy back then.

The police chief, Valarie now recalled in a sudden, terrible flash, was one of Merel's oldest friends.

She Drips

by Miriam H. Harrison

There's something strange that happens every night as I lay down to sleep. There, alone in my house, I hear someone. And she drips.

It started about a month ago, at a distance. I could hear the faint tap-tap coming from downstairs. Almost a loose faucet, but the sound was padded, softened. Water falling on carpet. For a while it was easy to forget, easy to ignore. But persistent.

I made my way downstairs, looking for the source. Walking through the living room, the kitchen, I found nothing. But as I returned to climb the stairs, I stepped through it: a damp patch on the hallway carpet.

That was all.

I stood and listened, but there was no sound, no dripping. I rubbed my feet dry on the carpeted stairs. Returning to my room, I slept in the silence.

But the sound returned the next night. And this time, I thought I could also hear the creak of the stairs. It was this new sound that scared me, filled me with a fear too familiar to women living alone. I crept from my room towards the landing. I peeked carefully down the darkened, empty staircase. I stepped down a creaking step, then another. I had almost reached the bottom when my foot felt wet carpet and pulled back. Standing still, I listened to the silence. There was nothing to see, nothing to hear, but I could feel it: a decided emptiness. I took in a breath of air and knew that someone else had breathed it before me.

This has gone on for many nights—all the same, but different. The sounds, closer each time, and me rising to find a new patch of wet floor. And that feeling. Standing in a hollow spot, an impression pressed into the air of my house. I feel the fabric of my reality rush in to reclaim its space, balancing itself, until I can't be sure if the thumbprint I had felt in that moment had ever been anything more than imaginings.

It is no longer fear that draws me from my bed. I'm not sure what I want this sound to be, yet each night I rise to meet it, only to find it gone. But there's something left behind in that closing space. An almost-warmth, so different from the cool, wet floor beneath. So different from the loneliness. As the sound comes closer and I arrive sooner, I can almost name a fragrance in that moment. A smell of sand, salt, seagulls. But only almost.

Last night, as I stood by my bed, the sound began behind me. I listened to the gentle tapping and breathed in the ocean's wetness that came and went with a warmth against the back of my neck. And I felt her—not as an absence, but a presence. I turned to reach for her and felt the subtle breeze of the shifting air, moving to fill an emptiness that had only just been carved away.

Tonight, as I lay in bed, I don't move. I don't even open my eyes. Not at the seaside scent, not at the creak of sudden weight on my floorboards. Not even as the first drop of water falls to my waiting lips.

Slave of the ~~Living~~ Dead

by Kasimma

Chidebelụ was creating a space for the cake on the overwhelmed dining table when she received a call informing her that her husband had been rushed to the hospital. It was Arinze's thirty-fifth birthday, a day so hot one feared balls of fire would rain from the sky. As she hurried out, she accidentally smashed her feet into the ice cream cake on the floor. The red "H" of the lettering rested right on the top of her cake-splodged foot as if in jest that the day was supposed to be "happy."

While barreling to the hospital, she wished she and Arinze had listened to her mother's advice and just stayed home. But somewhere in the loom of her brain lingered Aladiobiọma the slave, may he rot in hell, of the Kingdom of the Great Living and Greater Dead and of all other Realms unknown, First son, Head of the Obi, Defender of his lineage.

She knew the first sons in Arinze's kindred did not live past thirty-five. Her mother adjured her not to join that cursed family unless she wanted to be a young widow. But Chidebelụ's reasoning drowned in the pool of her love. Arinze's monolid eyes, and his square-shaped head as large as two pumpkins put together, kept her glued to him. Nothing else mattered to her, not even his bold smile like Morris Chestnut's or his stature like Burna Boy's. She was that child in school who always endured mockery for her small head. Adulthood saw her wearing big, wavy wigs to conceal it. So, Arinze's great head plus her small head would produce children with medium-sized heads.

Her family had suggested that Ikem, Arinze's younger brother, was most unlikely to die at thirty-five, and the top of his broader head resembled a ploughed field, giving him an added advantage over Arinze; and wouldn't Chidebelụ consider marrying Ikem since she found Aso-rock-heads sexy? Their pleas fell on ears stuffed with wax. Chidebelụ told everyone who cared to listen that she served a living God, and that generational curses would never have a hold on anyone connected to her.

Then, thirty-five-year-old Edozie, the first son of Arinze's eldest uncle, turned to ashes in a plane crash. Chidebelụ endured her crying mother's polemics as she reiterated her warning, and couldn't Chidebelụ see it manifesting?

But Chidebelụ had unshakable faith in Christ Jesus. It was a plane crash. It could have been anybody, for goodness' sake. Chidebelụ's mother howled loudest at Edozie's burial, as if she was Edozie's soulmate. But she knew, Chidebelụ knew, that her tears were for her son-in-law.

The next year, Izu, Arinze's cousin, a first son too, surrendered to a four-year-breast-cancer battle. He was thirty-five. Chidebelụ's mother called her again, crying. She imagined her mother seated on her favourite brown suede cushion, her phone on speaker, wiping her tears with the edge of her lappa. She did her best to explain to her mother that Izu's cancer was bull-headed; it licked mastectomy. But her mother was adamant. What business did a man have with breast cancer, for goodness' sake, her mother cried.

Akirika: aged thirty-four and ten months. It was as though Death could not wait to whisk him away.

Chidebelụ witnessed his final hours. She was in his house for a casual visit when Akirika went to relieve himself. Next thing, yowls! Chidebelụ and Akirika's wife tracked the screams to the toilet. Chidebelụ stood outside the door. She did not want to see Akirika in such a state. Akirika's wife called out for her help. Chidebelụ was hesitant, but she went in. And standing there was Akirika, his mouth wide open, tears streaming down his face, his scrotum neatly coiled in his trouser coil zipper all the way up as if it was part of the zipper. Some of his skin hung out as though the zipper passed through his scrotum like a train in a tunnel. His penis, as endowed as their great heads, hung there like a tree's breaking branch. His wife, now in utter confusion, cried with her husband. She stretched her hand close to Akirika's penis, but he screamed. She withdrew. Encouraged by the women, Akirika counted his steps, wince by wince, deep breath by deep breath, his legs spread apart, as if he had scrotal elephantiasis. His legs wobbled like a house shaken by earthquake by the time they got to the sitting room. He asked to lie down. Confusion frothed in the room: to zip down or not?

Finally, they decided to zip down so he could at least walk to the car. When his wife touched it, Akirika screamed so loud one would have thought droplets of molten magma landed on his chest. Chidebelụ fanned Akirika, patting his chest. His wife, her hands shaking like someone with hypothermia, counted one, two, three, go, and zip! The zipper came down, splashed with bits of scrotum and coloured in blood. Keep the open wound as clean as possible, Chidebelụ suggested. So Akirika's wife got methylated spirit and cotton wool and dabbed the rail on the scrotum. Akirika, by this time, whimpered like a dying dog. His labored veins plastered on his skin, so visible, so thick, as if the pain made his skin as transparent as wet silk. The women covered him with a lappa and got some men to help lift him to the car. During his surgery, Chidebelụ held Akirika's wife at her bosom, who in turn held the blood-stained lappa they had used in covering him. Akirika was wheeled out of the theatre, asleep, alive. Would he be okay, they asked the doctor? The doctor gave his confirmation. It was only then that Chidebelụ went home.

Akirika never opened his eyes.

Chidebelụ's mother called Arinze this time, as though she did not want to waste her wisdom on her daughter. Arinze and Chidebelụ were in their sitting room, resting on each other, wordlessly staring at a turned-off TV. Arinze answered the call and placed it on speakerphone. Would Arinze study Akirika's body during the funeral, she asked, because, in two years, he would be the one in the coffin with his nose and ears stuffed with blazing white cotton wool.

Before Chidebelụ could respond, Arinze hung up. She, however, observed a harangue of how dare her mother say that to Arinze, gbogbotigbo.

It might or might not have been his mother-in-law's words, but after Akirika's burial, Arinze gathered his cousins, who gathered their fathers, and they went visiting a diviner. He asked them to go home, that he would consult the gods, and come see them in five days. On the said day, they gathered on three benches arranged in a U-shape under a mango tree that was as old as, maybe, Jesus. Chidebelụ, as curious as a scientist, hid in their car that Arinze had parked behind the mango tree, and listened. If not for her rechargeable hand fan, she would have melted and poured out of the car.

The seven men waited until the diviner's voice and bell-staff pierced through their noiselessness. He sat on the blue plastic chair they reserved for him in their midst, between the eldest men, right under the tree behind whose trunk Arinze's tinted SUV sat. They asked if Abiankita would be so kind to receive their kola nut.

The diviner told them that this was not a matter of kola nut, and did he tell them that he came all the way from his house to beg for kola nut? Apologies rendered, the eldest man rolled out the reason for their invitation. He was a second son whose elder brother died at thirty-five. Their first sons died at their prime, and would Abiankita please tell them what was going on? Abiankita listened as though he was hearing the tale for the first time, chewing his teeth. It sounded as though he was chewing chin chin or kuli-kuli. He laughed, scratched his white goatee, and mocked them that ha ajụka n'oge. He pointed at the speaker and asked him his age. Ninety-two. And it took him ninety-two years to realize something was wrong? Silence. Abiankita went ahead to tell a tale, in his shaky voice, but with the ebullience of a storyteller.

Over two-hundred years ago, your forefathers allowed jealousy to get the best of them. Aladiobiọma was a man born with greatness at the tip of his tongue. The placenta that accompanied him is under this very mango tree where we sit. And as he grew, the gods favored him. He was handsome beyond measure. His eyes were as white as Amadiọha's ram and his pupils as brown as Ala's skin. The gods were partial towards him. Ala treated him as a favourite child. She blessed his farms with juicy crops. Because his harvests were so healthy, nobody bought elsewhere until he sold all his crops. His brothers got jealous. Things got out of hand when the king gave his only daughter to Aladiobiọma. Her refusal meant nothing. Nobody even understood why she would not want to marry Aladiobiọma. But her heart rested with Aladiobiọma's immediate younger brother, Njọku, a secret only both of them shared. Njọku poisoned his brothers' hearts against Aladiobiọma. So that when the white men came looking for slaves, Njọku and his three remaining brothers ganged up against Aladiobiọma, hit his head to hibernation, and sold him into slavery. The villagers combed their lands and rivers, searching for clues of Aladiobiọma's whereabouts or at least how such a hefty man vanished. The gods stayed silent. To compensate the family, the king offered his daughter to Aladiobiọma's immediate younger brother, Njọku. Their father cried to his grave. Before his death, he ordered that the mango tree should never be cut down. At least his useless sons adhered to that one.

Aladiobiọma suffered tremendously: first, from the inhumanities of slavery, and second from the hurt his beloved brothers set him up for such indignity. Like his father, he cried to his grave. He died an unhappy, unmarried slave. His body was chopped like wood, poured into a hole, and covered up. His lineage wiped off because he left no seed. In fact, his birth was a waste. Aladiobiọma still hovers, dead, living, unable to, at the very least, join ndị nna ochie. His blood cries for blood. He is responsible for the deaths of your first sons and will not stop until he is appeased.

The compound stayed mute. Even the air stood still, as though drawn to the story. They asked the diviner what they may do to appease the angry spirit. He told them two things, and, according to Aladiobiọma's instructions, they must occur in that order. First, they would marry Aladiobiọma to a wife who would bear him sons to keep his lineage alive. Second, they had to give Aladiobiọma a befitting funeral so he could join his ancestors.

The second one was not an issue, but for goodness' sake… for goodness' sake, would Abiankita be so kind as to tell them how to go about the first request?

An erected penis, the diviner responded, would find the vagina, even in the darkest pit. He began to sing. He had a nice voice for a man his age, but the words made no sense to Chidebelụ. The sound of his bell-staff faded away. It sounded like something coming from a far distance when the men's vocal cords returned from vacation. The big question was which family would marry out their daughter to a dead man. They decided to sleep on it and reconvene the next day. Chidebelụ was a boiling pot of sweat by the time she emerged from the car.

That night, Chidebelụ and her husband had a discussion so intense it almost started a fight. He opined that they did exactly as the diviner instructed. He accused Chidebelụ of insensitivity because it was not her head on the chopping board. She insisted that she served a living God so they should call a pastor who would use his anointing to break the yoke. Which yolk, Arinze wanted to know. Was it the yolk of akwa ọgazi, or the yolk of akwa ọkụkọ, or did she mean the yolk of akwa eke? Chidebelụ was still explaining that she meant yoke, not yolk, when he walked out and slammed the door in her face.

A crying Chidebelụ called her mother. Her mother only hummed and hemmed while Chidebelụ ranted. Why would Arinze, her husband, wear the rosary and the scapular on this neck when he lacked faith in their efficacy? Her mother chuckled. Chidebelụ steamed. Would her mother mind telling her what in the world was funny? What was funny, her mother responded, was that Chidebelụ had a small head because she forgot to fill it up with sense while she was in the womb. Chidebelụ threatened to ring off, but her mother apologized, three quick ndo that sounded like mockery. Then she went on to explain to Chidebelụ that should Aladiobiọma's spirit come for Arinze, it would first borrow the rosary and scapular on Arinze's neck and wear them to show Arinze na we-we. Then he would hold Arinze's hand and take him to where his cousins were chilling. Then, oh, Chidebelụ should not worry, Arinze would get a… Chidebelụ hung up.

Aladiobiọma's conditions were met in one year.

The marriage took place in the dead of the night, under the mango tree. The bride—the only female in attendance, dressed in black as a widow that she had become—held Abiankita's ikenga and vowed to take Aladiobiọma to be her husband. She pledged her love and loyalty and faithfulness to the dead man.

The bride, Azụka, was a twenty-five-year-old tailor from a family that had been flogged to humility by poverty. Her skin was dry and looked like an overused black shirt. Her blind father was a professional beggar. Her mother was a maize seller who only sold during the maize season. Azụka was the breadwinner of the family with the meagre sum she made from patching clothes.

It was not surprising that she and her family would jump at the offer to become a member of such a very wealthy family who promised to take care of Azụka's parents and to train Azụka and her nine siblings in school. All Azụka needed to do was pledge her loyalty to Aladiobiọma and bear children for him. Nobody cared who the biological father(s) of the children would be. Before the marriage ceremony, they knocked down her parents' bunk and built a small, cozy house in its stead. During Aladiobiọma's funeral, Azụka sat under the "Widow" canopy, receiving sympathizers' condolences.

Only a year after, Chidebelụ, whose brown face was smeared with mascara-tinted tears and feet sticky with cake, ran into the hospital asking doctors and nurses and cleaners and patients where her husband was. An elderly nurse took her to Arinze's ward. Plaster lumped at the left side of his head. He wore a blue hospital gown. He was asleep. The zigzag lines on the heart rate monitor, the nurse explained, showed that his heart was beating just fine. No problem at all. He sustained only a minor cut in his head which had been stitched. He was sedated so he could rest. All Chidebelụ could think of was Akirika.

As if the nurse read the worry in Chidebelụ furrowed brows and her sulky pouted lips, she placed a hand around Chidebelụ's shoulder and assured her that her husband would be awake in three hours. Her guarantee? She's been a nurse for thirty-five years, and she could tell a bad case from a good one, and she's never been wrong, ask anybody.

Chidebelụ sat on the visitor's chair, held Arinze's hand, and said her rosary while she waited for the said three hours.

What the Dead Whisper to the Living

by Mary Rajotte

If what Samuel Winslow did was so bad, surely the voices of the dead would diminish. But they lingered around him in all their splendor, so he built them a place worthy of their shine.

Up in the attic, on an old curio shelf stretching from floor to ceiling in a room no bigger than a broom closet, Samuel keeps a shrine filled with bottles of all shapes and colors. He tries his best not to go up there too much, to prevent all that magic from fading too soon. But when the night stretches out like a lonely highway with nothing so much as a whisper for company, it fills him with an ache so lonesome he just needs to hear a voice to soothe him.

Some of the bottles are wide-mouthed or squared. Others are stout or even rib-necked. Fancier, intricate ones in pale aqua and deep purple, the color of a bruised plum, have what looks like a peaked church window etched into the front. There are ones that used to hold bitters or ink, medicine bottle and flasks, stout amber tincture bottles the color of warm caramel, and some made from thick opaque glass that shimmer like moonstones. All do the job well enough, but there's one that's extra special. The brightest bluest bottle of the bunch, shapely like the female form, with a curved rim like a bee stung lip.

The moment he steps into the room, the atmosphere shifts, like someone else is already there. Floorboards groan. Dust motes take flight like sooty campfire ambers. A hint of blooming lilacs perfumes the air, the fragrance cloying with nostalgia so thick it tickles the back of his throat.

After a long day, he usually likes something high and light, like dewdrops plinking into the river beyond the house. But there's an earthy whisper of autumn outside that makes him crave something deep and smoky, like the smoldering maple down in the hearth. Perfect for this time of night, where the sunset doesn't so much as shine into the room but ooze through the window like honey.

In that moment, Samuel lifts a clear bottle made from thick glass so the light shines right through. Inside, the remnants swirl like a universe, like multitudes of stars, clusters of galaxies. And in the middle, a milky band of brightness so radiant, it aches to look at it. That's where they go when he takes them. A collection of all the best parts of a person, distilled down into a world made just for him.

Samuel pops the cork long enough to hear a few seconds of the voice inside when a car appears on the dirt drive, sounding its car horn on its way toward the house. Samuel drops the bottle. It hits the scuffed floorboards. The cork flies free and the low guttural groan Samuel stole some years back spews from the glass neck in a musty cloud. He pounces, shoving the cork in as well as he can before he flies out from the cubby, closes the panel behind him, and pushes it into place, so it's almost like it's not even there, praying to God it'll be enough to keep Lizzie from finding it.

For the last forty years, the voices have been his constant companions, billowing like the chimney smoke into the dark expanse of the Winslow farmhouse, unseen but felt around him. But he'd seen it coming for months, the way the chilly night air made his lungs ache. How even just going up the two steps onto the porch took enough of a toll, he had to stop and catch his breath before continuing inside. How his eyes got that milky look, like he was staring through a grease-fogged window. His time with the voices was running out. Soon, there'd be no one left to tend to his collection. No one to help it grow.

When Samuel gets to the landing and sees Lizzie's face at the bottom of the stairs, she looks up at him with trust and adoration in her soulful blue eyes, like she's done since she was a girl. That's when a tiny glimmer of hope flickers in his mind. She'll understand once he explains it to her. When she sees what he's done, she'll realize he didn't do it out of anger. Not even out of desperation. It was his way of keeping some spark of these damned souls alive long after he took them.

Lizzie peels off her coat and tosses it on the chair near the door before she comes into the foyer. "Dad, you all right?"

"Whatcha doin' here, girl?" Samuel says, trying to hide his harried breathing and his sweaty forehead.

"What's going on?" she says, gripping the banister.

Samuel rushes down before she can start up to meet him. His knees ache something awful and he nearly stumbles a few times, but when he gets to her, he forces a chuckle and wraps her tight.

"What kinda question is that to ask, huh?"

"I've heard some things."

Samuel tries not to glance upstairs. "How? You haven't come visiting in ages."

"I don't mean now. I—"

From the attic, a low groan filters through the gaps in the ceiling boards. Lizzie clasps Samuel's arm.

"That's..." she says, "still happening?"

"Just the bones of this old house. Creaky, like your dad's."

When the groaning surges, Samuel clenches his fists to stop himself from ushering Lizzie back outside. Why couldn't she have called first? He would have held off going in there until after she left if he knew she was coming.

When she edges toward the staircase and tilts her head just so instead of running out the front door like she used to, Samuel grips the banister to stop her. But then a kernel of promise blooms in his thoughts. Maybe Lizzie coming home after months of dodging his calls is a sign she's ready to see what being a Winslow really means.

She steps onto the bottom stair, but Samuel doesn't stop her. Not when she continues upstairs, past all the empty rooms that never got filled like Samuel hoped they would. He catches up to her by the time she's standing opposite the hidden panel in the wall that, in his haste, he didn't quite close.

The last remnants of golden sunbeams filter through the gap. She glances over her shoulder at him, her eyes as wide as they've ever been. Samuel gives her a nod. She edges open the panel and disappears inside. Samuel waits, praying she sees the beauty of what he's done. He gives her a moment longer, then shuffles inside to join her.

With the pinks and reds of the sunset at her back and the light illuminating her from behind, she reaches out with a shaking hand and trails fingers along the front of the bottles. Tracing gemstones and delicate class rings, earrings and dog tags pressed into wax, some of them decades old, others not so far gone.

But Lizzie's drawn to a tall, slender bottle in the middle of them all. Delicate and made of the most beautiful, rare, bright blue glass like summer skies, with a tiny pearl fixed to the front.

"Don't, Lizzie."

But her hand's on it already. "What are these, Dad? What have you done?"

"I said put that down now. You don't know how to handle 'em right."

"Handle what? I don't get it. This pearl. It's… it's…"

She clutches at her neck, pulling a delicate chain from under her sweater where a matching pearl dangles in the center. She raises the bottle, comparing her pendant to the other, but the bottle slips from her hands and crashes to the floor.

"No!" Samuel howls, diving for the bottle. He tries to clamp his hand over the opening, but hazy remnants of the voice escape in a thick curlicue around them like incense smoke, jumbled words so none of them make sense.

Lizzie clamps her palms to her ears, flinging herself back until she slides down the wall with her eyes squeezed shut. Samuel fumbles with the top just in time to trap what's left inside, his thoughts racing back to the day he made it. His first.

He'd found Ida with a thick coil of gnarled rope choked around her neck. She'd used his old work ladder to get up high enough to sling it over the king post in the center of the barn. It's like she did it on purpose, knowing she'd be the first thing he'd see in the pale dawn hours when he went out to tend to the horses. He couldn't save her from herself, but he could preserve the best part about her.

The bottle he chose was the exact color of her eyes, pale blue that turned violet at moonrise. Putting the glass to her lips wasn't even a thought. It was like those last gasping breaths of hers—not when he climbed up after her and cut the rope with his switchblade, but after, when he fell on his knees in the dirt beside her and she gasped and pushed Samuel away—told him to do so.

He spun from her, scrubbing the nape of his neck while little Lizzie wailed from inside, kicking up a fuss in her crib like she knew her mama couldn't love her enough to stay in this world. When Samuel turned back and saw the old glass bottle gleaming in the morning light on his workbench, something drew him to it. Something whispered to him to take it to Ida's lips. To make sure each gasp, every whimper, even her last words made it into that jar. Then, when he left her where she lay and let the Lord take her, he fished around for a cork to stop the top and preserve what little magic he managed to save. It was Ida's sin to bear. Not Samuel's. At least he had a token to commemorate her. The star of his collection. But it didn't take long for that shelf to look empty. All those cubbies with nothing else in them. All that space just whispering to be filled.

Lizzie's whimpering from the corner snaps Samuel out of his

memory to find her crouched against the wall. Her eyes are wide and her gaze darts from him to the bottle in his hand then back again.

"That was a voice. A woman's voice."

Samuel nods, pacing toward her with his hands in front of him. Lizzie kicks her legs out to keep him from getting too close. But the look in her eyes isn't alarm. The way her brow wrinkles and how her eyes narrow when she tilts her head to one side for a better look helps him see she's fascinated, even if she's acting scared.

"You recognize it, don't you?" Samuel holds out the bottle to her, noticing how her breath hitches in her throat when she leans toward him. "It touched a part of you, a part buried so deep, you aren't sure how you're connected to it. There's an invisible thread pulling you to it right now."

Her hand lifts ever so slightly, compelled to reach for it. "What is it, Daddy?"

"Not what. Who." Samuel edges closer. "Even though you were just a baby, even though it's been some twenty years, deep in your heart you know who."

Lizzie's mouth drops open and she shakes her head, blinking back tears even as she reaches out for the bottle. "Mama?"

Relief floods Samuel's senses. He staggers, steadying himself against the wall, losing a grip on the bottle. It drops into Lizzie's lap. She gasps but stays put, lifting it in her cupped palms to study it. Seeing it that way—more than half-emptied of Ida's shine—makes Samuel's heart hurt. But seeing Lizzie with the only remnants of her mama she's ever known is enough to soothe all the hurt of losing so much.

"I don't understand, Daddy. What… how is this… her?"

"The same way any of these are anyone," Samuel says, easing his way down onto the floor beside her. "I kept her essence with me 'cuz I couldn't bear to let her go. Now that you know, that missing piece of your heart is complete."

Holding the bottle out in front of her, Lizzie's forehead knits together with concern. "It can't be her. I… think you're confused, Dad. I think we have to do something. Call someone."

Samuel grabs her by the arm. "This is family business."

Lizzie jumps at his touch, scrambling away from him. "What did you do to her?"

"She did this to herself! I only… I tried to save what I could of her. For you! So you'd have something to remember her by."

A wounded sob escapes her throat.

"You were just a few months old, Lizzie! You don't know what it was like to be left alone like that with a newborn to care for."

She gestures to the cabinet. "And what about the rest of these? What… who are all these people? Why did you do this to them?"

"They didn't see just how special they were. Didn't appreciate their time on this earth. I know this is hard to take, Lizzie, but… it just seemed like a sin to see them squander what they had. Someone had to treasure their gifts, even if they couldn't recognize their own magic."

A low sob chokes in her throat and when she scrambles up with the bottle out in front of her like it's a threat, panic surges through Samuel's body. She pushes up so fast he can't do much more than flail his hands out to stop her, but he only catches her by the elbow. Lizzie yanks her arm free, but her grip on the bottle is loose. It flies from her hand, crashing to the floor where the cork pops out and the remaining essence seeps out.

It starts as a wheezing then builds into a shuddering gasp. A cough, then a choking sound brings tears to Samuel's eyes at how easily it stirs up those last moments. Ida's vacant eyes. Her last words with her final breath.

I can't, Samuel. I can't be the mother Lizzie needs me to be.

Lizzie wails beside him and it aches so much, it's like he's back there in that moment. Only Ida's voice is gone now and the suffocating sound of her fading away grows, echoing through the room, rattling the glass jars on their shelves, sending one then another careening to the floor. Their lids—some just screw-ons, others with a flip-top cap—pop open, billowing their captive souls into the air.

Samuel lunges to save them, but he only manages to scatter the bottles across the hardwood. Lizzie shrieks, spinning and kicking the bottles away. The air chokes Samuel with their essence. When he gasps for breath, the spirits surge into his mouth, forcing him to his knees with tears spilling down his cheeks.

Flopping on his side, he clutches at his throat. Lizzie hovers over him, trembling. Smacking his palm on the hardwood floor, Samuel fumbles for something, anything. When his fingers brush against one of the bottles, he snatches it up and thrusts it at her.

Lizzie backs away. Samuel shoves the bottle into her hand. He can't breathe. The light is growing dim.

"Lizzie, p-please!"

"I can't!" she sobs, sinking down beside him.

He grabs her by the wrist and wrenches her close. "So you won't be alone… like I was."

Wheezing, Samuel lurches closer, urging her to take up the bottle the way he's done so many times.

"Put it to my lips," he gasps. "Cup your hand 'round my mouth."

"Daddy, no!"

Samuel wheezes, his face burning hot. "Please."

Shaking her head, Lizzie squeezes her eyes closed. But after a moment, she takes several deep breaths and, when she opens her eyes again, she looks so much like Ida Samuel weeps.

Cradling her hand on his cheek, she leans over him. "Don't, Daddy. Please don't cry. It'll be okay."

Whimpering, Lizzie moves the bottle to Samuel's mouth. Her hands waver so it takes a few tries, but when she presses the glass to his lips, the cool smoothness is a comfort. When she uses her other hand to cup it over his mouth, Samuel huffs, exhaling deep into the bottle.

"That's my girl," he wheezes.

His vision blurs the longer she holds it there. With each exhalation, blackness seeps in from the edges and the air grows sweet. His lungs deflate, emptying more and more. In her eyes, she has that same look he saw in his own for so many years in the mirror. That emptiness of loss. The anguish that comes with taking the last breath of someone you love. That longing for solace before he came up with a way to conjure his own. Maybe now he can be that for her now, the way a good father's supposed to be.

Whirling around him, the air soothes, echoing his last words back to him.

Lizzie.

You won't be alone.

Lizzie… that's my girl.

With his heartbeat racing in his head and the room dimming, Lizzie is the glorious angel Samuel always thought of her as. His pride. His saving grace. The light in the presence of so much shadow. When she sits back, her shoulders shuddering with unbearable sobs, she's still a beacon of promise, with the bottles scattered around her shimmering gemstones in her light. They're empty. But they're hers to fill now.

Mercy

by Catherine McCarthy

Wherever Elias went, he carried The Bible in the crook of his withered left arm. No-one ever questioned why, for somehow it seemed inappropriate to admit the disfigured limb of a stranger caught one's attention long enough to realize what lay concealed within its fold.

Fleeting glances, flushed faces; over the course of forty years, Elias Edwards had grown accustomed to being greeted with something other than a handshake. Until people got to know him, of course. Or until he out-stayed his welcome and found it necessary to move on.

#

Elias arrived at Cardigan by train armed with only his Bible and a small suitcase, then walked three miles along the banks of the River Teifi towards the sleepy town of Cilgerran. By the time he stepped over the threshold of the Pentre Arms Inn on Church Street, rivulets of sweat ran down his spine and the pain in his left shoulder pulsed to the beat of his heart. The door lintel was low, yet Elias had no need to stoop.

The landlady stood behind the bar, drying glasses with a cloth as grey as the bun on her head. Elias recoiled. He was a fastidious fellow, and the thought of eating at that establishment made him feel a little queasy. A powerful odor of damp dog did nothing to alleviate his nausea, and for a moment he fretted that he might be the source of the smell, since the walk from the station had proved rather arduous.

"What can I get you?" the landlady said, feasting her gaze on

Elias's withered left arm with no hint of abashment. All eyes turned on him, and a hush fell about the place.

"I—I have a r—room booked," he said. "E—Elias Edwards." Stammering was not one of his usual idiosyncrasies, though he had many. He flexed his toes inside ill-fitting shoes and waited until she finished wringing the glass's neck.

"Come this way," she said, before marching off.

Elias gave chase, aware that as soon as he disappeared through the door, conversation once more thrived. He wondered if he was the subject, and thought it likely.

#

Later that evening, Elias squeezed himself into the furthest corner of the bar area and observed. An elderflower cordial stood before him, since he never partook of the devil's brew, and a napkin and cutlery awaited the arrival of his meal. He had asked if dinner might be brought to his room, as he detested eating in front of strangers, but his request was met with a disgruntled refusal by the landlady. He was famished, and so placing The Bible on the vacant seat beside him, he pinned the cutlery implements, one by one, beneath his withered arm and vigorously polished each with the napkin until his warped reflection shone on their surface. As far as what went on in the kitchen, he would have to adapt the old adage, out of sight, out of mind, since his hunger would not otherwise be satiated.

It appeared he was the only client who would be eating at the establishment, since all the others were either sprawled at the bar, shouting over each other in the native tongue, or scattered around the room, nursing half-empty pint glasses of bitter ale that suggested their reluctance to return home. Other than his, not a single table was laid for dinner. Perhaps the locals had little faith in the kitchen's standards of hygiene, too.

Elias scanned the room from behind his spectacles. The elderly man propped against the bar—sallow skin and broken capillaries on his nose—was not long for this world. Elias was as certain as he was that Sunday followed Saturday. And the landlady, too. She didn't know it yet, but there was something growing around the left ovary that ought not to be there. Elias wondered if he might end up giving either of them a helping hand in the future. That depended on two things: whether he took to the place and decided to stay, and how desperate they became once the grim reaper came calling.

#

The following day dawned warm and bright, and Elias woke with a stiff neck and an urgent desire to escape the confines of the dark and dreary letting room.

As he ambled through the town, breathing in the earthy aromas of slate and woodland, Elias believed the place grew on him, and so was pleased to discover a little cottage at the corner of Castle Street with a sign in the window which read, 'House for rent. Apply at Vicarage'. Elias peered in at the windows and saw that it appeared comfortably, if somewhat sparsely, furnished. He hoped he was not too late and set off down the lane towards the church with gusto. The vicarage had to be close to the church, they always were, and with his Bible tucked under his arm, he felt sure he would be welcomed.

#

Three days later, Elias found himself ensconced in the little cottage. Unpacking his belongings took him no longer than ten minutes, as apart from the small suitcase, which contained the most necessary of his belongings—his money box and a few items of clothing—the rest of his life's possessions arrived, contained within one large trunk. He did not consider himself a sentimental man and therefore held on to very few accoutrements. The money box and Bible were the only two things which Elias considered inseparable from himself, and one of those—The Bible—was a ruse; the means by which he was accepted into the fold, especially in these quaint towns and villages steeped in the old ways and beliefs. If only they knew. Elias had forsaken God at the age of ten, when he first realized his own power.

Whilst playing in woodland, he had come upon a fox caught in a poacher's trap. Hind leg snapped in two, it clung to life by threads of raw sinew. Foaming at the mouth, it pleaded for its end with a pitiful cry. Elias had been moved to tears. With his left hand, he reached out, instinctively, no thought for his own safety, and stroked the fox's white underbelly. "Sleep now, little one," he'd said. "No more suffering."

It was as simple as that. The fox closed its eyes and its foaming mouth relaxed into a grin. No more pain or gasping for breath. Just oblivion.

Elias had told no-one. He kept the fox's expression of peace in his memory for an eternity—the first of any new experience is always the most memorable—but that night, as he undressed for bed, he imagined his left arm felt a little weak, for it trembled and his hand failed to coordinate the undoing of his shirt buttons.

Stranger still, perhaps, was that as he was about to hop into bed, he saw that the mechanical money box which bore the nameplate Edgar the Esoteric now held a shiny silver florin in the palm of its right hand, ready to devour. A small fortune to a child, and certainly nothing to be sniffed at. Since it wasn't his birthday, Elias could think of no reason for the reward other than the fact he had put pay to the fox's misery, so he dutifully pressed the lever and watched in awe as its painted eyes rolled back in their sockets before its gaping mouth swallowed the coin.

The money box had resided on his bedside table since as far back as he could remember, though really it oughtn't to have, since it was one of the most macabre specimens Elias had ever seen. Cast in iron, it resembled the top half of a magician: jet-black cloak, wicked eyes, and a long moustache which curled at the ends. In place of a left arm was a lever, which one turned to allow it to operate. Its sturdy build offered reassurance that it would outlive Elias, though he was just a boy.

#

Over the course of his childhood, Elias put several animals out of their misery, and all it took was the laying down of his left hand and a few words of wisdom. On each occasion, he returned home to find a shiny coin waiting in the mechanical conjurer's right palm. By the time he reached the age of thirteen, he had amassed the princely sum of two pounds four shillings, which equated to no fewer than twenty-two lives mercifully ended. He did not do it for the money, though he had to admit it helped compensate for the ever-increasing discomfort in his left arm. Payment in kind, though from what source Elias had no clue. It wasn't God's doing, though. Of that he was certain. Throughout history, too many had suffered for it to be God's doing.

#

It wasn't until Elias reached the grand old age of sixteen that he experimented on his first human, and by then he had not the slightest doubt his method would work.

His experiment happened to be an elderly aunt, pious to the core; Welsh chapel and all its shenanigans. Elias accompanied his mother to pay their last respects, having been forewarned that Aunty Lil was approaching the end. Elias did not fear death, only suffering. That gasping, rasping breath that tainted the air with its incomparable stench.

Aunty Lil lay in bed, mouth gaping like a baby bird, oblivious to the fact that both her sisters, her niece, and her grandnephew—the one she'd plied with pear drops since he'd had a full set of teeth—stood over her with thoughts they couldn't verbalize. And it was whilst the aunts had retreated to the parlour for the Welsh cure of all ills—a nice cup of tea—that Elias slipped back into Aunty Lil's bedroom and carried out the mercy killing. The only difference between seeing off Aunty Lil and seeing off the animals was the slight hesitation regarding which part of the body he should lay his left hand on. Somehow it felt unseemly to stroke the swollen abdomen of a female relative. Nevertheless, he decided against altering his method in case something should go wrong.

As soon as it was over, Elias returned to the parlour and devoured no fewer than three slices of buttered bara brith. For some reason, mercy killings sapped his strength and whet his appetite.

By the time the women returned to attend to Aunty Lil, there was no longer any need, and Elias was certain his left shirt sleeve hung a half inch lower than it had done previously.

Thinking the situation might have upset him, Elias's mother had picked up Aunty Lil's Bible, from where it lay prone on the night-stand, and handed it to Elias, saying, "The Lord has seen fit to end her suffering, Elias. It is He alone who decides when the time is right, and it is not our fault that she spent her final moments alone. Here—she would have wanted you to have it."

Elias had smiled, though not for the reason his mother assumed, before muttering words of thanks and hitching the bible under his left armpit, where it gradually warmed.

Once home, Elias retreated to his bedroom to gather his thoughts, surprised to see that instead of a florin, a shiny half-crown lay waiting in the hand of the mechanical conjurer.

That night, the throbbing in Elias's left arm was more acute than ever before. He failed to make himself comfortable in bed, no matter how he lay. And by morning, when Elias held both arms out in front of him, the fingertips of his left hand barely reached as far as his right palm.

Still, Elias considered it a small price to pay for the relief he felt at having terminated the suffering of the dying. And in any case, it was addictive; he simply couldn't resist.

#

As time went by, Elias was no longer able to assist the birds of the air or the creatures of the woods because he feared that doing so would speed up the deterioration of his limb to such a degree it might one day disappear altogether. And what would he do then? He had never attempted to carry out the act of euthanasia with his right hand, nor any other part of his body come to think of it, since he felt certain it wouldn't work. No: there was something powerful about that left arm. A contradiction in terms, since it retained very little physical strength these days.

Elias refused to worry about what might happen should it one day disappear altogether, nor did he ever question where his unique skill derived from. One thing he knew for certain: it was not God given, and therein lay the rub, because wherever he went, and whichever town he chose to reside, he was expected to conform to the ways of the church. He felt obliged to attend weekly sermons at whatever religious establishment dominated the town, and carrying his Bible led others to believe him a devout Christian. In a way, he believed it was the cross he had to bear so he might continue to raise no suspicion as to his true calling.

#

Several months passed by before Elias felt at home in Cilgerran, but once settled, he began to feel as if he belonged. The little town had everything he wished for: a superb countryside setting, walks from the doorstep, even a ruined castle. A paradise for the solitary. He found the townsfolk amicable, and of course there was the inn, though he never frequented it. On Saturday afternoons, however, he partook of a pot of tea and home-made scones at the cafe known as The Buttered Muffin on the corner of Church Street, where he passed the time of day with one or two locals whom he grew to consider acquaintances.

Whenever anyone enquired about his background, Elias gave them the same spiel he had practiced for years: he had spent his youth in mid Wales before studying law and becoming an articled clerk to a firm of solicitors in North Wales. And this was all true, though he knew what they really wanted to hear was how he came to have one arm less than half the length of the other. On occasion, the bolder among them would ask and Elias would explain it was an affliction from birth; the arm had failed to develop correctly in the womb. This prevarication was always accompanied by a nervous tic whereby Elias repeatedly stretched his jaw to one side, so much so it left him with an ache.

Elias had the feeling his backstory spread from house to house, street to street, like a dose of influenza, but once heard, people began to accept him for what he was: a newcomer with a deformed arm and a warm heart. He even managed to find employment at the local solicitor's office where he was taken on as a part-time copywriter; an unlikely profession one might think for someone with a disability such as his, but Elias's penmanship skills were impeccable. And part-time work was all Elias required, since not only did he live frugally, but over the years his savings from the contents of his money box had amassed to a substantial amount.

For the first time in a long time, Elias believed life might be taking a turn for the better. He intended to carry out his special work there in Cilgerran with due diligence, and only when absolutely necessary, so past mistakes were not repeated. Doing so would require great discipline, since the urge to end the life of those who suffered was a raging bull. However, he would not be able to bear it if folk thereabouts became suspicious as they had done back in Caernarfon. There, as word had spread about how Elias was able to help the suffering of the dying with no more than a few words of comfort, too many had called on him, and rumors had rumbled about how both the doctor and vicar were intending to have words with the peelers. Thus, Elias had fled, and it had upset him a great deal since he had been content there.

Still, he was settled again now, and not only that, but there were celebrations to look forward to, since the turn of the century was right around the corner. Cilgerran had all sorts of events planned: street parties, a bake-sale, and the one Elias looked forward to most—the travelling circus was coming to town.

Now, Elias was not usually one to thrill at the thought of such a public event. However, the colorful advertisement, which had been pasted to the billboard on the town square, read, 'Edgar the Esoteric, Conjurer of the Dark Arts'. Elias spotted it the day after it was posted and it stole his breath.

How was it possible? It had to be a coincidence. Didn't it? That evening, Elias sat soaking his feet in a bowl of hot water infused with peppermint oil, which not only soothed the ache but also helped clear his head. He came to the conclusion that once upon a time, there must have been a famous magician named Edgar the Esoteric, and that was why the moneybox he'd had since childhood bore the same name. The conjurer who was due to visit Cilgerran must therefore have adopted it. Nevertheless, Elias's curiosity was piqued. He would purchase two tickets, one for himself and one for his friend Charles, who owned the Buttered Muffin, and they would visit the circus together.

#

The day before the circus, the son of the landlady of the Pentre Arms called upon him to pay a visit to his mother, who was writhing in agony. By then, the tumor on her ovary had grown to the size of an orange and she could no longer bear the pain.

As Elias stepped through the door of the inn, memories of the first time came flooding back: the same dog-like stench, the same grey dishcloth. Elias swallowed hard, biting back the bile in his throat before following the landlady's son upstairs.

Afterwards, he did not experience his usual hunger pangs. Instead, he walked the short distance back to what he now thought of as home and went straight to bed. Alas, a nagging, throbbing ache in what remained of his left arm kept him awake half the night. Such discomfort was nothing new, but the pain and loss of appetite accompanied a sense of foreboding, an instinctive feeling of impending doom. And the money box magician, perched on his bedside table, curled the corners of its moustache a little higher.

#

The circus was held in the castle grounds. Elias considered it a marvelous venue for such entertainment. The white peak of the big top could be seen billowing in the breeze as Elias and Charles descended the hill, its red and white candy stripes tempting them inside.

The Ringmaster did a stupendous job of whipping the crowd into a frenzy. First up were the jugglers. Although entertaining to some, they bored Elias. He fidgeted in his seat, unable to find a comfortable position. Next came an alley of clowns: chalked faces, painted-on grimaces, slapstick humor. Not Elias's cup of tea at all, and what was more, the noise from the crowd as the clowns frolicked about the ring was deafening. Elias's head pounded, and were it not for the anticipation of seeing the conjurer, he would have taken leave of the place.

Meanwhile, Charles appeared to be having a whale of a time. He guffawed at all the right moments and drew breath whenever there was apparent danger. Elias wished he had come alone, since Charles's enthusiasm was grating on him.

Finally, the moment he had been waiting for arrived. Lights dimmed, and eerie music floated through the ring as Edgar crept from behind the curtains. Elias held his breath. Draped in a cloak of black, in the dim light the conjurer appeared at first as a floating head, one which Elias instantly recognized as that of his mechanical money box. The likeness was uncanny, but then if Edgar had modelled himself on a famous magician, he would have copied the detail: jet-black hair, parted down the center and pomaded to his head until it gleamed; heavy moustache, twisted upwards at the ends; brass buttons and chain fob on the front of a brocade waistcoat. He certainly cut the mustard. Elias leaned forward in his seat, drinking in each and every detail.

"Good evening, ladies and gentlemen. Tonight, I shall beguile you with my bird cage, enchant you with the sands of India, fascinate you with the fire-bowl, and I have one more trick up my sleeve which has never been performed before."

The whole audience, including Elias, gasped with delight. For the next few minutes, Elias did not remove his watchful gaze once. He was transported to another world: one where reality and trickery melded into one. Hypnotic. Edgar's magic made him forget his immediate surroundings and instead his mind focused on the magic that had dominated so much of his own life.

Suddenly, he was awoken from his stupor by the prodding of Charles's elbow. From the stage, Edgar beckoned to Elias, dark eyes fixed on him.

"He's chosen you as his assistant," Charles hissed. "Don't keep him waiting."

Elias was appalled. He hated being the center of attention and shrank back in his chair, cowering.

"Come, sir, you have nothing to fear," the conjurer said, grinning from ear to ear.

Elias found himself obeying. Forty paces it took to reach the center of the ring. One for each year of his life, and each step labored with acute embarrassment. By the time he reached the waiting magician, his face flushed red and perspiration pooled in every crevice. The men shook hands, right hand to right hand, and Elias felt a shock of static electricity shoot along his arm.

From the pocket of his waistcoat, the conjurer produced a shiny coin and held it aloft to the audience. "Ladies and gentlemen," he said. "Before your very eyes, this silver coin will appear and disappear into thin air, but first I invite my assistant to examine it so that you may be assured it is genuine."

He handed the coin to Elias, who received its warmth into his trembling palm. Compelled to do as instructed, Elias squeezed and prodded the silver crown before mumbling in agreement. He planted both feet firmly on the ground, feeling himself sway. He worried he might faint and the thought of doing so in public made him feel even more light-headed. He swallowed hard and attempted to focus on the coin in the conjurer's right hand.

The words Edgar spoke to the audience went unheeded by Elias, because with a shake of his cloak sleeve, the conjurer displayed his left limb.

Elias's mouth fell open. Two-thirds the length of the other, the left arm which deftly moved the coin from a visible to invisible state, was not fully formed. In fact, it resembled Elias's some twenty years earlier. His faint forgotten, he focused hard on the limb and had to stop himself from grabbing it in order to examine it more closely. This was more than coincidence. This was dark art. How else might the uncanny resemblance be explained? Why, if it were possible to take what remained of Elias's left arm and join it to Edgar's then it would make one complete limb. Simply astounding!

The coin was at rest now in the palm of the magician's right hand, and the audience went wild. Whoops of joy and lots of nudges, but from Elias nothing more than a slack jaw.

The conjurer bowed to his audience, then to Elias before handing him the coin. "Sir," he said.

"Over the years, I have taken what was rightfully yours." He nodded toward Elias's withered limb. "And you have received what was rightfully mine." The coin in Elias's right hand glinted at the magician's words. "If in future you wish to grant me a little more, I will be eternally grateful, and of course you shall continue to reap the rewards." And with a shrug of his black cloak, he once more hid his withered limb, leaving Elias in no doubt about what he desired: the remaining stub of Elias's arm.

Elias stumbled back to his seat, blurry-eyed and heart throbbing. Edgar the Esoteric's words would have meant nothing to the audience, but to Elias they meant the world. Each piece of the puzzle had fallen into place. All this time he had thought himself all-powerful, only to discover that the power to take a life was not granted by him after all, but by the magician and his familiar in the shape of a metallic money box.

And The Bible? A keepsake, nothing more.

Picture Perfect

by Patricia Miller

It was one of those isolated, rambling country houses that spoke of old money, bloodlines, and generational trusts. My parents had one just like it. I had never understood the appeal of our family's summer home—it was too isolated, too crowded, too overwhelming with the sheer volume of noise and drama. This house seemed different, though, more alive than lived in.

The portico covering the front entrance dwarfed my car. It was from an era when horse-drawn coaches needed to be sheltered from the weather, not ten-year-old Hyundai wagons. I parked under its granite arches and mounted the stairs leading to the massive front door.

A clock inside chimed the hour as I rang the buzzer. He opened the door almost immediately and waved me in. We did not exchange greetings. He led me upstairs and showed me three rooms, each with nine empty easels set up to display my work for his perusal.

"You may choose which room you think would suit them best. Will you need assistance?"

"No. Thank you."

He nodded. "Take whatever time you need."

The sunny, glass-lined room on the south side of the house was the perfect venue. I made nine round trips to the car and back, careful not to bump the oak wainscotting or, more importantly, the canvases. Some of them were still slightly damp.

I pulled out my new cell phone, used the camera to document the original positioning of the easels, and checked sight lines, sunlight, and shadows. The portraits were grouped, arranged, rearranged by age of the subject, by size. It took just over an hour before I was able to step back, satisfied to watch the play of light across the monochromatic faces in front of me.

I left the room and peered over the carved balustrade. He was waiting patiently downstairs in the foyer. I cleared my throat ever so softly. At that signal, he climbed the stairs with an enviable ease and grace, joining me on the landing outside the sunroom. The easels were arranged in a serpentine fashion toward the west end of the room, displayed in chronological order from right to left. The head of the lineup greeted us at the door, the last was turned toward the windows.

Silently, he approached the first portrait. I held my breath. A tilt of the head, a bend at the waist to look more closely, a blink. He shifted left to the next canvas, then the next, moving at his own pace. Some of the faces received no more than cursory acknowledgement, others took long minutes of close examination. I was certain no detail was overlooked. He did not take notes, nor did he offer any comment or ask any questions until he'd viewed them all.

"You were asked to paint the truth."

"Yes."

"Then, if I may, let me tell you the truth as I see it in your work."

I nodded agreement, and we started at the beginning, a full three-quarter portrait of a flawlessly maintained, fifty-something woman, pretending she wasn't a day over forty.

"Your mother, if I'm not mistaken." It was a well-known face to anyone familiar with the social register. "Did she ever see you?"

"I was a trophy, trotted out on special occasions as proof of her beneficence until I outgrew the cute orphan phase. Once that happened, I was invisible to her." It's amazing what you can see in someone when they don't see you at all.

"And your father. Practically a blank canvas to everyone." Three thin slashes on gesso—a bare shadow of a profile.

"A means to an end. He had money to add to the family fortune and a good gene pool."

"Meaning his genes wouldn't overwhelm hers, I imagine. The family likeness has always been striking."

My sister, classically beautiful, barely rated a second glance. "America has no need for princesses anymore."

Her husband received a closer inspection. "Dear God, what an ass! I keep hoping the Homo Americanus Frat Boy will die out, but they still roam amongst us."

"He was my brother's college roommate, a perfect match for my sister. She worshipped him and he quoted romantic poetry to her."

"All while trying to corner you in the dark."

"Yes." He and my brother had a bet. Neither of them managed to collect on it.

"And this then is your brother—what's his head count?"

"His third wife left him two months ago." She was willing to put up with the other women, the drugs, the alcohol. It was the temper that wore her down.

The next three portraits were of my uncle and two cousins. They received wordless shakes of his head, but no comment.

He stared at the last portrait for some time, moving from one side to the other to view it from different angles, even pulling out a magnifying glass to examine the brush strokes. Finally, he straightened up, took a deep breath.

"She hated you. Hated your very existence. Why?"

Why indeed? I never understood my Aunt Brendell until it was too late, although I learned early on that even to call her that made it worse. She never spoke of me without adding 'she's adopted, you know,' to my name.

"She hated the idea of me. Hated the idea of my questionable heritage polluting the family bloodline. Always said blood will tell, and in my case, it wouldn't have anything good to say."

And she made certain that would never happen. The surgical scar was nearly invisible to the eye, but it echoed inside the hollow where my uterus should be.

He backed away from the easels to the long bank of windows along the room's southern wall, leaning on one of the marble sills. "The subtleness of the shading, the play of sunlight on the features—you picked the right room for your display."

"The details would have been lost in shadow."

"True. It's an impressive body of work. Although they are different in style, they are the same in substance. Any unbiased observer would agree the same hand painted each portrait."

"Thank you. As an exercise, it was more cathartic than I expected."

"And is the series complete?"

"I would say so, yes."

He reached out, and, taking hold of my right hand, slowly unwound the bandage which encased my palm. He raised my hand to his lips, pressing a gentle kiss on the barely closed cuts scoring my lifeline.

"Then welcome to my atelier—I'm looking forward to seeing you work with a more expansive palette."

He grinned, and I smiled for the first time. The monochromatic faces had no more power to hurt me. And I no longer had to suffer for my art, although it turned out they did. It was a shame their blue blood only came in red.

Down With the Holly, Ivy, All

by Jessica Lévai

Richard Carrington was cold when he arrived at his aunt's home at noon on February 1st, 1874. He would be colder still when he departed the next day.

He had received a letter from her in late November, inviting him to celebrate Christmas. Even though her country manor was reportedly as elegant as any could hope for, he found its moniker, Colley Castle, pretentious. And even though he was her last blood relative in all the world since the death of his father seven years ago, he had only met her once in his life, and that was enough. He declined her invitation.

Cynthia Abershire, his father's only sister, was now the widow of a count whom she had married at an age advanced for both of them. He had died, leaving her Colley Castle and little else, but little else did she require. Cynthia, an actress in her youth, had made her own money—and Richard's mouth soured at the thought—as a novelist in her maturity. Richard had never read one of her books. His distaste at their fantastic subject matter, not to mention their success, was enough to gum the covers closed to him forever.

A second letter from his aunt arrived in late December. In this she mentioned, with subtlety and restraint even Richard had to admire, that she was neither so young nor so healthy as she had once been. "As I look around me at Colley Castle, which shall be my tangible legacy on this earth, I think it would ease my worries over its future to see you at least once before I come to my end." This line convinced him to make arrangements to travel. While any respectability Aunt Cynthia had gained from her marriage was squandered with her writing, he now gave serious consideration to where her fortune would go once she was gone. He wrote after the

New Year to inform her he would accept her invitation after all.

He had been delayed by snowfall and the demands of business but, at long last, he was here. He stepped from the coach and took his first look at Colley Castle, stark and gray to rival the stark grayness of the sky behind and above. It was modest, he supposed, but could be imposing with the right owner. He imagined himself standing at the main door, ready to receive guests.

His reverie was broken by the arrival of Mrs. Pomme, his aunt's housekeeper. She was a ruddy, talkative woman in her middle years. She chatted with him as she led him to the entryway and other servants collected his luggage. He noted, with disdain, the absence of a butler.

When Richard entered Colley Castle, he gasped. This was not a reaction to its size, which still underwhelmed, nor to its warmth, which was wasted on him, but rather to the volumes of holly and ivy garlanding every wall, nook and corner. Fires crackled in the hearths, and servants lit candles against the early nightfall. It was all, he thought, a bit much, and he said so to out loud to Mrs. Pomme.

"I'm not sure as I agree with you, sir," she replied. "Of course, it is all your aunt's wish. She does so love this time of year."

"It's February," Richard noted, dryly.

"So it is, sir, so it is. Only just. Won't be much longer now."

Their conversation was interrupted by a loud "Hullo!" from somewhere behind them. Richard turned to see his Aunt Cynthia, striding toward him with a smile on her face. Striding, that was, as best she could while leaning upon an elegantly carved cane. He feared for a moment that she might embrace him and flinched.

Whether she noticed or not, she stopped and stood beaming at him. "Richard, it is such a pleasure to welcome you into my home," she said. "I hope your journey was relaxing."

He could not find the words to answer her. From her letter, he expected to find his aunt close to death, or at least bedridden. Yet, despite the cane, she looked as if she might begin dancing any minute. He stammered, "You look well, Aunt."

"Oh, you are a dear," said Aunt Cynthia, "I do feel rather well today." She tapped her cane on the floor. "We have so many things to discuss, and we will, but surely you will require a bit of rest before the party tonight."

"The party?" Richard was still taken aback by her appearance. "Tonight?"

"Why, yes," she said, smiling again. "Did I not mention it in my letter? We'll have a grand do tonight, to see out the season properly. Tomorrow, you and I can talk business." She winked.

He blushed, fearful that his purpose in coming here had been found out so quickly. He made himself smile at her, holding his breath until she was gone. Once Mrs. Pomme showed him to his room, he collapsed on the bed with a loud, rattling sigh.

#

The dinner party was intimate and cheerful, and Richard hated every minute of it.

He noted bitterly that his aunt had not seated him next to herself, but rather between two of her local friends. On his right sat a woman nearer his age and not unattractive, who was a passionate fan of his aunt's books. He guessed the reason they were seated together, and did not appreciate it, no more than he appreciated the beef joint, the wine, or the dessert. His companions, finding their efforts to engage him blocked by a wall of polite, disinterested responses, simply spoke around him.

After dessert came sherry in the salon and music from the phonograph. His aunt danced with a fellow actor, her cane forgotten in the corner. She was blooming and, despite her age, the picture of health.

Left to himself, Richard watched the clock. When it struck ten, his aunt stood and the rest of the guests hushed. Mrs. Pomme appeared at this signal with bundles of cloth in her hands.

Aunt Cynthia spoke, "My dear, dear friends and family." This last word could only have been directed to him, so Richard sat up, expecting an announcement in his interests. "Mrs. Pomme informs me that your rooms have been prepared. But before we may take our rest, there remains but one last ritual to perform. So if you would, please, pair off and we'll begin!"

Eagerly, the guests rose to take sacks from Mrs. Pomme. Richard, puzzled, dutifully joined their line. The company sorted themselves easily into pairs and chuckled at him for being the odd man out.

"Never fear, Richard, never fear," said Aunt Cynthia. "Mrs. Pomme will be your partner. She will appreciate your height and reach!" More laughter. Richard reddened as Mrs. Pomme took her place beside him.

"A song?" Aunt Cynthia asked. She began in a clear contralto, and the other guests joined in.

Down with the rosemary, and so
Down with the bays and mistletoe;
Down with the holly, ivy, all,
Wherewith ye dress'd the Christmas Hall.

Richard had never heard this song, but hummed along with false good humor. He was already impatient with it as he was with festivity in general. He hoped this signaled the end of the night's events, reckoning without his assignment to Mrs. Pomme.

"Come along," she clucked, taking him by the wrist and leading him out the door. "You can help me with the taller shelves in the library."

Soon they arrived among the books. Mrs. Pomme, still humming, quickly moved from shelf to shelf, plucking bits of holly and ivy from where they lay in decoration. She balanced precariously on her toes, reaching for boughs high above her head and stuffing them into the sack she carried. At last comprehending, Richard stepped beside her to help. She chuckled and took the branches he gave her, all the while singing:

That so the superstitious find
No one least branch there left behind:
For look, how many leaves there be
Neglected, there (maids, trust to me)
So many goblins you shall see.

Richard took the sack from her and grunted under its weight. "Does my aunt always wait so long to remove the decorations from Christmas? Surely it makes a mess."

"It is a bit messy, sir, certainly." Mrs. Pomme had tied off the sack and produced from nowhere a broom and pan, into which she swept some loose, fallen leaves. "But she does so love Christmas. And if it makes her happy, what's the trouble to leave them up a little longer?"

"Then why not take them down tomorrow, when the guests have gone and the festivities are quite over?"

Mrs. Pomme looked at him as if he were cracked in the head. He resisted the temptation to look at her the same way.

"Why, you must have everything down by Candlemas, sir. As the song says."

"Yes, the song." For the life of him, he could remember none of the words he pretended to sing twenty minutes ago. "Is that all?"

"Well, sir," and her voice dipped to a whisper. "You know what they say. If anything's left up longer than midnight tonight, even a bough or a berry, there'll be death in the coming year."

"Oh, come now," said Richard, exasperation getting the better of him. "Surely in any collection of humanity there is bound to be a death in a given year."

"I suppose there might be, God preserve us."

"And you think it has to do with a few holly branches? That's not very logical, is it?"

Mrs. Pomme appeared to think on this, folding her hands primly over the dustpan. Then she shrugged. "The mistress in such health as she is, it doesn't do to take chances, does it?"

"She does not seem so very ill to me," said Richard, all but sneering.

"God bless you, sir." Mrs. Pomme turned to perform a final check on the shelves in the back. That was when Richard saw the small red spot on the floor beside the bag. Once the housekeeper was out of sight, he crouched to the floor and picked it up.

It was a large holly berry, like a blood-red gooseberry, fallen from its mother bough in the cleaning. He held the berry in his palm and waited for Mrs. Pomme to re-emerge. When she did, with a satisfied dusting of her hands, he put the red ball in his pocket.

"That's all done in here," she said. She glanced at the watch pinned to her apron. "In plenty of time, too. Thank you kindly for your help. Now, the rest of the guests will be finding their way back to the salon, so you might hurry along and join them."

"I might not," Richard said. Mrs. Pomme's face fell like wet paper. "I have had an exhausting day of travel, Mrs. Pomme. I should like to retire for the evening, so I may be fresh tomorrow. My aunt and I have hardly had a proper visit yet, wouldn't you agree?"

The housekeeper smiled sympathetically. "As you like, of course. You must be dead on your feet. You know the way?"

"Yes. Thank you."

She lifted the sack and swept her glance around the floor beneath them. The berry in his pocket burned. Once she was gone, he took it out to look at it.

Holly berries were toxic, but not enough. It would take many to kill someone, even an old woman. He shook his head at the thought. The melody which Mrs. Pomme was still singing as she left the room bounced wordlessly in his skull and would not leave. He pondered her words to him. If a death were to occur within the year, well, that may happen for any reason. Indeed, one death in particular was to be expected, anticipated, hoped-for. He grimaced. Was he so impatient to be master of Colley Castle? Not really. But he chafed at the sentiment that was the basis of tonight's gathering, and the superstitious nonsense that was its errand. He hated it as he hated his aunt, whose fanciful writing was surely its source. When he came into his inheritance, such nonsense would cease.

He pulled out his watch: ten minutes until midnight. He listened for the sound of the other guests rising in gentle waves from the salon. He would not join them. He desired nothing more than to be alone, which he could manage. His other desire, well, that was out of his hands. Mostly.

He listened again to make certain no one was coming, then stepped like a cat over the carpet and placed the berry on a prominent bookshelf. Pleased, he saw himself into the empty hall and up the stairs to his room.

#

Richard awoke with a start to the blackness of his room. His sleep had been fitful, host to images of holly turned to green blades and its berries to blood, while song became smoke. He awoke coughing. It was three in the morning, announced by the chiming of a clock somewhere downstairs. This was the witching hour, for those accustomed to thinking in those terms. It bothered him that he even knew this.

Once the chimes faded, Richard stared at the ceiling for a few minutes before deciding that if he was going to be insomniac, he might as well do it somewhere more interesting. He pulled on a dressing gown and stepped to his door. He opened the door a crack, listened for any other movement, but heard none. Nothing human greeted him as he continued, candle in hand. His foot rocked against a loose board on the stairs. A disapproving creak echoed against the halls, which now yawned cold and empty and, he thought, hungry after the ebullience of the party. He shuddered and decided to help himself to a book from the library.

The door was ajar as he approached and he entered cautiously, his candlelight flickering across the shelves. He had a sudden need to find a fellow guest at reading, but there was not a soul in sight. As he glanced over the shelves, he noticed the holly berry he had placed so carefully was now missing. He frowned. He looked below, bent to examine the carpet. The little red ball was nowhere his eyes could see.

He smiled grimly. Doubtless Mrs. Pomme had made another pass at the library before midnight. He had to admire her industry. When he was master here, it would be put to better use.

A sort of scraping, rustling noise came from behind an armchair. His candle wavered as he called into the room, "Is someone there?" No response. But the rustling continued. He stepped deeper, looking behind furniture, breathing slowly to steady his nerves and ignoring the prickling sensation in his palms. Rats, he suspected. Perhaps they had discovered the food from the celebration and were having their own. He revised his opinion of Mrs. Pomme's industry. He left the library, but the sound followed him. He spun back so quickly the flame of his candle was nearly extinguished. In the space between shadows, he saw its fluttering light reflected back at him. Twice over.

The candle dripped hot wax onto his flesh and slid from his hands. He swore, but he was also grateful. What he had seen on the carpet, before the flame was gone, was nothing he ever wanted light shed on again. For it was not a shadow, but substance. It had glowing eyes, pointed ears, and flesh like a plucked chicken's. It was no rat. And it had smiled.

He stumbled by feeble light coming from the moon through the windows. Behind him, the scratching intensified. Feeling his way along the walls, he cursed as he struck his toe against a corner. He limped on. It would be all right, if he could get to the stairs, and from there to his room. He would be safe there, with the door between him and… that.

At last, he gained the stairs. He dared not look back as he began his climb, his feet pounding. But he had forgotten the loose board, which twisted fiendishly underfoot and threw his balance off. He reached for the banister, but his sweating hands slipped. He fell backward, landing hard on his back and head at the bottom of the stairs, his wind gone.

Once he had his breath back, he moved his limbs and found them sore but whole. He took his time before attempting to rise. He listened. The scratching noise was gone. He had imagined it. The house got to him. But it would be all right. He would go to his room and no one need know of his folly, as long as he moved quickly.

He rolled over and bumped into something clammy. There sat the creature from the library. There grew its smile. And there shone the holly berry in its claws.

#

Mrs. Pomme discovered Richard at the foot of the stairs the following morning; servants heard her scream out on the grounds. Aunt Cynthia summoned the doctor, and when he had completed his examination of the body with a sad shake of his head, he pronounced it an accidental death, the victim having fallen and struck his head. The doctor did note, with surprise, a holly berry lodged in the dead man’s throat.

Aunt Cynthia mourned her nephew for the appropriate amount of time. When she died, ten years later, she left her entire fortune and estate to a nearby theater company.

The Lake in Winter

by Emily J. Cohen

The tires of the Chevy pickup truck crunched over gravel and a thin layer of snow. The rusty beater barely crested the hill as Jen pressed down on the gas pedal. Groaning and creaking, the truck finally rumbled to a stop beside a snow-covered trailer.

The trailer looked familiar yet alien. She had been there every summer as a child, but she had never seen the pine trees of White Birch trailer park covered in snow. It covered the fire pit, the picnic table, and the barbeque grill under its tarmac.

Jen's breath misted the crisp air. The normal pine smell of Naples, Maine was subdued, buried like everything else beneath three inches of snow. She stretched and touched her toes in her warm L.L. Bean boots. It was a six-hour drive from Batesfield, Connecticut and her muscles were aching.

The lock to the trailer was stiff with ice and she had to throw her weight against the door to push it open. The kitchen was the first thing she saw, décor straight out of the seventies, faux-wood paneling and yellow linoleum floor. The kitchen table was a booth along the far wall which also converted into a bed. As a child, she slept on that bed while Laura slept on the small couch in the "living room" to the right. She had loved turning the kitchen table into a bed, folding down the pole and rearranging the cushions. The trailer was like one of those Transformer toys—everything became something else.

Inside was dark and cold. She got to work opening the propane tank and starting up the trailer's diminutive heater. Then Jen took the cleaning supplies out of the back of the truck and started dusting everything, wiping down each surface and taking cushions outside to shake them out, watching dirt and dust fall away into the snow.

As she waited for the trailer's small heater to kick in, she walked farther down the gravel road past the truck she had borrowed from her parents.

There was a deep silence to the woods, a silence she had been unable to find in Connecticut. The only sound was the crunch of her boots on the snow. There were no birds or squirrels, no sign of life at all. It felt like walking across the surface of the moon.

The Wilson's trailer came into view around a bend. There were no cars parked in front of the modern vehicle. It looked like a small house, like something out of a fairytale compared to their old ugly trailer with the sagging roof. She and Laura had played with Andrew Wilson—Andy—when they were kids. His parents had a sailboat they would take around the lake, through the lock into Sebago. Andy could swim, and fish, and start a fire. Back then, he had been tan and never wore a shirt. She had been half in love with him. She wondered where he was now, if he was married, with kids. Divorced maybe. She wondered if he remembered her.

She wondered if he remembered Laura.

The next trailer belonged to the Millers, nice people from Maryland. They had a long drive up every year to escape the heat. An older couple, they had no kids, but they had a Portuguese water dog named Sussy. She used to walk Sussy for them for a dollar. The dog would drag her all around the trailer park, wagging its black curly tail and chasing the red squirrels that were everywhere in the summer.

Sussy must have been dead by now. She hadn't seen the Millers in a long time. Perhaps they were dead, too. A lot of the trailers in the park had been owned by retirees back then. Maybe they were all dead now, their trailers mausoleums.

Past the Miller's was the rec center, a red-painted barn where the kids used to gather to tell scary stories and where she had smoked her first cigarette at age twelve. She had choked on the smoke, hacking as the others had laughed. She had even gone to third base for the first time in that building. Sitting on the back of an abandoned John Deer tractor, she had let Andy's cousin Mark put his hand down her pants as they drank White Russians with Kahlua they had pilfered from the Wilsons. They had gotten sick, succumbing more to the expired milk than the alcohol.

Jen kept walking, crunching through the thin layer of snow and ice as she passed the rec center. A gentle slope led down past a few more trailers to the beach at the edge of the lake. She paused, almost able to make out the glint of the cold water through the snow-crusted boughs of pine trees. Then she turned and headed back up the hill of the gravel road. She wasn't ready to face the lake. There would be time later.

The trailer was infinitely warmer by the time she returned. Although the heater was small, it didn't have a lot of space to warm up. Jen peeled off her winter coat and set about unpacking her bags.

She had packed light, a duffel bag of clothes, long underwear and fleece pullovers, and her laptop bag with her notes and a few novels for when she needed entertainment. There was a small television in the corner of the trailer they called the living room. It was black and white with rabbit ear antennae and a dial instead of a remote control. There would be no internet up here, and just a few fuzzy channels—news and sports, mostly. There would be little in the way of amenities.

What there would be, though, was time and solitude to work on her writing. Her memoir had sputtered out after a few dozen pages. Maybe here the words would flow more easily, among the silence and the snow, and the memories.

Here, where every rock and stick reminded her of Laura.

Jen took out a can of Spaghettios and heated it up in the microwave in one of her grandmother's old ceramic bowls. Grandma Annie had passed away four years ago. She realized she hadn't talked much about Granny Ann's passing in her memoir. She had been too focused on Laura's story. She ate while watching the television. The weather was on and the red low-pressure and blue high-pressure systems all looked the same.

After her meal, Jen took her laptop out of her bag and flipped open the screen. Her MacBook booted up immediately, illuminating the trailer more than the weak overhead light.

The words on the screen blurred together, the black of the letters against the crisp white like her black boots in the white snow. It made her head hurt and her eyelids lower. There was no point in trying to write at the moment. She was exhausted from the long drive and cleaning out the trailer.

Instead, she got out her toiletries. The trailer's bathroom was more a broom closet than an actual room. The toilet pulled out from under the vanity and had a foot pedal flush. She brushed her teeth and bent over to get her spit in the tiny sink.

It felt odd sleeping in the master bedroom at the front end of the trailer with its folding vinyl door. That was always where her grandparents had slept when Laura and Jen spent their summers in Maine. She should have changed the sheets; she sneezed at the musty linens.

She stared at the ceiling, at the skylight covered by a white blankness of snow. It reminded her of the empty page. The empty pages that had been taunting her for weeks.

Her mother had told her not to come here. That she was crazy for driving out to Naples in the snow. But she needed to be here, in the midst of the emptiness, in the midst of her past.

That was the only way she would be able to write Laura's story.

Jen drifted off to sleep just as the snow began falling again, softly covering the woods, the lake, the trailer, and her rusty pickup. Covering everything with more whiteness, more blankness.

#

The water was warm, the muddy lake enveloping them like silk as their white arms cut through the water.

She kicked hard like she had been taught, turned her head for breath, and kept her arms cutting forward urgently. Laura was ahead of her, always just beyond her reach. Laura, her younger sister, moved like a dolphin, her body rhythmic in its agility.

"Wait!" Jen tried to call, but her mouth filled up with lake water. Laura was moving farther away. No matter how fast she swam, her sister grew more distant until Jen was alone, bobbing in unfamiliar water, no land in sight. Her arms and legs were tired, leaden.

The water closed over her head.

#

Jen woke with a start, kicking off the dusty covers. Her heart was racing. With the blankets thrown off, Jen started shivering immediately. She got up and moved to check on the heat. With a sinking feeling, Jen realized the propane tank that fueled the trailer's small heater was empty. Without that tank, the trailer would soon grow too cold to be livable.

Jen sighed and pulled on her flannel-lined jeans. It seemed she would have to go into town immediately.

The inside of the Chevy truck felt somehow colder than the outside. Jen shivered as she started up the engine, turning the heat up.

The truck rattled back down the hill towards Main Street. The road was empty. She put on her blinker and turned left towards town. Across a bridge over the lock between Long Lake and Sebago Lake lay the heart of Naples. Most of the surrounding shops were tourist traps, closed for the season. There was Rick's on the

Causeway, a restaurant that served kid's meals on frisbees, and next to it the arcade where her mother used to dump her and Laura with a handful of quarters while she went grocery shopping. They would spend an hour playing Teenage Mutant Ninja Turtles or Street Fighter 2 until their pockets were empty. Connected to the arcade was the crappy miniature golf place, with its prosaic windmills and its unconvincing water hazards, just blue-painted concrete. There was the ice cream parlor and comic book shop, a few clothing stores that sold beach cover-ups and moose tee-shirts. Those storefronts were all empty and dark.

Farther down Main Street, she found a gas station with a mart next to it. Inside, an older man was reading a paper with his feet up. He didn't look up as she entered. Jen's face ballooned in the store's overhead mirror. She wondered if this place had ever been robbed. Seemed unlikely.

She grabbed some food; hot dogs, more Spaghettios, anything that was simple and would not go bad easily.

"You got propane tanks?" she asked the man reading the paper.

He pointed with the toe of his shoe out back.

As Jen paid for her supplies at the register, she paused, hand halfway to her wallet. Laura's face was looking out at her from the refrigerated section.

It was a milk carton. A face on a milk carton. Not Laura's after all, not up close. But a young woman—girl really, with the same oval eyes and upturned nose. The same constellation of freckles across the bridge of her nose. Similar but not identical.

"That's fifty-six thirty-five," the man said, annoyed. Jen pulled herself together and handed over her credit card.

With everything in the bed of the pickup truck, Jen drove back down Main Street. This time she did pass a car or two. Naples was not a ghost town. Not quite.

The truck made it up the steep hill that led into the White Birch trailer park. It was not a sure thing as the old engine sputtered and the tires flung up ice crystals and gravel. She parked as close to the trailer as she could and manhandled the propane tank over to replace the old one. Just when she had gotten the new tank hooked up, she heard the sound of an engine.

Jen looked up and wiped her hands on the back of her jeans as an SUV crested the hill. It was black with tinted windows. Rather than continue down the poor excuse for a road, it pulled up alongside her truck. The door opened and a familiar face looked out at her.

"Is that little Jennifer Crowley?" said Frank. Silver-haired Frank Carvalho was her grandfather's friend and the sort of unofficial leader of the White Birch trailer park. She had known Frank since she was a little girl. He had probably known her before she was walking and talking.

"Hey Frank, nice to see you."

"What are you doing up here? Didn't expect to see any of the Crowley gang until the season starts. Are you checking on the trailer for your parents or George?"

"No, I just needed a bit of space, a bit of quiet and thought no one was using the trailer," Jen said.

"Quiet you'll get out there all right. Quiet as the grave," Frank said, scratching his scalp. She wondered if something registered on her face because Frank immediately blanched.

"Oh listen, I heard about Laura, I'm so…"

"So what are you doing out here? You still live in Massachusetts, right?" Jen said, cutting him off abruptly. She couldn't stand the pity. Even after a year, it was still nauseating, the concerned hugs and hand pats. The condescending fucking sympathy.

"I usually pop by a couple times over the winter just to make sure there's no leaks, no vandalism, that kind of thing. I also told the Wilson's I would check on their place. Believe it or not, last autumn a couple of squirrels got into their trailer and chewed out their couch and made a nest in it. By the time the Wilsons' came back to open the trailer they had a whole family of squirrels eating their place, making nests everywhere. It was a real mess."

So the Wilsons were still alive, Jen thought to herself. She found the thought comforting. Marilyn Wilson was a sweet old lady who used to do crosswords and play cribbage with people in the rec center. Her husband Will was slightly deaf and a big marine enthusiast. He liked to watch the sailboats cross the lake, though he never seemed to go on the water himself.

Maybe if she came back during the summer, she would see the Wilsons, just older, deafer. If she came back, maybe she would see everyone. After all, she hadn't been in the trailer for years, hadn't swum in the lake for years.

Not since Laura had gotten sick.

"You know, it's not such a good idea to be out here all by yourself, a young lady on her own," Frank said scratching again, his gesture for pensiveness. Jen tried not the bristle at the gentle chauvinism. She knew Frank meant well.

"There's a nice warm Econolodge up the road a ways, should still be real quiet."

"Don't worry about me, I'm only staying for a few days. I'll head back home soon."

Frank scratched again. "Well, if you say so. I don't feel quite right leaving you out here all alone. I know your folks; don't think I could look them in the eye if anything happened to you. I might stop by on my way out to check on you if that's alright."

"Please don't worry. I'll be fine."

With that, the septuagenarian got back into his SUV and continued down the gravel path towards the lake.

The trailer was toasty with the new propane tank, though she had no idea how long it would last; the heater was not meant to be going full blast twenty-four hours. Still, she had bought two tanks at the market. She would drive back and buy more. Whatever it took.

Jen pulled out her MacBook again. For an hour or so, she wrestled with a few more pages, eking out another thousand words. She was trying to describe Laura's first swim meet.

That first meet was in Fairfield Connecticut. It was an hour's drive. Cousin Drew and a few friends came as well. Laura was nervous. She looked paler than usual, her hair tucked up in a cap, wearing not the polka dot two piece she lived in over the summer but a sleek competition uniform, blue with silver up the sides. *If I close my eyes, I can picture it still.*

No one had expected much out of Laura, the one girl swim team out of Batesfield, Connecticut. But after that first meet they all took her seriously. She came in first in free style and butterfly and third in the back stroke. Her free style was a pool best. It was the under 14 division, but already Laura had attracted the attention of college scouts.

There's a picture of us, somewhere, blurry and out of focus, hugging Laura, still wet and slippery as a seal after her last race. I remember the feel of wet denim clinging to my leg as we posed, Laura's coach gamely telling us all to smile.

Those were the days when anything was possible.

Jen leaned back from her keyboard. She needed a break. After rooting through some cabinets, she came across Grandpa George's hidden stash of alcohol.

"Good old Gramps," said Jen, taking out a few bottles of vodka, a bottle of Scotch, and Spiced Rum. She had picked up some Orange Juice at the mart and she poured herself a glass, then added an equal measure of vodka.

"Cheers!" Jen said to herself, throwing back the drink. It burned in the most delightful way, warming her up from the inside more effectively than the trailer's heater. She knew she shouldn't start drinking, it was still only early evening, but she figured she'd earned it with her five new pages.

There was a knock on the trailer door which startled Jen. She got up and opened the top half of the trailer's divided front door. She shivered immediately at the blast of cold air.

It was Frank again, of course. Smiling and scratching in the weak light of her trailer.

"Well, I'll be heading out now, just wanted to say if anything happens, I'm only a few hours away. Here's my number." He handed her a scrap of paper. "I'm closer than your folks, so let me know if anything comes up. And again, if you get too cold out here, you can always stay at that motel. The weatherman said the temperatures are going to be turning frigid soon. Maine winters are no joke. Neither is frostbite."

Jen nodded and thanked Frank. She didn't feel cold at all thanks to the vodka in her bloodstream. She stepped outside and waved as Frank's black SUV lurched and disappeared into the surrounding pine.

She was alone once more.

That night, she didn't get any more writing done. Each time she opened her MacBook her head swam and the letters didn't stay in one place. Too much vodka.

She tried watching TV instead, monochromatic Wheel of Fortune, but found her head nodding once, twice.

#

She was standing in front of the lake, but something was wrong. The colors were wrong, or rather, there were no colors. The edges of her vision dissolved into static. Snow of a different kind.

Jen knew she should be cold, but she felt nothing, not even curiosity as to why she was standing on the beach of Long Lake, looking at the winter sunlight dancing on colorless waves.

There was movement then, on the surface of the water—ripples, like muscles flexing beneath a snake's skin. And a white arm, a familiar white arm, cut through the water. It was Laura, swimming towards the shore.

Come on, Jen thought. Just a bit farther. But then the white arms faltered, the shape disappeared beneath the gray waves that were suddenly treacherous.

"Laura!" Jen called, stepping closer to the shore. "Laura? Where are you? Answer me, Laura!"

There was no sound, no motion in the water.

"No," Jen said. She took a step forward, then another. Her feet met the edge of the lake.

And now, finally, she felt something. Coldness. Wetness.

Jen stood barefoot in the snow. She blinked and looked around as the winter wind pulled suddenly at her long, dark hair. Teasing her.

She was only wearing jeans and a sweater and standing outside in temperatures in the single digits. She shivered uncontrollably, and she dashed back to the trailer. The front door had been left wide open and a fine layer of snow had blown onto the linoleum kitchen floor. Jen closed the door and locked it. She moved to the bathroom to run her feet under hot water in the claustrophobic shower. Her toes were numb at first, but the hot water hit them like a thousand knives as the sleepy nerves woke up. She rubbed her feet vigorously, trying to get the blood moving again. The skin of her toes was pruned and white, as if all the color had been leached away.

Frank had warned her about frost bite. Still, Jen was sure her toes would be better in a few hours. She moved to the bedroom to grab a pair of woolen socks from the drawers built into the side of the trailer.

When she was a little girl, Jen used to sleepwalk. Her father had to put an extra lock on the front door for fear she would somnambulate around the neighborhood. But it had been years since she had had an episode. What was it about being here that had brought it back? Was it the memories? Or being alone? Or was it simply a side effect from drinking too much of her grandfather's vodka?

That night, in bed, she pulled off the woolen socks to check on her feet. Her toes were still white, as colorless as her dream.

As colorless as the snow.

#

Her mother called the next morning. The beeping of her phone woke her up.

"Hey Mom."

"Have you frozen your ass off yet?"

"No, not yet," Jen said, moving to the kitchen to microwave a mug of water for some instant coffee.

"You know, I keep thinking about the Shining, that you'll end up like Jack Nicholson, grinning and frozen to death."

Jen cradled her cell in her neck as she spooned two tablespoons of instant coffee into her mug. "There aren't any hedge mazes here."

"Well, I still think you're crazy, that trailer is not winterized—it must be terribly cold. Listen, there's an Econolodge just a mile or so down the road. You could write there."

"So I've heard. But this is where my memories are."

"I know your writing means a lot to you, Jen, but have you ever thought that maybe it's too soon? She's only been gone a year, maybe you need to grieve and not try to relive it all."

Jen put down her cup of coffee on the kitchen table and slid into the booth that had served as her bed as a child.

"This is how I'm dealing with it, ok? We talked about it, you said you would let me find my own way."

There was a long pause on the line.

"Mom?"

"Yeah, I'm still here. I know you aren't a little girl anymore, but you don't have to deal with everything on your own. You aren't alone."

"I know, Mom," Jen said, ending the call.

But looking around the cramped trailer and seeing through the windows the snow had started again, she did feel very alone. The only living thing for miles, alone with the pine trees and the ever-falling snow.

#

The next few days Jen spent working on her memoir, slogging her way through the years and the memories. She subsisted off a diet more fitting to a college student—Spaghettios, instant ramen, and hot dogs she cooked up on the electric stove with her Granny Ann's old pans.

The writing came, but it came slowly. First, it was Laura in high school, the way her swimming career took off. The offer of a scholarship to Stamford. Jen had already been in her sophomore year at UConn but everyone was talking about Laura's scholarship to Stamford. It was in the local paper in Batesfield, alongside a black and white grainy picture of Laura in her swimsuit.

But it was when Jen tried to describe Laura's last high school meet, the day everything changed, her fingers froze over the keyboard. She had another stiff drink. There was no more OJ in the fridge, so she just drank straight from the bottle. It was too cold to face the night sober.

#

The last meet was so different from the first. We all knew now that Laura would easily take first in the free style race. So different from that first competition, when no one had any expectations at all.

The murmur was how I knew something had gone wrong. People in front of me stood as Laura's coach dove into the water. He hauled her out, her fingers bending and unbending quickly, spasmodically. Laura's cap had fallen off and her blonde hair was plastered across her face; her chest was not moving. I pushed through the crowd, nearly falling down the steps of the bleachers.

Laura was already coming around by the time I got down there. Mom was at her side, not crying, but her face tight with concern.

"It was just a cramp," Laura said. "Please, don't make a big deal, it's so embarrassing." But she hadn't looked anyone in the eye. She was lying. Laura had always been a terrible liar.

Later at home, I confronted her.

"What really happened?"

"Jenjen, don't make a fuss, ok? I'm fine," Laura had answered, calling me by my old childhood nickname. Jenjen. She hadn't called me that in years.

#

Jen leaned back from the computer, tears burning her eyes. She took a long chug of vodka, letting the burning of her esophagus distract her.

That night, when she went to sleep, she stacked her backpack in front of the door to the trailer. It was going to be below zero out there tonight. Too cold to wander around.

Under the covers, Jen waited for sleep. The trailer's heater was no longer keeping up with the dropping temperatures, and she hugged her knees for warmth. She would need to pick up a space heater if she was going to stay, or she really would get frostbite. She checked on her toes and they were still pale, but a bit more flesh-colored.

"Laura," Jen said aloud to the snow-covered skylight. She thought about that day, seeing her sister's prone body, pushing past strangers to get to her, to see if she was alive or dead. The way her wet hair stuck to her face, how deathly pale she looked.

As she shivered beneath the covers, she could almost hear her sister's voice in her ear, calling her Jenjen.

#

It had been days since she'd spoken with her mother and she hadn't talked to another living soul since. Her life consisted of waking up, having a cup of bitter instant coffee, and working on her memoir. She would go for a walk before lunch, then she would work on her memoir again with the television blaring out monochromatic news, or weather, or sports. She would stay up late at night, drinking vodka to take the chill off until she passed out more than fell asleep. The last two nights she had fallen asleep on the couch rather than the bed. She woke disoriented, her mouth cottony, and the cycle repeated itself.

The first thirty pages had been easy enough to write: their childhood, their summers in Maine. Now, though, she was getting into it, finally. She was writing about the moment they got the diagnosis at Temple Hospital in New Haven. That first incident at the swim meet was not the last, of course. Since that fateful day, Laura had fallen several times. Her knees buckled unexpectedly and with little warning. Her hands began spasming more frequently. Some days she was fine, other days she couldn't walk half a mile. Laura, who was as fit as some professional athletes, couldn't walk a mile without her legs giving out, couldn't write her name with how her fingers trembled and her hand clenched up.

We had been sent to several specialists, ping ponging around the state, desperate for an answer. Training, of course, had been postponed, and we hadn't contacted the people at Stamford. We were sure there would be a simple answer, an easy solution, a potassium deficiency, something like that.

Doctor Parik was kind and warm to us. He welcomed us into his office and ran through a battery of tests. After a week, he called us back. As soon as we walked in and I saw his face, I knew it was bad. The whole family sat there in his office, Mom, Dad, and Laura. I stood in the corner feeling like an interloper.

"Whatever it is, we'll face it together," my mom said, stubbornly dragging us all around to each of the specialists. I had midterms to study for. I missed classes, missed seeing my friends. I felt put out. How selfish I was then, looking back on it now.

"So, what's the verdict?" my dad asked, jokingly.

"We have a diagnosis," Dr. Parik said.

There was some sense of relief that we would finally know what was going on.

"It's not what we were hoping for, but it's important to move forward with every possible treatment," Dr. Parik said. We could tell he was stalling, not wanting to say it. Finally, he took a deep breath. "It's ALS."

At the time, to me, ALS was a string of letters that meant nothing. My parents knew, though, immediately. My mom started crying. My father's face froze up, like he had forgotten how to look human.

But we both learned that day in Dr. Parik's office, Laura and me. ALS— Amyotrophic Lateral Sclerosis. Lou Gehrig's disease. Untreatable, incurable, completely fatal.

Laura and my mother sobbed while my father tried to ask important questions. And I—I just stood in the corner of the doctor's office, over by the cotton balls, secretly glad it wasn't me.

Jen stood up from the couch where she had the computer

balanced on her knees. She rubbed at her eyes with the back of her hands and went to the broom closet bathroom to splash some water on her face. Then the wracking sobs came, rattling her. Jen slid down to the floor of the bathroom, unable to stretch out. There simply wasn't enough room. Instead she crouched, her back pressed against the door, sobbing, chest heaving, breath coming raggedly.

"Laura," Jen said to the small wall mounted mirror over her. "I'm so sorry."

#

For a minute it was a television screen, black-and-white picture fuzzy and distorted. But then she moved through the picture until she was there, standing on the rocky shore, staring out at one lonely swimming platform bobbing on the surface of the lake.

There was wind, although it felt neither cool nor warm. It moved the boughs of the pine trees but curiously there was no sound, no gentle rustle of branches in motion.

There was no snow either; with everything in extreme black and white it was impossible to tell what season it was.

There was someone standing on the swimming raft. The figure had not been there a moment ago; it sprang into existence from nothingness. At first it was just a person-shaped blur, but then the image focused.

It was Laura. She was not wearing a bathing suit. No, instead she was wearing the hospital gown; her standard uniform in the last two years of her life. Her hair was long and unkempt, not tied up or tucked into a cap as it always had been when she went swimming.

"Laura..." Jen stepped closer to the shore.

Laura held her arms open wide, as if in prayer or exultation, then she let herself fall forward into the water. There was no sound of a splash, she just disappeared.

The surface of the lake became placid once more. No sign of a struggle, no sign of Laura trying to swim or tread water.

Jen charged into the water. There was no sensation as it rose over her ankles, then her calves, her thighs. She dove forward, kicking, propelling herself ahead.

Under the surface of the water the world looked different; blindingly white. She couldn't see anything. She reached out to find her sister—she would find Laura and use the crawl to drag her back to shore. Jen had been trained in CPR. This time, she would save Laura.

She wouldn't let her drown again.

#

Cold was the first sensation Jen was aware of. Then nausea hit. Then roughness, her hand pressed against something.

Consciousness crept up on her slowly. She was leaning against a towering pine, her palms pressed against the bark. This time she was not barefoot, but the wetness of the snow had long since soaked through her woolen socks. Jen trembled with the cold and sickness that had taken hold of her stomach.

She looked around. The last sleep walking episode had ended within sight of the trailer. This time, she was not so lucky. There was only darkness around her, the wind that whipped her hair obscuring her sight. She had no idea how long she had been outside. Her feet were numb already, but that wasn't surprising given the temperature. The forecast had said the low tonight would be eight degrees. The rest of her was not numb, just shaking uncontrollably. Not knowing which way to go, she set off boldly in one direction, hoping for the best. She had to get back to the trailer before she froze to death. Jen thought about the conversation she had had with her mother about Jack Nicholson dead at the end of the Shining, a mad grinning man-cicle. She moved faster, hugging herself for warmth.

A building loomed out at her. She moved around it until she found a door. Stumbling inside, she turned on a light switch and was greeted with a big space full of stacked chairs, old odds and ends, bits of fencing, and an old lawn mower.

It was the rec center. She hadn't walked too far then, thank God.

She turned the lights off as she left through the front door, orienting herself and heading back up the hill towards the first trailer plot.

Her Chevy was still sitting by the front door of the trailer, covered in a finer layer of snow than everything else. The door to the trailer had been left wide open.

Just as she was walking up to the door the nausea hit her again, harder this time, bending her double. Beside the front tire of a tractor, Jen heaved up her dinner. The vodka burned half as much on its second trip through her esophagus.

Jen wiped her mouth with her shirt. Too much vodka.

Once in the trailer, she shut the door and turned up the heater. Then she moved into the bathroom to soak her feet in the bottom of the shower with hot water.

"I'm so sorry," she said to her toes, massaging feeling back into them. Jen sat there for twenty minutes until the hot water and the steam had removed the chill from her bones.

She put on fresh clothes and locked the front door of the trailer again. This sleep walking was getting out of control. She could die wandering around in a Maine winter with no shoes, no winter coat.

But worse than the sleep walking was the dream. It was still fresh in her mind, the feeling of horror as Laura's body fell motionless into the lake. The panic as she tried to move through water that felt like concrete.

Once out of the bathroom, Jen wrapped herself in a comforter and sat on the couch. She was exhausted but afraid of falling asleep;

afraid she would wake up in the woods, or standing in the middle of Main Street, or in the lake. Things were starting to unravel. She was starting to unravel. It was a combination of things; being isolated, working on the memoir, drinking too much.

I should just go home, Jen thought. It had all become too much. Whatever her intentions were, it wasn't healthy to be up there by herself. The cold, the woods, the silence; it was all pressing down on her.

And there, sitting at the bottom of the hill, the lake waited for her, a crouched monster. Beckoning, waiting to devour her.

Jen flipped the television on and tried to lose herself in late night game show reruns. She tried to remain awake all night, tried to focus on Pat Sajak and Vanna White and forget about her dreams, forget about the terrible whiteness of the snow. Forget about the silent lake at the bottom of the hill.

Jen stayed up until dawn, too scared of sleep walking into a frozen lake to shut her eyes. Finally, she drifted off watching colorless infomercials.

#

Her mother called that afternoon. Jen didn't pick up the phone. The face in the bathroom mirror didn't even look like her anymore, that pale ghost with the dark circles and the unwashed hair.

She had a few packets of ramen left and not much else, but she didn't feel like going to the market. Being around other people was beyond her.

It had been two days since she had written anything. She just stared at her computer screen until the black Times New Roman type swam around in her brain.

When her cell phone battery died. Jen didn't bother recharging it. What was the point since she didn't want to talk to anyone?

On walks, it seemed like things were constantly swimming in the corner of her vision. Maybe it was the lack of sleep, or the near steady stream of vodka. Alcohol was one of the few things she was well stocked with. Sometimes it was Laura's blonde hair, or the glint of water where only pine trees stood. Sometimes it was a cruel sterile hallway, harsh with fluorescent lights. Sometimes it was the kind, pained face of Dr. Parik.

Sometimes, less often, she thought she saw her parents standing in the snow and the trees.

Jen knew it was all in her head. She knew that, but it didn't seem important. No more important than showering or putting on fresh underwear.

She could no longer tell how long she had been in Maine. Some days she was worried her mother would show up to bring her home. Some days she wished she would.

And whenever Jen actually did sleep, Laura haunted every one of her dreams, white arms beckoning to her from under the surface of the lake.

#

One morning, before the sun had risen, Jen put on her bulky winter coat and walked purposefully down to the lake.

The lake she had spent her summers in for years had morphed, mutated these last few days into something else. Not a familiar, safe place, but a lurking menace, the black epicenter of her fears and guilt. She couldn't ignore it any longer.

Jen walked down the hill, trying not to slip as she made her way through the snow that was at least five inches thicker now than it had been, no longer a mere covering. She struggled not to lose her footing.

The shore was clear of snow, the precipitation melting away to add to the already swollen lake. Ice crept up at the water line of the artificial beach.

There was a floating platform about thirty yards out from the shore at the end of the swimming area. That had been the first real test of their childhood—trying to swim out to that raft. The youngest children stayed by the shore where their feet could still touch the leafy sediment at the bottom of the lake. As children got older and more confident in their swimming prowess, they would strike out for the floating raft. It had a ladder on the far side to pull yourself up.

Laura had been three years younger than Jen but she had still reached the dock first, Jen struggling to keep up with her pale arms that cut through the water like rotor blades, even and unrelenting. Laura had always been precocious, always ahead of her time. As tall as Jen; her blonder, more able shadow.

Of course, Jen had been envious of Laura. Her early growth spurt, her confidence, the attention everyone showered on her because of swimming. Somewhere in her grief was a poisonous seed of guilt that she had wanted this to happen.

Past the snow-covered basketball courts and picnic tables she walked, rounding the shore to the boat docks. It took a moment to find her footing as she stepped onto the wooden docks that swayed with the motion of the water underneath. As a child she would race Laura down those docks, or go fishing with her father, pale feet dangling out over the water. The boards beneath her feet now rolled over the swollen waters. The lake was deceptive; it looked serene, but underneath there was frantic motion and unrealized power. It made her nervous in a way it never had as a child.

All the White Birch residents had dry docked their boats for the winter. Jen walked down the empty dock, over the skin of the water, to the boat house on the far side.

It was a big building, much like the rec center, only faded and peeling green paint covered its clapboards. It wasn't locked, as there was nothing of worth inside. A few old kayaks, a bicycle rusted beyond use. There was the Wilson's canoe, though. Jen had used it once or twice to row around Long Lake with her father, or with Laura. It was upside down and wedged under a kayak. Jen hauled it up, coughing as dust and spider webs flew up to assault her.

She dragged the small boat across the dock, wondering, as she slid it into the water, whether it was still seaworthy. The canoe rocked but did not sink. After a few moments, there didn't appear to be any water gathering in the bottom. Carefully, Jen stepped inside, nearly falling as the boat shifted under her weight.

It was colder on the water. The wind cut through her and she could feel the icy lake beneath her, the cold seeping through the bottom of the canoe and creeping into her.

Paddling slowly, deliberately, Jen made her way to the floating dock. The plan hadn't really been formed before she started paddling, but on the water she realized that was where she was heading the whole time, from the very moment she had woken up. She needed to stand there, where the ghost of Laura had called out to her and fallen into the lake.

It only took a few minutes, as the dock was only a few dozen yards away from the boathouse. She grabbed hold of the metal ladder of the dock, shocked for a moment at how cold it was in her bare hands. It was a messy process, hauling herself up onto the dock. One foot was soaked before she had clambered up. By the time she stood tentatively on the roiling swimming dock, the canoe had begun to drift away, pushed by waves towards the shore. Jen reached out to grab it, clinging to the ladder, but the canoe was too far out of reach.

She found herself stranded, alone with the lake, and the cold, and her thoughts.

Maybe this was always where she was headed. Why she had come to Maine all along. She thought it had just been for some solitude, some space to think. How untrustworthy her own mind was.

The guilt was unbearable. She hadn't killed Laura, of course. Jen wasn't self-absorbed enough to think sibling rivalry could strike down her sister with ALS. It was a fluke, a genetic game of roulette.

But it was how Jen had reacted that made her a monster. The way she had come to resent the hospital trips that pulled her away from her friends at UConn, the way she couldn't look Laura in the eye when her face spasmed. The way even at the end, she was still glad it wasn't her.

Laura should have lived. Laura was the talented one. The bright star. Why had Jen lived?

She was cold and tired. There was no finishing the memoir. No coming to terms with any of it. It was too much, and she wasn't strong, like Laura was strong, like her parents and Laura's friends had been strong. She hadn't known what to say, couldn't pretend there was a higher power, a greater meaning behind it all. Because there wasn't, it was all a lie. Laura died from ALS and for nothing.

Jen thought about the dream again. The way Laura had spread her arms and fallen from the dock. Jen had wanted so badly to dive in and save her, not to let her drown, not this time.

That was the biggest joke of all. The ALS had slowly corrupted her lungs, filled them with fluid.

Laura had drowned, on dry land, in a hospital bed. Laura the star swimmer had drowned.

Jen inched closer to the end of the dock, moving slowly to equalize her weight. Tears were rolling off the slope of her nose, dropping into the lake below, their saltiness and warmth disappearing into the cold purity of the water.

Jen spread her arms wide and let herself fall forward.

The cold hit her like a brick wall, knocking the air out of her lungs. There was no wetness, only the cold, like a knife cutting through her, wrapping itself around her in icy tentacles. She was falling slowly like snow. The world was frozen. After a few moments, the pain subsided into a paralyzing sleepiness, closing around her mind like a veil.

Her face was pressed against something soft. It was the sediment at the bottom of the lake. Here, by the dock, it was only about fifteen feet deep; she had already reached the bottom.

Some small part of her was screaming, burning—not freezing—burning for air and for the surface, but it was a small fist beating against a closed door. It meant nothing.

Jen opened her eyes. The cold sent daggers into her brain, numbing her mind. There was a dark square above her—the dock—and a small weak light overhead. The sun rising over the lake. But its light and its warmth couldn't penetrate down here.

Consciousness was slipping away, either from lack of air or from the cold. Jen was drifting away, slowly, softly. She wasn't glad to die, wasn't happy about it—but she was resigned.

Just as she closed her eyes again, she felt a disturbance in the water around her, a wake created by movement. Before she lost consciousness, she could feel something pulling her, tugging her upward.

#

The sky was white. For a moment she thought it was a dream, the sky like that crappy old TV back in the trailer. But then the pain hit her, the stabbing knives in her lungs. She turned on her side and coughed cold lake water onto the shore.

How am I alive? Jen thought. She sat up, surprised to find she still had control over her muscles. She was trembling, but she could still move, still think enough to be confused.

In her head, she could see herself, from afar, spreading her arms and falling off the dock into the frigid lake. But she couldn't for the life of her remember why she had done it.

She hadn't killed Laura. Maybe she wasn't the perfect sister, but she loved Laura. Grief, loneliness, and vodka had twisted up her thoughts.

One thing was clear now, she was very glad to be alive, even if every inch of her that wasn't numb was screaming in pain. But if she wanted to stay alive, she needed to get out of the cold.

Jen stumbled away from the lake, not even daring to look back.

#

Once back in the trailer she ran the shower for several long minutes and then stepped into the hot curtain of droplets. The pain was excruciating, worse than her white, frost-bitten toes. The tax for being alive, Jen thought. She stayed in for half an hour until her fingers had pruned. Then, she put on the warmest, cleanest clothes she had left in the trailer and packed up her laptop and the last sad remains of her food provisions. It was time to go home.

She packed up the truck, but when she hopped into the driver's seat and turned the key in the ignition, nothing happened. The engine sputtered a few times but stubbornly refused to turn over.

Jen took out her cell phone. She had no charge left. She could plug it in and call her parents, or call Frank, but they were both hours away, and she didn't think she could stay there another moment alone among the snow-covered pines. Instead, she packed her laptop and her clothes into her duffel bag and started walking.

It was only two miles to the Econolodge on Main Street. It was cold, but the sun was up, and her legs still worked. If anything, the fresh air felt good on her face, and moving for the first time in days felt liberating.

At the turn off to White Birch, Jen stood looking down. There was only a sliver of the lake below visible from the intersection with Main Street; it glinted like the blade of a knife catching the light. Jen raised a hand to it in farewell.

#

If any cars had passed her as she walked, she might have considered flagging them down, even though she had never hitchhiked in her entire life. But the road was empty save for her. Her only company was the sound of her boots crunching over the snow on the side of the road. She trudged for nearly an hour before the red neon sign of the Econolodge was overhead. Jen had never seen anything so beautiful.

The man at the reception desk looked askance at her, appearing from the woods like a phantom, but her money was green.

Jen was the only guest. The heat was blasting in her modest room. Twin beds huddled under rose-colored, starchy bedspreads. She took another shower, trying to wash the chill out of her bones. She ordered a pizza from the only place open and ate it while sitting on one of the beds.

In all honesty, it wasn't all that much better than the trailer. Except the television was in color and the heat was more effective. She was still alone. Jen did not open her laptop, and she waited until it got dark to call her mother. Her mother asked surprisingly few questions after she asked for a ride. She would pick Jen up the next day.

That night, as she lay down, Jen finally felt at ease. Memories of Laura were not draped all over that place. The motel room with its faint disinfectant smell was neutral territory.

She thought about the lake. Right before she had lost consciousness in the water, someone had been swimming towards her, grabbing her, dragging her back to the surface. Someone must have come along, some passerby must have saved her, though who else would be out there at the lake was a mystery. Was it Frank come back again to check on the trailers? Unlikely the seventy-year-old could have dove into the lake and saved her. No, it must have been someone else, someone who didn't want to stick around for some reason. But who? And why?

A memory nagged at the back of her mind; a soft voice that had whispered into her ear just as she was on the cusp of wakefulness. A familiar, feminine voice had said, "Jenjen."

Just that. Just an old childhood nickname.

Jen would have to think of it more in the morning, her mind was overwrought. Her breathing slowed, and she fell into a deep sleep, the first real sleep she had had in days.

A dreamless sleep.

The Door to Other Places

by Kathleen Palm

The jingle of my keys sounds lonely in the long hallway. I walk along the orange, blue, cream, and dark gray striped carpet. Past silent doors. Past sconces that drip a weird yellow glow down the cracked walls. Walls that try to be white, but the decayed past seeps through.

Renovated, the landlady said. And it was. Nice. Shiny. But it didn't last. A fresh layer of new wouldn't erase the old. Won't hide it forever. Won't keep it from lurking. Won't keep it from being real.

A plastic grocery bag hanging at my elbow, I stop at my door, the one at the end of the hall. Plain. Brown. The numbers 317 sit like black scars. Quiet. Uninviting.

But it wasn't always.

After my parents died, I took what money they left and moved. I didn't want their house, where the way they ignored me hunkered like monsters in every room, where their looks of disappointment haunted each corner, where their worry draped over the furniture. I needed a home, and this grand apartment building called to me, offering a place from the too many memories. It looked so nice, all freshly painted and colorful, reminding me of a long-ago happiness. A happiness I wanted back, even if it was only in my imagination.

The click of a door creeps into the silence. I glance down the hall, hope rising at the prospect of seeing someone, anyone. Of not being alone. I'm always alone. In a cubicle at work. In the store where no one acknowledges me. In the street, where people walk, but don't see.

A light flickers.

A shadow crawls across the hall.

"Not real." I fumble in my pocket to get my phone, which is always there, ready to show me the truth.

A slam.

I jump, nearly dropping my phone as I unlock it and flip to camera mode. "Not real."

Quiet clicks and creaks work down the hall toward me. The dark form stands. It grows. It reaches for me. Corinne.

The sound of my full name sends my nerves leaping from unease to pure fear. No one calls me that. No one but…

I aim my camera at it, gazing at the screen, which shows nothing but a long hall. The camera doesn't lie, a trick I learned from one of my many therapists, my last therapist, one I haven't seen for two years. Because I was coping.

I lower my phone and stand in the empty, quiet hall. Because it's just a delusion.

I juggle my keys, find the right one, and slide it into the lock.

I hate being alone.

Such a big apartment building. I thought there would be people.

I had imaginary friends for years to fight the solitude. And one of those friends was my very best friend. Always there to play, to chase away the loneliness.

Lily.

I glance down the hall, the sound of my name lingering there like a stain. Lily. Who called me Corinne, not Cori like everyone else. Corinne. Like the voice.

Strange. I haven't thought about her in so long.

A soft flutter, like paper, tugs on memories, and I look down at a black square that slides out from under the door. It wavers as if not solid, dark wisps squirming at the edges as if it will fall apart.

A note. Just like the ones Lily used to send, slipping them under doors and from under my bed.

Only she didn't. Because she's not real.

I struggle to get my phone as bright white letters twitch across the black.

Come find me.

With hands shaking, I hold my phone over the note and check the screen. Nothing. I reach to put my phone back in my pocket, but the note lingers. Threatening me. But it should be gone. I whip my phone back into place, so it can do its job. The job it always does. The camera screen shows nothing.

I close my eyes. And breathe.

Opening my eyes, I clutch my phone to my chest and look down.

The note is gone.

With a shake of my head and a shiver of hopelessness, I turn the key.

Because it's not real.

The quiet of home settles around me. Empty soda cans on the kitchen counter. The scents of dirty laundry and bitterness creep from under the rug and hang from the ceiling.

I've been so lonely lately. That must be triggering all this. My mind remembers her, remembers what she used to call me. Just as I manifested her then, I'm doing it again.

There's been more shadows lately. More voices. But they disappear when I use my camera.

Except for the note.

I shudder as memories shift in the blackness of the past. The bag on my arm crinkles, reminding me of the sweetened marshmallow-y goodness I'm about to have for dinner. My favorite.

Lily and I always had cereal. Not a memory, though, just an imaginary childhood romp.

I need to get her out of my head. Lily isn't real.

I kick my shoes off in the entry, a place defined by the back of my couch and a few hooks on the wall. The painfully off-white wall.

We had so much fun.

I pass the gray couch and the hall and head to the kitchen. The bag hits the card table, which wobbles, unsure if it can hold the box of cereal. Pushing aside the mismatched chairs, I flip on the overhead light and go to the cabinets, the white paint barely covering the old brown.

It didn't always look like this. I swear it was wrapped in happy colors when I moved in a few months ago.

Or maybe it wasn't. Doesn't matter.

A bowl. Some milk. And sugary cereal full of rainbows…

Rainbows. Like one of the Other Places. We had so many. Places filled with colors. Places where we would laugh and swing through the sky on clouds. Where we would fight dragons and sit in our clubhouse, our crooked tower.

Me and Lily. It was magical, and the best part was that I wasn't alone.

Even though it wasn't real, the memories have weight.

Taking my bowl, I sit on the couch, then reach for the TV remote. To end the quiet. To try to dispel the loneliness.

Corinne.

My fingers drag over the remote as I look at the hall behind me, where the whispery voice lingers. Years of therapy taught me not to pay attention. To understand they were just part of my imagination. To make them disappear.

The shadows were always there. The monsters. The spirits. My only friends. I could see them when no one else could; so many waiting in my closet and under my bed. And no one believed me. My parents worried. My teachers sighed. My peers giggled and pointed.

At eight years old, I was sent to therapy, to people who tried to listen, to hide their worry and their sighs.

But I didn't ignore the shades and lurking things, because without those friends, I was alone.

Maybe that's why I look now. Maybe that's why I stare down the hall. Because those past visions, images, and feelings burn bright. Those times when I had fun, fill the emptiness.

My only friends.

And Lily was the best one.

Only I was alone. I made it all up. The couch creaks as I set my bowl on the end table, then turn.

The hall stretches into shadow.

I push myself to my feet. The weight of my phone in my pocket comforts me, waiting to help, to save me.

Lily and I had so much fun. I remember it. It hasn't faded like dreams.

Ready to prove my sanity, I stomp to the hall. "She wasn't real."

I hit a switch and the two hanging lights awaken, illuminating the almost white walls, the bathroom door, office door, my bedroom door and…

My thoughts jumble into a knot of shock. That can't be there.

A door on what is… what should be a blank wall. An ornate, arched door that doesn't fit. So tall, like the ceiling is afraid of it. So dark that the light won't touch it.

But the door is familiar.

Cold oozes from it and sinks into my soul.

"Not real." I grab my phone, ready to see the truth.

A black note creeps out from under the door.

Lily? I don't say her name out loud. And there was a door, wasn't there? A door like the one at the end of the hall. One we went through. Maybe.

Or maybe not.

I was a kid. A lonely little kid. Of course I made it up. All of it. All of them.

Whispers crawl over the dark wood floor, mingling with the cold and shifting shadows. Hands shaking, I lift the phone, open the camera, and check the screen.

Just a blank wall with a crack and some peeling paint.

Relief knocks the edges off my unease. As I lower the phone, the lights flicker and go out, leaving me squinting into the shadows. Is it still there? Like the note? Or has it gone like it should?

The lights come on with a spark. And the door is there, only—Colors swirl and dance as if to enchant me. And they do. I know this door.

My door. The door to Other Places. I'd forgotten it.

The sight erases all my worry, all my need to hold on to what is real. The colors fill my soul with happiness, and I hurry to the door at the end of the hall. Laughter stumbles over a gasp of delight, of shock.

How could I forget? That door. Shiny and glittery and painted like a rainbow.

That brilliant portal appeared for me when I was six. It offered magic and an escape from loneliness, opening to countless places of my own where I could be anything, create everything. Lily and I played in all those worlds.

My fingertips hovering an inch from the door, I pause, my excitement fading to doubt, to fear, to strange blurry memories and thoughts.

Because I stopped going. Something made me embrace the notion it was all imaginary, what the therapists, teachers, and my parents kept repeating. I take a step back, readying my phone to help me hold on to reality.

As much as it feels real, it's not.

A rasp, like paper sliding over the floor, cuts the silence like a blade. Not again.

I gaze at the square shadow at my feet. Black with wispy, jagged edges and white letters that jerk and squirm as if they hurt. Letters that ask a question.

Why did you forget me?

Shaking, I pick up the note, so cold it burns my fingers. Sadness collects in every corner of me, gathering until I can't hold it in, because it still feels so real, because I want it to be real. As I cry, my tears drop onto the note with awful hisses. "Lily? I didn't forget you… I…"

Another note slithers under the door. A simple phrase in bright white.

You left me.

"You're not real!" My sobs warp the words, maybe because I don't quite believe them anymore.

Another note. Black with words so bright they scream.

Of course I'm real.

Emotion twists through my thoughts, distorting them, cutting away at the reality I cling to. It can't be, but…

What if it's real?

I stare at the notes as they sizzle against my palms. It hurts, but I don't care. I wipe tears from my face, then glance behind me. The space beyond the hall hovers as if sitting in another dimension. The edge of the couch, where I sit and watch mindless TV. My bowl on the end table. The fridge, which holds nothing more than milk and boxes of carry-out. My apartment. The lackluster paint hiding years of rot.

I don't want to be here. I don't want to be alone.

I shove my phone in my pocket, its reality a burden, then laugh, a high-pitched sound full of nerves and fear.

Because in my rainbow place beyond the door, I was afraid. But I don't remember why.

Does it matter?

If it's there. If it's not. Does it matter?

I step to it. The cold is almost unbearable, and yet welcome. What if it's all in my mind?

What if it is? It doesn't matter. As long as it makes me happy.

I put my hands on the door, the bright happy colors swirling at my touch. Glowing. Shining. Inviting. A keyhole appears in the middle of the portal, right between my hands.

A key?

Of course.

I locked it. Had to be ten years ago. I did what everyone wanted. I found friends, new friends, real friends. I lived in the world of high school. I coped just as they all wanted, then stopped going to therapy. As I navigated college, then work, the darkness returned, little by little. It followed me. I tried not to react when the shadows touched my friends. I stayed quiet when it wrapped around their heads and flowed behind their eyes.

I was only slightly surprised when, one by one, my friends faded from my life. I was only slightly sad. Then Mom and Dad died, surrounded by darkness. And I went back to therapy. Where I accepted the diagnosis, that the shadows didn't kill Mom and Dad, it was a terrible accident. That I drove my friends away. It was my fault.

But why would I drive them away? No one understood how much I did not want to be alone.

Lily was the only one who understood. But I didn't have her.

Because Lily wasn't…

The door and our adventures weren't…

I press my fingertips to the door and scream. Because it isn't real. I fought to keep the happy memories, the adventures, the fun, but finally I let the idea of Lily and the door become imaginary. I let it go, then forgot it.

But I need it to be real. I need to get out of this apartment. I need to go where there is more, where all the things I can see and hear exist. To the Other Places.

One after another, I pound my fists against the door. "Let me in."

My hands ache with the cold and the impact. "I need in." My voice wavers with sobs as I slump forward, my cheek pressing to the icy door. The colors fill my vision. "I'm sorry I forgot you."

Fire erupts in my belly. I cough and heave as pain travels to my chest and into my throat. Struggling to breathe, I stumble back and scratch at my neck. My fingers bump over sharp points as something hard moves under my skin.

Panic bites at my mind, nibbling away at every thought except my desperate need to not be alone.

My lungs burn as air won't go in or out. My gagging and retching invade the silence like unwanted guests.

Hands at my throat, I bend over, my stomach heaving. Something cold presses at the back of my mouth. I force my fingers past my lips and over my wiggling tongue until I touch metal.

My muted whimper turns into a scream as I jam my fingers farther back, slipping and sliding over the smooth surface of the object lodged in my throat. My body bends and twists as I work to get it out.

My fingernail catches on an edge. Hacking and crying, I pull. With a final heave, a long, twisted thing falls to the floor with a clank.

I stare at it. A flat end in the shape of a triangle with a spiral in the center. A thin line of black links it to a set of jagged teeth. I place my hands around my neck, still throbbing, and stare in shock.

A key.

More shadow than metal, but a key.

I can't help it. I grab my phone and open the camera, my one link to what's real, what I'm supposed to believe. And all it shows is the scratched wood floor.

So I lower my phone.

And the key remains. Of course it does. I can't stop from reaching for it, from picking it up. It's as long as my hand, heavy, and as cold as ice. A key. A key that isn't real.

My key to my door.

A door that isn't there.

I put my phone in my pocket and look behind me at what I hold onto as reality. The terrible loneliness that I would rather not be real.

A scrape. A whisper. I look down at the base of the door as a note appears.

Come play in the tower.

With a cry of excitement and uncertainty, I slide the key in with a click. The tower. All that matters is to find my friend.

The door opens without a sound. Glowing dots of color slip out from beyond to creep and crawl over the floor...over my feet.

With nervous laughter, I walk into the light, into the huge round room of the tower, ready to leave the sad apartment, to leave the nights of staring at the TV, to leave the silence of just me. I forgot my friend, but I found her again, just when I needed her.

Glass windows sparkle in every color. Statues of unicorns and faeries and cats sit around the edge of the first floor. As an eight-year-old, I loved old castles, where I imagined knights clanking in their armor. Shadows lurk at the edges of the brightness, but I ignore them. Lily, my friend, waits for me at the top. I know it. I rush up the stone stairs, around and around the curved walls of the tower, my hand sliding and tapping along a railing made from twisted tree branches. Out the windows, the world is full of rainbows, colors of laughter and friendship. Glowing lights dance in the sky. The world I created in my mind.

But it isn't real.

A burning tightness sits in my chest. I reach for my phone, a habit created over the years. As I slide my fingertips along the smooth edge, my urge to check what's real lingers like a red-hot coal in my mind.

I struggle to breathe as I race up and up, as my mind screams for me to retrieve my phone, to use it. My lungs burning, I don't grab my phone. I can't. I won't.

My fingers spasm in disbelief. Empty hand pressed to my chest, I pause at the top of the stairs and stare at the handle of the great door guarding our secret place.

"Corinne." Made of ice, the hollow voice creeps under the door. The frayed, black corner of a note trembles.

I slide it out, the jagged letters jerk and convulse.

Don't ever leave me again.

"I didn't mean to…" Did I? Why did I leave this wondrous place?

I have a vague memory of running, of not wanting to go back, of being scared. I stare out the window. Scared of what? Rainbows? Fun? A friend? Whatever it was, I left. I stopped believing and locked her away. With a trembling hand, I touch the door. Maybe not a door at all, just a wall in my apartment.

I give the door a push and it opens with a sharp cry. I step into our circular room where secrets linger, stuck to the rough stone and wood. They whisper from the darkened edges. They crawl through the cracks and seams.

Comfy chairs surround bright-colored tables with games. Dazzling chandeliers hang from the tall ceiling, sending dancing lights on the walls and floor. Suits of armor stand in line with swords and spears and shields decorated with my drawings.

Because knights are better than princesses.

We became the best of friends, Lily and I. Except, it was only me sharing secrets. Only me wishing and hoping. Only me.

Because Lily isn't real.

But she must be.

The colors flicker. Out a window, cracks form in the sky, black jagged marks that cut across my dream. The color drains away.

The crystals in the chandeliers turn black, dripping with goo. The tables break, falling over, spilling moldy game pieces. The knights rust, their beautiful armor eaten away.

This is not what I made, but I remember this. The black. The cracks. The strange place lurking underneath my world of happiness.

The place that made me let my parents and therapist convince me…

That it's not real.

And I ran from it.

Shadows gather at the windows and spread down the walls and floor.

A whimper drips from the darkness, as if caught in cobwebs from years of neglect. The soft sound sharpens into a shriek as a figure steps into the room. Not steps, but floats. Her toes drag on the stone floor.

She's pale. So pale. Her neck crooked. Her eyes black holes. Her mouth open as she screams. I reach for my phone, so it can show me that it's not real. Please don't let it be real.

"Hello, Corinne." The voice is just as I remember. Soft and lilting like a song. A voice coming from the ghastly thing in front of me.

"Lily?" It can't be. I step back, fear dropping like hailstones in my gut. That's not the Lily I remember. Always smiling. Eyes bright and filled with fun. Brown hair in a long braid. I put my hands out to stop her as she hovers closer and closer. "I'm sorry." My apology bursts like fire into the cold gray of the room.

I stare at the odd version of my friend. My imaginary friend. And I remember when I first saw her. How she hovered in my closet and skulked under my bed with all the others, but she was different. She emerged from the shadows to be the best friend I wanted, to show me the most fantastic things. "You showed me the door."

Like in my apartment, the first door existed in my childhood home. The portal stood tall and dark, an entry to an empty void. One I painted. But like old buildings, paint doesn't cover the stains that spread and rot.

"You needed me. And I needed you." Lily groans, her hollow eyes staring. Her musical voice gone.

"Needed me?"

"You can see the door."

"I can."

"And you can open it… pass through it." Lily spreads her fingers, the tips long and black. "Then you left. Without warning. You left me and locked the door!"

I locked it. I ran from here and let it become mere imagination. Because the darkness broke through my place of joy and friendship, the decay and terrible evil showed itself. Maybe it was always there. When I was six and seven, I didn't care. But at twelve, I saw it. Really saw it. And I ran.

I tremble as the tower shakes, the walls cracking and crumbling. The Other Place wails as if in pain.

Lily grins, wide and wicked. "But you couldn't keep me away."

I back up until I hit the wall. "I just wanted to not be alone."

"And I needed you to be alone."

But I wasn't. For a while, I wasn't. "You drove my friends away."

"How could you return to unlock the door if you didn't need it?"

I glance out the window. The lights are gone, swallowed by clouds that burn and rumble. I turn to Lily. "Who are you?"

She floats closer to me, her fingers twitching. "I want out. You were supposed to let me out."

"Out?"

"I died trapped in the dark." Her voice echoes through the room, filling it with ice. "And I'm still here!"

She used me. All I wanted was a friend. To escape the world where I was nothing.

Or maybe it's not real.

I reach for my phone, again. Hands shaking, I hold it up. The camera shows darkness. What is the place beyond the door?

I don't want to know. And I don't want it to be real.

I run down the stairs. The cold nips at my heels.

Lily's shrieks chase me. "I won't let you leave without me."

I stumble to the bottom of the tower, the exit a dark blur through my tears. Still trying to escape. Still alone, and maybe trapped in my mind.

Because it's not real. Except I don't believe that.

Lily's raspy laugh trips down the stairs. Her long fingers scrape along the walls. "You need me."

Maybe. Maybe I do. But she's not the Lily I remember, not the friend I want.

The door. I need to get to the door, get through, and lock it. To dismiss what I know—think-is real.

I slam against the door, a thing of ice, a slab of darkness.

Lily screeches and howls. "You shouldn't have locked me in. I was your friend."

I glance over my shoulder. At Lily, a twisted version of the girl I knew. She reaches for me, her face a mask of anger and determination.

I turn back to the door as her cold fingers stretch over the back of my neck. Her roar of victory moves to inside me. I hear her in my head. I feel her moving in my thoughts, changing them. All those years. Had she planned this all along?

Maybe. But then I left and didn't return.

I push against the door, which opens without a sound.

"You'll never be alone again." Her voice echoes in my mind, darkens my thoughts.

I fall through the door with a sob and turn, looking at Lily's black eyes and screaming mouth. Her voice fills my head. Her hand clutches my neck. I struggle to pull the door shut, pushing her away. It closes with a boom, cutting through her arm, which disintegrates.

With hands pressed to the door, I search for the key to lock her in.

There's no key. No keyhole.

I press my forehead to the cold door. I can't lock her in.

But she's not real. So it doesn't matter. And I'm home.

But wasn't I always home?

I slide to a seat at the base of the door.

But my dim hallway doesn't stretch out before me.

Under a swirling sky, black ground falls away at my feet, dropping to a landscape of fire and shadows. A hoard of creatures crowd on the cracked rocky mass. Twisted horns and black claws. Yellow teeth and red eyes. I know them. They used to talk to me. Now they snap and growl. Lily let me cover the darkness with my colors and light, lured me here with my dreams come true. Like a coat of white paint on ancient walls. Like a mantra of "not real" to chant when sanity is questioned. Like a friend to chase away the loneliness.

But they're… "Not real." My voice is small. But I put all my longing and hope into the words.

My phone still clutched in my hand, I stretch out my arm.

Through the camera lens, my quiet, lonely home waits. The dim hall. The edge of the couch. My cereal bowl. I fall back, collapsing against the door, and flip the camera's view. Me. Me leaning against a blank wall, the white paint peeling to show the color of the past.

But when I lower the phone, I see them. The monsters.

"You're not real."

Bringing my device to my face, I stare at the image of home on the screen.

That's where I am. I'm huddled in front of a blank wall at the end of the hall.

Maybe I can believe I'm there.

Alone.

Except I'm not. Because they're real.

Hello, My Name is Goya Wyeth

by Evelyn Maguire

I am writing this letter so that whoever may find it may know the truth of what happened to me. I am from Chadds Ford, Pennsylvania. I am seventy-five years old, and will turn seventy-six on Tuesday, although I fear I will be dead by then. Murdered, as it happens.

Here are the facts: Beginning a few months ago, I started to receive a barrage of strange letters. These missives escalated in the past few weeks to strange items left on my porch. Final-ly, this morning, I woke to a horrendous discovery—evidence that my stalker had entered my house in the night. So, I've taken my cat Enoki and fled to my old cabin here, where I presume you will discover this letter.

For the purpose of your subsequent investigation:

THINGS I KNOW ABOUT MY STALKER

1. My stalker is a woman. I know this is unusual, but read through the strange correspondence I have received (find the letters enclosed with this box) and I'm sure you will concur with me on this point. On that note, smell the letters themselves. It is possible that they will have lost their potency by the time you find my corpse, but I tell you that upon their deliverance they were perfumed with rose oil; a hint of sandalwood.

2. She… Perhaps I will suggest a name for my stalker. When we name things, we expose them to scrutiny, wouldn't you agree? Before my retirement, I was a biologist, more specifically a mycologist, the majority of my career spent as a field classifier of fungus, and so the art of naming holds a great deal of significance

for me. Once we can label something, once we can classify its subgenus, once we can understand its specific nomenclature, then we can anticipate its subsequent behavior. So, were I to classify my stalker I would take into account these attributes:

i. A pleasant smell, as aforementioned by the scenting of the letters.

ii. A delicate touch, as evidenced by my peaceful sleep while she entered my home and rearranged my belongings.

iii. Increasing potency as exposure is prolonged, as evidenced by the increasingly volatile nature of her communications.

And so, with those attributes in mind, I will name my stalker Amanita suaveolens, combining the poisonous genus with the subgenus of an unassuming, yet pervasive tooth fungi, quite known for its pleasant, soapy smell. That name is a bit of a mouthful, of course, and so we may call her Amma, colloquially.

3. I fear Amma is someone from my past, or someone I've come into contact with through mutual acquaintances. In her letters, she frequently mentions aspects of my life, from my childhood to my collegiate years to my current, advanced age that seem impossible for a stranger to know. How could she possibly know these hazy details of my past? I suppose it's your job to discover that, investigator.

4. I suspect Amma lives nearby to my Chadds Ford house, for how else could she have become so interested in me? Proximity breeds interest, and, in some instances, resentment.

While I've been writing you this letter, dusk has fallen on my cabin and must confess I am nervous. Even Enoki is anxious, tail flitting as he sits upon the window ledge and looks out for Amma. Will she come? Will she follow us hours into the Poconos mountains? My instincts tell me yes. Perhaps it will take her some time to locate us, but she will come. She will.

#

It is morning. No news of the night, apart from the realization that the lock on one of my windows has rusted to the point of snapping off when I tried to secure it. I note that here so that you may consider the compromised point of entry in your reports. For my own part, I will attempt to secure the window by utilizing plywood as a wedge, and, as added security, applying duct tape along the edges. Only time will tell if my defenses will hold. I have enough food here to last me for at least a week, perhaps two if I venture into the attic. I have the faintest memory of my husband Howie storing cans up there. Cans of what, who could say. He often bought things in bulk.

It's cheaper that way, Goya! He always told me when I nettled him about it. In the basement of our Chadds Ford house you could find hundreds of bars of soap, enough cat food to keep all the strays of Istanbul fat, mountains of individually wrapped toilet paper rolls arranged like a marshmallow castle, a gallon drum of mustard from which Howie would scoop out globs of the Dijon to refill our small squeeze container. He was funny like that, my Howie. An unusual compass of practicality.

Howie died, of course. That's the way these things happen. He was old. There isn't much more to the story than that; he was old and his kidneys were old, and one evening they failed and now I live alone. No children. Perhaps it's important for you to know that, as I'm sure someone will be tasked with calling my next of kin upon the discovery of my murdered body. And who should be called? I suppose my brother Blake would care to know. I hope the notoriety of a murdered sister will boost his book sales. Perhaps he could even take up writing the tale of my demise. I expect the story would be quite the thriller. Yes, in fact, please do send this letter along to Blake after the police are through; I'm sure it will help with his writing.

But back to the matter at hand. Since Amma is still making her way towards the cabin, I find myself with more time to clue you in to this mystery.

I suppose the thing to say on the topic of the letters is that they began arriving on a very momentous day. Whether Amma was aware of the occasion is unclear. I received the first letter on May 27th, the anniversary of Howie's death two years prior. I was returning from the market—I like to walk, it's only a half-mile and the path takes me past this ancient oak with a very interesting slime mold—and upon my return, there was a slim envelope resting on my welcome mat. No stamp. It was placed there while I was out, not mailed.

On the envelope it read: Ms. Goya Wyeth. Now this was interesting because Wyeth is my maiden name; to everyone in the neighborhood who knew me, I had been Mrs. Goya McManus for forty years. Queer, then, for this missive to be addressed in such a fashion, and so I opened it at once, right out on the porch, the sweating milk bottle left forgotten at my feet. I won't recount the whole letter here, but I would care to call attention to two lines.

First, the very first sentence: It has come to my attention you could be in want of a friend.

What an unusual way for a person to write! So formal, it leads me to believe that Amma is well educated, and perhaps of an age similar to myself. Furthermore, the statement "It has come to my attention," invites a shiver down one's spine—for she has been watching! Watching when and how? My trips to the market, always alone? Is that all? Or had she been observing closer—very little mail outside of the electricity bill, no guests to speak of, or even closer still—her face pressed up to my window, noticing that I cook dinner for one, take weeks to work my way through a single wine bottle, watch the same three films over and over for comfort. And to suggest that she, this unnamed letter-writer, could be a friend to me… how curious.

Second, the signature: Sincerely yours.

Of course, there was no name after the signature, but that's not the only unusual tidbit. Sincerely yours is how Howie, without fail, would sign his own letters. Whether to his mother, or to the bank, or in Valentine's Day cards to me, you would always find: Sincerely yours, Howie. What do you have to say about that, investigator? I suppose it could be a common enough sign-off, but all these details taken together—the date of the letter's arrival, the peculiar knowledge that I was alone, the lack of a name, and the use of my late husband's phrasing? I knew at once I had a stalker on my hands.

That's all for now. I'm going to make myself lunch. If these are the last words written, I would like it to be noted (for the purpose of Blake's novel) that my last meal will be a can of albacore tuna, two pickles, and saltine crackers.

#

Dusk again. Still alive, and no sign of Amma, although I anticipate we will see evidence of her pursuit by dawn. Where did I leave off?

The letters signed Sincerely yours continued for a few weeks, arriving every third day. I was growing more and more unsettled as they grew more and more specific to my life, although I must admit a part of me enjoyed a little thrill seeing them on my mat, waiting for my notice, much in the way we enjoy a scary film or a rollercoaster reaching its peak before the fall. I tried to catch Amma in the act; I would wait by the upstairs window, hidden by my curtain, peering down over my front stoop to spy on my stalker. But she was too clever for that.

After the first few missives, I decided to write back. I enclosed my letter in an envelope and left in on my front mat in the same way I was receiving her correspondence. I wrote to Amma that I did not understand how she could know so much of my life, and that I viewed her intrusions as unscrupulous and bordering on eerie. The next morning, my letter was gone, and in its place, a package. Hesitant, but far too curious, I brought the package inside. Curiosity killed the cat, Goya! Howie would've reminded me. But what is a scientist if not curious?

Investigator, did you know that fungal spores make up the largest percentage of living particles in the air? In fact, did you know that fungi produce fifty megatons of spores each and every year? And that the weight of said megatons is equivalent to five hundred thousand blue whales? All around you are fungal spores and I bet you've never even spared them a passing thought. It was much the same with Howie, never interested in the most fascinating life-forms on this planet—which reside in neither the animal nor plant kingdom!—nor in what I had to say about them. But fungi are in a class all their own. Most people, when they think of fungi, simply think: mushroom. A mushroom is, in fact, just the fruiting body of a fungus; it is merely the fellow who answers the phones for an exceedingly complex office building. Now, that's not to say that fellow can't be dexterous, for he could be a balm to your ailments or a quick ticket to a violent end. I apologize for this tangent, but you'll see how it relates in a moment.

Back to the package. With a sharp knife, I sliced through the packing tape and carefully opened the cardboard. Out slid a sealed plastic baggie. I opened it and turned it upside down, and can you imagine what came out? To the untrained eye, it would appear as though someone had sent a delectable gathering of common field mushrooms worthy of sautéing in butter and serving up alongside a ribeye. But I knew what they were at once—Amanita bisporigera, also known as the Destroying Angel mushroom. Elegant white stalks, milky gills and an ivory skirt near its top. It looks quite like a fairy's parasol. Just a pinch ingested and death is a near certainty. Following consumption, symptoms of poisoning begin to appear in six to twenty-four hours in the form of violent vomiting and suffering extreme stomach cramps. Because of the delay, doctors often don't ascribe the symptoms to a fungal poisoning but rather to a more benign stomach flu.

If the victim is well hydrated, there is a honeymoon period of remission, where the symptoms lessen, usually inviting a hospital discharge. The victim may even be driven home, tucked into bed, unwittingly ensuring death later in the night when the lethal fungus returns for its final act. Organs shut off one by one, typically one step away from a coma—an eternal sleep, which, to an untrained eye, could appear as peaceful as a midday catnap.

The mushroom told me a few things: First, I knew for a fact that Destroying Angels grew on my very property. I had classified them years ago sprouting up underneath a fallen tree and periodically checked up on them. I felt sure these mushrooms were from that very cluster. Amma had been lurking through my woods, sampling knife in hand. Second, Amma knew I would be able to classify such a mushroom immediately, and so their delivery certainly was not intended as a murder attempt. What was it then? A warning.

I've poured myself two fingers of whiskey which I've discovered in the cabinet above the stove. Howie must've put it up there. Howie had a kind heart, that's the truth, but when he had a drink… No use ruminating over the past. I am aware of the fact I am writing this letter for two reasons. One, of course, is to provide as much context to my murder as possible so that you may apprehend Amma. But secondly, I must admit that writing to you, investigator, is calming me during what must surely be my last few days spent breathing. A chore is a blessing, Howie would always say—idle hands and whatnot.

I've never been much for writing. That's probably the biggest reason my career in mycology never led to much more than an offhand mention in someone's thesis, no major publications to speak of. I was never invited to guest lecture or lead a research team. Well, that and Howie. I guess there's no harm in saying it, now that he's gone. Howie impeded my career. Whenever there was a conference I should've attended, Howie came down with a fever. If a colleague asked me to join on a paper, Howie reminded me of all that needed to be done at home. Once, not so long ago, I was offered a teaching position at my alma mater, but to move across the country was inconceivable to Howie—never mind that he was already retired. Even my own experiments, my own inquires which I conducted at home, had to be done outside, or in the garden shed if it were chilly, as any sight of my research in the house sent Howie into a fit. More than once I found my specimens in the trash, I thought it was dirt, Goya, how was I supposed to know? Of course, when the house was actually dirty, you wouldn't find Howie cleaning it. Oh my. The whiskey has gone to my head, I'm afraid. Howie was a good man at his heart. Truly, he was.

#

Amma is here. Not in the cabin, not yet, but she has made her presence known as I knew she would. This morning, after checking all the locks on the doors and windows and finding them unmolested, I believed myself to be in the clear. It was not until Enoki starting sniffing and meowing at the front door that it occurred to me to check outside. There, lying on the front porch, a letter. My heart turned cold, investigator, my hands started to shake. I did something quite unlike myself: I walked back inside, grabbed my pack of matches from the drawer, picked up the letter, slim as usual, addressed to Ms. Goya Wyeth, and I struck a match and lit it on fire! As it burned on the stoop, I called out: "Are you happy now? Show yourself! I'm not afraid of these games any longer! If you want to talk, then let's talk!"

My hands still shake as I write, pardon my messy penmanship. Of course, there was no answer, for Amma operates in the shadows. I locked the doors and checked the broken window. Secure. I suppose I should tell you, while I still have time, of the final incident, the one that sent me running up here hoping to delay the inevitable. Amma's letters and packages were becoming more and more alarming. Following my reply asking for the letters to cease, her writing had departed from its friendly, if overbearing, tone to one drenched in accusation and threats. In one such letter (see letter labeled 16 included in the box) she alluded to her reasoning for pursuing me—claiming, terribly, that I had something to do with Howie's death. Her exact turn of phrase was: The guilty will not live free.

Now, how could she make such a claim? Howie's death, though sudden and rather disturbing in its nature, had never been investigated for any foul play, and even if it were, how could this person, this Amma, assume it had anything to do with me? Feeling quite distraught after this letter, I took a sleeping pill and fell into a fitful sleep. But oh, if only I could've remained asleep. Picture this, investigator: where the night before I left an orderly home, that morning I found all of Howie's stockpiled items strewn around. In the kitchen, paper towels and soap and toothbrushes and shampoo. In the foyer, green beans and canned corn and black olives and piles upon piles of Spam. Peeking out of the closets, batteries, gallons of water, drums of motor oil, biscuits and fruit preserves. I shrieked. I was beside myself. Not waiting to see if Amma was still in the house, I picked up Enoki, my car keys, and now I am here. Waiting… for what? My own death? I suppose so. I suppose it is inevitable.

I have helped myself to more of Howie's whiskey. If it is indeed soon to be my end, I may as well try to understand the appeal it held for him all those years. You may be wondering, investigator, why I haven't phoned the police to report Amma. I've been wondering that myself recently.

These past fraught weeks have invited much self-reflection. As a little game to pass the time, I started to consider how I would classify myself if I were a fungus in need of naming. I believe my own mushroom may be defined by rapid growth following a long period of dormancy. For years, the Goya mushrooms lay paralyzed, shrouded in too much shade, given too little water. But now, it is as though a cloud has passed, and my stalk shoots up; new attributes are sure to follow, and if one such newly developed attribute is a bulb of poison, is that so wrong?

Investigator, I must stop writing. I feel a cold draft coming from the hallway. I fear the window has been compromised. Please forward these notes to Blake and take care. Don't trouble yourself over my fate. I am sure it was quite inevitable.

Like-Minded

by Cindy O'Quinn

The edges of my life were there as a form of protection; window dressing for those who kept their eyes on me, odd little Yarley Stone. A girl so small, I never concerned myself with being chosen for games requiring much strength. It was just a trick I played on their minds to hide what actually lived inside of me.

Beyond those decorative edges, my life often bled, undisguised. I heard older girls than me refer to the bleeding time as the 'Red Rooster'. I wasn't sure if it was the same thing I was experiencing. I had my doubts, so I kept it to myself like the other things I found which differed from children my age.

I learned to live in my world, divided. Years would pass before I knew there was something more than everyone else, and me, the other.

It was dead of winter; the time I didn't notice just how cold I was until the blood which streamed from my eyes froze on my cheeks and around my nose. I couldn't breathe, so I opened my mouth and tried to scream. Exhaling air that was dense as frozen steam. Death tried to take me like an early frost on fruit, not yet prepared to be someone's food. I told no one, not Momma or Poppy or Brother Alex. I couldn't swear it actually happened.

I remained quiet. Some people ate their entire weight in pies. I desired to eat my weight in silence and savor every morsel without guilt or bloat. Most people talked, even when they tried not to. That's how dumb kids my age behave. Some adults, as well.

Silence was something I considered beautiful, almost sacred. It caused me to choose my words carefully, no need for frivolity. I made my needs known, and they were met. Return to silence made all the sooner. There was more than enough chatter inside my mind which was out of my control. I looked ahead for a day when I did have control.

I knew I was unlike most, but I nurtured my otherness. No one else did. Classmates avoided me, and my family pretended all was as it should be in our quaint home. I was fairly certain Momma and Alex were afraid of me. They stared only when they felt it safe to do so, but I saw them. The look of horrific confusion bubbled in their eyes as if I was a yet to be identified primate. I was otherness personified.

Nights were welcomed. My room was lit by one lone candle. I was protected by collected pebbles and stones arranged in a horseshoe just beneath my bed. An authentic dreamcatcher slowly turned above my head, moved along by the occasional breeze pushing its way through the window screen. I watched for the candle to flicker three times in a row, beneath the framed portrait of a redhead with skulls placed near her small feet. That was how I knew it was safe to sleep. Most people have rituals to be one with sleep, don't they?

After surviving high school, I was tempted to cry out for help. It was what I learned in Abnormal Psychology I, which pushed me to do so, knowing it was a mistake, especially in my family. It was a self-diagnosis after barely touching on the subject of mind illness during the last quarter of school. The puzzle pieces fit. I knew if I didn't get help, I wouldn't return to myself. Was there ever a time when I was myself? Haven't I always been—other?

I was slipping into the murkiness of insanity. "Should I let it be?" I answered the question but kept it to myself.

It came natural for me to seek out the like-minded. I was intelligent beyond my years, according to all the tests. But, at the same time, I knew there was something wrong with me. I was unwell in mind, if one could make sense of that. Please, do try to keep up.

So, I became educated as a psychiatric nurse and planted myself among—you guessed it- the like-minded. It was the one place where I could safely observe those who were unwell like myself and gain the inside scoop on how best to treat or even cure that which ailed me. The bad thing which kept me separated from everyone else had a name.

Mental Illness.

I did not seek treatment or allow anyone to know of my problems, because it would have been frowned upon by my family and their circle of friends. I considered myself smarter than any disease or disorder that invaded my person. I knew without a doubt I would win. It was easy to blend with the afflicted, regardless of the authority I held over them. And, of course, the blinding white uniform I wore, which let people know I was not one of the others. The afflicted.

There was only one mirror in the facility, and I passed it every day I worked. It hung just inside the lobby doors, so employees and visitors alike could stop and primp. As for myself, I avoided looking in the long-outdated mirror. Smoke and mirrors.

It was the building itself which caught my attention. The Luca Ciotti Asylum, built in 1896, was named not after a psychiatrist, but after the architect who donated the land and drew up the blueprints, free of charge. His wife suffered from illness of the mind, and he wanted the very best facility for her, so he helped construct it.

The asylum was five stories high, not counting the small attic room, which was thought to have been Luca's room, so he could be close to his wife at all times. It was my favorite room on account of the window; a bull's eye window with cobalt blue glass at its center. I imagined it to be the color of Mrs. Ciotti's eyes. It was the only room with normal eight-foot ceilings. The rest of the asylum had twelve-foot ceilings. Was that wasteful, or did the architect know that cramped spaces increased anxiety, especially for the paranoid?

I eventually acquired a key to that room and spent my dinner breaks there. The sun and moon hit the window's center and cast a spray of blues across every part of the room, which I felt in my soul. A rollercoaster ride for the mind much better than psilocybin mushrooms or an acid trip.

I learned all I could about the people within the asylum who were so like me, yet they were in a mental institution and couldn't simply clock out at shift's end and go home. It was their secret language I had yet to decipher. Don't look so fucking surprised, of course they have their own language, just like all other groups of people.

I knew if I learned the language, I could pull myself out from under the darkness which harnessed my will and kept me from happiness. Bystanders who observed only noticed a twitch here, a tic there, or maybe continuous movement of a hand or finger, a grunt, or a bleep. Those things combined made up their language. Being a fast learner, I had no doubt I would catch on quickly. Always have. Always will.

There were occasions when lessons were taught. The strong hands of my past kept me from falling on some mishaps. Most lessons were learned the hard way. Some of the rules abided by were written in blood. I considered myself lucky during those times when the blood spilt wasn't my own.

Just as when I was a child, I kept all my anger inside of me, hidden from my family. The anger became deceptive as it tried to find its way out. It grew razor-sharp claws and had a stinger on the tip of its tail. One layer at a time, it began slicing its way free. I was where I needed to be, to be kept safe. My surroundings of the like-minded served as my private laboratory. My disease hidden among those like me. Yet, I came and went as I pleased.

The wheel of the year turned four cycles by the time I knew their language well enough to speak it forwards and back. Both ways necessary, because the like-minded were that advanced. Had you been paying attention, you would have known that already.

I looked at the other nurses gathered around the doctor and allowed the sonder to sink inside of my very being. I didn't care about the complexity of their lives, because they were unlike me. They were frivolous and unknowledgeable when it came to the depth of knowing.

My angst was no longer stomped upon as though it burned like a wildfire. I was allowed to let the feelings simply flow and be true to their creator. Me. The like-minded knew I held their secrets and left me be. I continued to do my time among them and learned who was faking and who was not. I often pondered the idea of letting the like-minded free, but thought it a dangerous idea that would lead my family to really see me.

It was time to move on with my life, free of my family, and free to control, if not cure, my disease. I contemplated whether to apply for the Nurse Manager position at The Boston Institute of Mind Ailments. I laughed at the name. Gone were the days of asylums and sanatoriums.

The bell rang at Luca's door. All the staff knew I spent my lunch hour in Mr. Luca Ciotti's room. They usually left me in peace for that one hour. Some days were trying indeed. I called for them to enter and turned to see who the invader of my quiet reflection was.

Mother, Father, and Alex stood in the hall looking more confused than I was to see them.

"Oh my! This is quite out of the ordinary! Is there some family emergency which brought you all to my place of employment in such a disruptive manner?"

Mother stepped forward and started to explain, but Father put a firm arm on hers, and she stepped back.

"Darling, we always come to see you on Sundays!" he said. "It's the only visitation day which coincides with my day off from work. And you know Mother doesn't like to drive alone. Alex has his hands full with work and his own family."

A fellow nurse walked by, pushing a patient in a wheelchair. All I could focus on in that moment was the state-assigned, mint-green hospital top and bottom the patient wore. It held that morning's oatmeal stains down the front. I felt disgusted. It forced me to check my crisp white uniform, out of habit, to make sure it was spotless, as always.

My mind screamed as that putrid, fucking mint-green color echoed back at me like a vicious slap! But then, I remembered my uniform was soiled and being laundered... wasn't it?

A Kindness of Ravens

by April Yates

They're fiercely protective, you know.

Ravens.

And ever so dexterous, both in intellect and the use of their talons.

You'd do well to remember this as well as you read my tale.

#

The groundskeeper always told me that ravens were pests, they destroyed crops and seeds and, given the chance, they'd maim and kill lambs.

"They go for the face. And I dare say that if you were any smaller, Miss Clara, they'd 'av at you too."

It would have mortified my parents to learn I was escaping from my lessons to roam about the grounds, but I can't abide the stuffiness of the indoors. I want to be outside, to feel the whipping wind, the sting of the ice-cold rain. Inside, I'd have never been allowed to feel much of anything. Out here, I'm free.

I've been merrily making my way along the boundaries of our land, the dry-stone wall crumbling where the root of a sapling had taken hold.

It pleases me to see this bit of nature reclaiming that which had been forged by man. It's there I see the raven fluttering desperately around the base of a felled tree, trying to get something from between its roots. I approach carefully, curious as to what it's so intent upon.

Seeing my approach, it hops back a few steps, its dark eyes firmly on me.

Assessing.

Finally, it hops forward again, nipping at my skirts, urging me to follow. Allowing myself to be led reveals a nest wedged under a branch. Next to it, another raven lays with its head at an impossible angle.

The live bird looks from the dead one to me, then back again.

"Your mate?" I don't know what had possessed me to ask, but the raven's head bobs in affirmation. "I'm sorry."

I'm surprised by my own sincerity, but not nearly as much as the fact she understands my words. She pecks at my hand, gently urging me towards the nest.

Miraculously, a single egg seems to have survived.

I cup the nest in both hands and straighten up from my crouched position. My new friend flies up and settles on the edge. I tip it forward slightly at the sudden extra weight.

"Careful."

She nods before gracefully hopping to my shoulder.

We walk a while looking for an ideal spot. None meet with her approval.

"Listen, you'll have to pick somewhere. And I really don't understand what was wrong with these last five trees."

We've reached the house; dare I take them both inside? They'd be easy enough to hide.

"Don't fly off," I whisper, "or make a sound." Head down, I barrel through the house, ever careful not to lose the precious cargo I'm carrying.

The window is the perfect spot, she lets me know with a nod.

I place the nest on the sill. I keep the window open so she can come and go as she pleases, but she doesn't move from the last of her clutch, and with her mate dead, it falls to me to feed her.

Weeks pass and the egg remains an egg.

Eventually she seems to realize this and leaves. I fear my only friend is gone forever. I shut the window. It's late at night when I hear the gentle rap on the glass. I let her in. She perches atop the mirror, and that's where she remains, my nameless companion until I'm forced to leave home for boarding school.

#

It's my sixteenth year when I first dream of her.

We meant it to be a lark, a sprig of rosemary and a crooked sixpence beneath your pillow on Hallowe'en night, and you would dream of your future husband.

An old Derbyshire custom. When I told the girls who shared the dormitory, they insisted we all try it. It was nice that they were so adamant; I hadn't been home in two years, summers now spent with my aunt, and it would be fun to have this reminder of home. However silly.

Susan harvests the rosemary from the school's garden, but each girl provides her own sixpence. There's giddy excitement that night, whispers in the dark, till one by one we succumb to slumber.

The woman I dream of is dark-haired, with ivory skin, and clad in black under-garments that cling close to her. Her eyes are carved of azurite, so dark as they regard me with a strangely familiar curiosity.

When I awaken, my heart beats wild in my chest and there is a strange ache between my legs. I kick the blankets from me, my body on fire despite the November chill creeping through the stone walls, pervading the air.

I lie there as the windows turn from black to grey and the soft snores turn to whispered good mornings.

"Did you dream?" Susan asks, padding silently over to sit on the end of my bed.

"Yes." Then quickly, before she can ask me for further details, "Did you?"

"No, well, yes, but no handsome eligible man paraded through my head last night."

"I think it was a lot of old nonsense to begin with," Myrtle says, also plonking herself down on the bed, leaving scant room for my feet. "And I had to bend my own six pence because it weren't already crooked."

"Never mind you," Susan says. "You're doomed to be a spinster anyhow. It worked for Clara. Was he very handsome?" They both look at me expectantly.

How can I say that the person I dreamt of is not a man? Although I don't know what it means, instinct tells me that the whole truth is best left hidden.

"Oh, they were certainly very handsome." Which is true.

"Look, she's blushing," Myrtle says.

I feel the embers within me being stoked anew, flames licking at my face and neck.

"Leave her alone." This from Susan. "It's all rather sweet, I think. Is it someone you already know or a stranger?"

I open my month to answer but Susan ploughs excitedly on.

"How exciting for him to be a stranger to you. You can tell your children you met in a dream. It's all so very romantic."

"Yes, very romantic," I mutter. "I think we ought to be getting dressed now though."

They'll have hopefully forgotten about it by the end of the day, and I won't have to think about it anymore.

There's a gentle tap on the frosted glass of the window and I can just make out the hazy outline of an enormous bird.

#

I dream of her again the following Hallowe'en, though I made sure that no sprig of rosemary or sixpence rested beneath my pillow.

The feelings she inspires in me are all too familiar now. During the previous year, I had noticed the other girls more and more; how soft their lips looked, the curve of hips and breasts.

During that last summer at my aunt's before I am to be welcomed back home, I shared a chaste kiss with the head groomsman daughter. She smelled of sweet hay and lavender.

#

I welcomed her in that third year, sure I'm not dreaming, she feels so real.

She takes my hand, and lays me down amongst silken pillows, every touch bringing absolute pleasure. I cry out when I finally come undone beneath her fingertips, as the maid comes barrelling through my bedroom door.

I frantically bring the covers up to hide us, but I am alone.

"You must have been having a nightmare Miss, I could hear your cries from all the way down the hall." She brings a cool hand to my brow, hot and drenched in sweat.

I bat her hand away.

"I'm fine."

"Your breathing, Miss." She puts her hand to my chest. "And dear Lord, your heart."

"Really, that's enough. If you want to make yourself useful, get me some water."

"Yes, Miss." She returns swiftly with a glass, watching as I drink deeply from it. Despite my anger, I'm grateful for it. I hadn't realized how parched I was.

Once she has left, my hand drifts down, and this time I am sure to bury my screams into the pillow.

#

My nineteenth year and I am to be married. My suiter is a solicitor whose firm handles my father's concerns.

Both mother and father assure me he is a kind man, a good man. He will provide for me and when the time comes, my marriage will secure my inheritance.

I cannot argue against the sense of this.

We are walking in the great conservatory at Chatsworth when he makes his formal proposal. During our brief times together, always under the watchful eye of a chaperone, I have witnessed no malice in him.

He does not kindle passion in me, but I could do much worse for a companion.

We shall be happy.

#

"I didn't hurt you, did I?" Jonathan asks when he rolls off me.

"No," I lie. "It was lovely."

Satisfied, he kisses my forehead and gets up from the bed. His long pale limbs glint in the firelight and I have to look away. Everything about his body is sharp, hips and clavicle threatening to tear through his skin.

I had desperately hoped my wedding night would be a new beginning. I had lain beneath him while he had grunted and thrusted. Thankfully, it hadn't taken long till he was spent.

He pulls a nightshirt on. "I'll leave you to get some sleep. The day has been a long one and you must be tired."

I reach out for his hand. "Thank you," I whisper, aware of how lucky I am to have a man as gentle as him.

He smiles and kisses me again, "Sleep."

I turn over. A raven sits on the window's ledge bathed in moonlight, its dark eyes boring into me.

#

When she comes to me that night, there is a thin current of anger in the woman's stream of emotions.

I have betrayed her by laying with another and she intends to reclaim me.

Her caresses, always passionate, have an urgency to them.

"You'll always be mine."

I freeze beneath her. She has never spoken before.

"Always."

Her tone is wistful, and when I look into her dark blue eyes, they are wet with tears.

"Always," I say as I kiss her. "I'll be yours always."

#

Our honeymoon is brief. Jonathan can ill afford to be away from the office for long. We are to remain at my family home. Already he plans to take over a study for his own use.

"Why set up a home of our own," he says, "when we will inherit this estate upon your father's death."

"I should like to think of him living for a great deal more years,"

He looks at me and for the first time I see the embers of ambition; he did not wrangle a marriage to a woman of higher class in order to pour his earnings into the purchase and upkeep of a house when I could provide one ready done.

This flaw I can allow, Jonathan remains kind and invites himself to my bed only when his urge for relief grows too great for him to endure. He works hard, attends his social clubs, and leaves me to my own devices.

In my mind, it is the perfect marriage.

#

Nine months had passed since my wedding day when the accident occurs.

A startled horse, a broken wheel, and both my parents are gone. Jonathan can barely contain his delight, finally he can spread his influence upon every aspect of the house.

Everything that was my fathers has bypassed me and become his to do with what he wishes.

#

"She comes highly recommended," Jonathan says. "And I believe the girl could do with a guiding hand."

"How do you know of her?" I ask.

"She worked for Lord Firth." An old friend of my father's, another client of Jonathan's.

"And why is she in need of a new situation?"

"No real reason. But I believe some of the girls are less than kind to her."

"And why might that be?"

"Jealousy," he says simply.

Jealousy over what, I wonder?

I do not wonder for long.

Jacqueline is the most beautiful creature I have set eyes on, bar of course, the woman in my dreams.

Shining fair hair, emerald green eyes, and a healthy tawny complexion. I can see why all the girls would be jealous of her, and it is clear to see that Jonathan is captivated by her beauty.

I don't blame him.

Had my heart not belonged to another, I would have found myself drawn to her as well.

#

She comes to me every night now; I sit bleary-eyed at each morning at breakfast. They attribute my lethargy to grief; who would dare to suggest nocturnal passions of the sapphic variety?

Jonathan sits across from me, examining his newspaper.

"Busy day ahead, darling?"

He looks up, noticing me for the first time that morning, "Yes, quite busy." He folds his paper and smiles. "I've arranged a treat for you". He rings the bell, summoning Jacqueline. Jonathan points to a spot in front of me. She sets the teapot down, steam billowing from the sprout. "Pour it," he says.

I follow his instructions and pour.

"It's purple!"

"Violets. I thought they might prove soothing."

I gaze into the cup, mesmerized by the vibrant color. "Hearts ease," I murmur.

"Pardon."

"The Greeks called violets hearts ease. They believed them to cure heartache. Thank you."

"Are you going to try it?"

I bring the cup to my lips, feeling the warmth radiate from it. Just as I am about to drink, a mighty thud startles me, and I drop the cup.

"What the devil was that?" Jonathan exclaims.

Jacqueline goes over to the window. "Just a bird hitting the glass," she says. "I'll pour you another cup, Miss."

They both watch me take a deep draft of the liquid. It's sweet and floral and instantly I'm taken back to the days when my father would bring home boxes of Charbonnel et Walker Rose and Violet Creams.

"Sweet flowers, for my flowers," he would say to me and my mother.

"Would you like a cup?" I ask Jonathan.

He raises his coffee in answer; he takes it black and strong, how he stands the bitter taste I'll never know.

"No, thank you," he says with good nature. "I'm afraid that would be rather too feminine for my tastes, but please you enjoy."

I finish my drink, pleased that he cares so much for my well-being.

#

I spend the evening violently ill, my stomach contorting, and I cannot keep any food down.

I try to remember when Jonathan last visited me in my bed. Seven weeks ago. The last time had been a week before Jacqueline's appointment. Never has he stayed away from my bed for so long, and I wonder if he is warming Jacqueline's, instead.

My mother told me that men are wont to have a mistress; this would suit me well. I appreciate Jonathan for his companionship, let Jacqueline tend to his baser needs.

I've bled since the last time with Jonathan; my nausea, thank the Lord, must be down to something I ate.

Sleep does not come easy. There're brief respites from the pain during the night, but the sleep I grasp during those times is fraught and dreamless.

I pray for the night to end. It does, but there are many more nights like it to come.

#

Some days are better than others. On those days when I feel well enough, I take my tea at the breakfast table, other days I take it in my bed.

This is one of those days when I must take it in my bed. Jacqueline brings it to me with a smile.

"Thank you," I say.

"You're welcome, Miss." She gives a slight nod of her head and turns to leave.

"Please stay!"

Jacqueline's eyes dart briefly to the door and then, somewhat reluctantly, she stands by my bed.

"If you wish, Miss."

"You can sit if you like." I indicate the chair.

She sits, looking somewhat uncomfortable. I hadn't meant for this. My only intention is to perhaps a strike a kind of friendship.

I wonder again if she is sharing Jonathan's bed, which would explain how guilty she looks. I wish I could tell her I truly do not care. Most consider my persuasion to be unnatural, crooked, and wrong, and as such, I consider myself unworthy to pass judgment on others.

"I know it's not considered proper, but I hoped that if we got to know each other a little better that we might become friends."

Jacqueline shifts uneasily in the chair. I decide to throw societal conventions out of the window.

"Are you sleeping with Jonathan?"

Jacqueline immediately reddens. I take this as a yes.

"Jacqueline, I don't care. Really, truly I don't. In fact, if you were, I'd be happy. Jonathan is a good man and there are certain things I can't give him that you obviously can."

What she said next, though, I could never have foreseen.

"Yes, I understand that. There are whispers about your inversion." She looks at me pointedly, challenging me to deny these aspersions.

"And what is it exactly that they say?"

She laughs. "Your tryst with the groom's daughter at your aunt's is well known."

"An innocent kiss between friends," I say, my nervous laugh betraying me.

"And you have visitations. During the night."

Her gaze remains steady on me, and this time it is I that reddens. Is it that obvious?

"They say that's why you're so ill. Wasting away. This creature is draining the life from you. And what's more is that you enjoy it."

My heart pounds in my chest.

"You're very loud," she adds for clarification. She gets up from the chair, smoothing her skirts as she does. "Will that be all?"

She does not wait for an answer. She leaves, slamming the door behind her.

#

Her hands, soft and cunning, run up my thighs, parting them ready for lips and tongue.

I want it—want her so badly, but Jacqueline's words resound in my head.

"Stop!"

She halts immediately, blue eyes looking questioningly at me. She crawls up to lie beside me, pushing the hair from my brow.

Would a demon bent on corruption act so tenderly?

I was always taught temptation would take a beautiful form.

Devil or angel, her visits to me are a tonic and whatever illness has plagued me passes.

After she leaves, I do something I have never done before in my life; I go down into the kitchen in search of food.

I expect the kitchen to be empty, the hour having passed midnight.

"Mrs Jones," I exclaim. "Shouldn't you be in bed?"

"I could say the same to you," she says, spooning an indigo

powder into a bowl of soft white fat. "We have a rodent problem, Miss; I find it best to deal with it late at night when people are out of the way." She mixes the powder and fat together vigorously.

"I'm sorry to have disturbed you, but for the first time in forever, I feel hungry."

"I can find you something, Miss?" She goes to the basin to wash her hands. "Mind you don't touch that. Nasty stuff."

"What is it?" I ask, peering cautiously into the bowl. The mixture inside resembles whipped cream, although coloured a pale blue.

"Arsenic, Miss."

"I thought arsenic was white?"

"It can be if you have a good reason for it to be. Otherwise, they dye it indigo, makes it harder to sneak it into somebody's food or drink. Rats, however, don't care what color their food is, greedy little blighters."

A thought crystallizes. "Would someone not be able to taste it?"

"No, it tastes of nothing, smells of nothing. Strychnine, on the other hand, is very bitter. You'd know if you had a dose of that in your porridge. Works a lot quicker too. We keep some in but I've no call for it. Arsenic does the job well enough for rats." She pauses, looking at me curiously. "Are you alright Miss? You've gone awfully pale."

"I'm fine, thank you. I've changed my mind, though. I'll wait until breakfast to eat. I'm sorry to have disturbed you."

I go back to my bed, leaving Mrs. Jones to mutter about 'bloody time wasters'.

#

She's waiting for me, naked beneath the covers; she stretches cat-like as I sit on the bed beside her.

"It's the violet tea, isn't it?"

She doesn't reply, but the answer forms in my mind, regardless.

"Of course, why bloody else would they give me something that color?"

I know what I must do, though I am loath to do it.

"I need your help."

She nods enthusiastically, causing her raven hair to fall over dark blue eyes.

#

I have made my way to the table this morning feeling refreshed.

It surprises Jonathan to see me. He and Jacqueline were deep in conversation, one hand stroking the back of her head, the other on her hip.

He breaks away from her. "Darling." He strides brazenly over to kiss me. "You are looking exceptionally well today."

"I feel well."

Jacqueline lingers close to Jonathan.

"Jacqueline, your mistress will be wanting her tea," he says. "Sit down, darling, I don't want you to tire yourself."

I sit down. On cue, Jacqueline places the teapot before me.

"Jacqueline, I meant what I said before about us being friends. So, as your friend, I would like you to sit down with me and share a cup."

She looks nervously over at Jonathan, who has sat down in his usual place and is drinking his own bitter concoction.

"No thank you, Miss, I've other duties to be getting on with."

"Nonsense," I say. "Is this house not my own? Sit down, I insist."

She sits down beside me. I pour two cups and push one over to her.

"Let's drink a toast to friendship."

Jacqueline looks with horror at the indigo liquid.

"Whatever is the matter?" I ask. "Surely there is nothing wrong with it? My husband would have ensured that only the finest flowers were used in its making."

Jacqueline brings the cup slowly to her lips, no doubt thinking a single dose of it would cause no lasting harm. After all, the campaign against me had been a long one, and, as yet, I am not dead.

"Enough!" Never have I heard Jonathan raise his voice, and I am slow to register the bellow that comes forth as being his. He would not risk one grain of the poison to pass her lips. He does indeed care for her.

"So, you do intend for me to die. Why? You both could have lived here in this house and I would have said nothing. Jonathan, you've even the right to will my money to any children the two of you might have."

They remain silent, Jonathan's mind no doubt rapidly working towards a solution. I have to be quick.

"The fact of the matter is," I press on, "that you tried to do it all too slowly. I can see your reasoning. It'd be much less suspicious for me to waste away rather than die suddenly. That would raise troublesome questions."

I notice the slight twitching of Jonathan's neck. Had I not known better, I would think it a nervous tick.

The spasms spread quickly through his body. He drops to the floor, his back arching with such violence his whole body lifts off and falls in a sickening rhythm.

"What have you done?" Jacqueline falls to her knees beside him, attempting in vain to pin him down by the shoulders.

"I have done nothing. I can imagine the newspapers now, though. An unhinged maid slowly poisoning her mistress with arsenic in her tea before putting strychnine in the master's coffee."

I smile at the raven, my constant companion, sitting watching intently with dark eyes, a twist of paper at her talons.

A raven's beak and talons are ever so cunning and clever. Certainly more than capable of lifting the lid of a coffee pot and dropping something within.

"You won't get away with this. I'll tell them everything. They may gaol me for the rest of my life, but you'll hang."

"Oh Jacqueline, I don't take any pleasure in this, but who would believe you? Jonathan won't be able to attest to your story."

Jacqueline sobs, knowing what I say is the truth. I hope she believes me when I say I take no pleasure in it all.

I take a deep breath and scream for help.

Something After

by Erica Ruppert

Felice gazed up at the front of her father's house. It was dingier than she remembered it, the brick front eroded, the landscaping overgrown, the lawn gone to seed. She sighed. At least it was still almost as big as it had seemed in her childhood. She could just barely remember when they had first moved in, the surprise of it after the limits of the apartment. It had been vast, then, and unexplored.

A shadow crossed one of the wide picture windows that flanked the front door. Amira had beat her here, despite her reluctance to come. Felice looked around for her sister's car, but didn't see it. She pulled out her phone and scrolled through for Amira's number, but she didn't see it. She scrolled again. She didn't remember deleting it.

Amira was always just beyond her reach.

She tried the number for her father's old land line. The grating mechanical pulse meant a receiver was off the hook somewhere. It didn't surprise her. There had been no one to answer it for weeks. Not since he had died. She drew a deep, shuddering breath, refusing to cry.

Felice knocked to warn Amira, then let herself in. Her own shadow stretched in a long band before her until she shut the door against the light.

"Hello?" she called into the stillness.

"Back here," Amira answered. "In his office."

Felice shrugged out of her coat as she walked down the long hallway. Of course that was where she would be.

#

He was still here, somewhere. She knew it.

Felice ran her hands over the damp, papered walls of the old office, spreading her arms wide until her cheek pressed the brighter spot where a picture had once hung. She closed her eyes, imagining the room as it had been when he was here, furnished and cluttered with work and with life.

She stepped back from the wall and opened her eyes.

The thin sunlight seeping in through the high windows made the room seem even emptier than it was. The dulled Persian carpet was pitted where chair legs had rested too long without moving, and the scattered scorch marks before the fireplace were too many to be hidden by the pattern. The only piece of furniture remaining was his desk.

"Well?" Amira asked.

Felice shook her head, coming back from her reverie. "I smell him," she said. "His cigarettes."

Amira moved slowly toward the door. "It's just your memory," she said from the threshold. "It smells of nothing but mold and dust in here."

Felice smiled thinly. "My memory," she said quietly. "What else could it be, but memory?"

Amira watched her sister closely for a moment, her eyes narrowed.

"I'll leave you to it, then," she said at last, and swept away down the hall.

#

The desk's dark wood was mazed with scratches and scarred with years of cigarette burns. Felice pulled open one of the drawers. The faint smell of rubber erasers drifted up. She remembered how fascinating the soft, kneaded erasers had been to her when she was small, how much she liked to play with them instead of plain clay.

She reached up to touch the scar above her left eye, a souvenir of when she had run into the sharp edge of her father's drafting T-square when she was two. She couldn't remember it happening, but she knew the well-worn family story.

She remembered how he said she had screamed and screamed.

#

Upstairs in their father's room, Amira stood amidst the piles of his possessions, sorted into what might be worth something and what was pure junk. It was the last room to clear out, the last of what was left of him. Felice could not stop touching the pile of discards, picking up worn belts, old ties, half-used bottles of aftershave.

"This is your inheritance," Amira said, her jaw clenched around the words. "His leavings, all for nothing."

"Don't you miss him?" Felice asked, surprised at Amira's anger.

Amira braced her feet, as if she leaned into a heavy wind.

"No," she said. "Not after, I don't."

Felice put down the shirt she held and looked away. She didn't want to remember.

"I miss him," she said to her sister's silence.

#

As Felice bent over the sink to brush her teeth, she caught a sideways glimpse of a figure passing the open doorway. She spat out the toothpaste and stepped into the hall.

It was empty. The shadows were too thin to hide anyone.

She listened for the creaks of Amira getting herself ready for bed, but the house was still.

She smelled the acrid tang of wet ashes, a breath of it, then gone.

He was here. She knew it.

She finished washing up and padded back to the bedroom she had shared with Amira when they were children. Her father had never changed it. The dusty familiarity was less comforting than Felice thought it would be. She slid under the covers of her narrow twin bed and tucked her arms behind her head, watching the play of moonshadow on the ceiling.

"I wish we could live here again," she said into the silence. "Put it back the way it was."

"You really think that's possible?" Amira asked from the darkness beside her.

Felice caught the scent of a snuffed-out cigarette, carried on a draft.

"I don't know. I think so," she answered, distracted. "Do you smell him? Right now?"

"I never smell anything, Felice."

Amira shifted position with a dry swish of sheets. Even in the dark Felice could feel her sister's eyes on her. She knew Amira's pinched expression from the tone of her voice.

"I know you need to believe he's still here, that you can still find him all around, but it isn't real. And the more you tell yourself it is, the more you try to make me believe it is, the worse it is for you."

Felice kept her eyes focused on the ceiling.

"I like being back here. With you. Even like this," Felice said.

"I just want to go home," Amira answered. She sounded so far away.

"This used to be home," Felice said, pleading, turning to face her sister's dark shape. "Remember when he made us the rope swings?"

"Stop it," Amira said. "He's gone. Everything's gone. Everything changed years ago. Stop trying to keep some imaginary past alive."

Felice remained quiet, waiting until her sister eventually sighed and rolled over to sleep.

The rustle of her sheets released the faint sting of cigarette smoke.

Amira had never smoked.

Felice breathed in deeply, welcoming the smell.

"I'm here, Dad," she whispered into the night.

#

Felice rose before dawn. Despite the strange hour, Amira's bed was unused.

Felice crept quietly down to the kitchen, in case Amira had slept in a different room. She put up a kettle of water and opened the jar of instant coffee she had brought with her. She drowsed on her feet while she waited, looking out the window at the dark expanse of the yard. The kettle whined, and she lifted it to pour. As she turned, she thought she saw movement through the glass, and glanced up again at the window.

At her shoulder, her father's face faded into view, reflected against the failing night.

She jerked and the boiling water splashed out of the cup, spraying her hand. She shrieked and dropped the kettle. It clattered off the counter and onto the floor, a pool of hot water spreading from it.

"What have you done?" Amira shouted just behind her, stepping back from the steaming puddle.

"I saw him!" Felice cried, gripping her scalded hand.

Amira kept her distance from the mess.

"You did not see him. He's not here to see. It's not even five o'clock yet and you're still half asleep."

"Amira, I saw his face in the glass, just before you came in."

Amira shook her head. "Stop trying to convince me. Let me see your hand."

Felice held her hand out to her sister, flinching against expected pain. Amira's fingers were ice cold where they stroked the rising blisters. The chill felt good against her burns.

"Thanks," Felice said. "That helps."

Amira let Felice's hand go and stepped back into the darkened hallway.

Felice took off her robe and used it to wipe up the spill. As she knelt on the worn linoleum, she sighed.

"He told me once that one of us was unplanned," Felice said. "Did you know that?"

"Unplanned?" Amira asked. "Or unwanted? Mama was never very warm toward either of us."

Felice looked at the wet fabric in her hands. It was already cold.

"No, she wasn't."

Felice tossed the robe into the corner near the sink and climbed to her feet.

"Dad was," she said to Amira, and paused. She swallowed before she went on. "You don't believe that I know things, that I can tell things," she said. "But I can."

"You don't know anything," Amira said, moving away. "You just need to feel special. But it's magical thinking. You should have grown out of it. None of us are special. None of us. Not really. No matter what we're told."

#

Later, Felice went back into her father's office. It felt less empty without Amira there, reminding her. She lay her cheek against the damp wallpaper again, closing her eyes, remembering how the room had looked when he was alive. When the world was a safe place. When she didn't know so many details.

When she hadn't been alone.

She stood at the desk and ran her hands over the damaged surface, hoping to find something she'd missed before. From behind her came a rustle of papers and a burst of sharp cold. She spun around, wanting.

As she watched, the ashes in the fireplace curled and crackled as they unburned, smoothing out into the dull squares of faded photographs that had fed the long-ago flames. Felice startled, delighted. She was right. She had known. She reached in gingerly, expecting heat. Instead, her hands sank into a pool of bitter cold. Her eyes teared as she leaned into it. Shivering, she scraped the reformed photos into a rough pile and pulled them out onto the hearth to look at.

The first few were baby pictures of a chubby, smiling infant in her crib, on a blanket on the lawn, in her mother's arms. Her mother. Their mother.

Felice looked at the picture in shock. Her mother smiled weakly at the camera, squinting against the summer sun, propping up her daughter at an awkward angle against her chest. Was the baby her, or Amira?

Why would her father have burned them?

Felice flipped through the rest, any joy draining from her. There was the one of her and Amira in matching crochet-lace dresses, taken when Felice was four and Amira two. There was the family picture taken one bright spring day on the wide back lawn, the year before her grandfather died. There was her high school graduation portrait. There was the photo of Amira with their father, the one she wanted to forget. It was taken that day.

Her mother left, after that day, that unforgiven day, and left all the silences after.

The questions remained.

Felice stood up and kicked at the photos, scattering them across the rug and back into the fireplace.

The room grew bitterly cold around her as the freezing air billowed from the fireplace. Frost spread in a froth across the stone hearth and up the fireplace bricks. Felice heard the tiny pings of the mortar cracking under the sudden chill. Breath froze in her throat as she cried out. She slipped on the icy floor as she tried to turn away and fell heavily against the desk. Crushed against the sharp edge, her arm went numb.

She shoved herself up and ran for the door. The room seemed to stretch out before her like a bolt of cloth unspooling. She was out of breath when her hand closed on the door frame. She clung to it.

"What are you doing?" Amira called from upstairs.

Felice sagged against the frame, letting it hold her up.

"Felice?" Amira called again.

She tried to answer, but her mouth was suddenly too dry.

Amira's footsteps sounded quick and light on the stairs, growing louder and more solid as she came down the hall. Felice lifted her head, her face as stiff as a mask.

At first she could not see Amira. Her eyes would not focus. She shivered from the cold at her back. Then Amira was there.

"Why are you in here again?" Amira asked, reaching for her.

"You're lying if you say you can't sense it," Felice replied angrily, pulling away from her sister's hands.

"You don't know what you're saying," Amira said. "You don't know anything at all."

#

Felice waited until she thought Amira had to be asleep. She couldn't hear her breathing, even when she held her own breath.

She rose silently and tiptoed out of their bedroom, making her way by moonlight down the hall to her father's room. She eased the door closed behind her.

The moon stained the room with a wash of blue light. Felice walked forward into the abandoned space. There were no sorted piles. The room had been emptied. Felice rubbed her eyes, knowing she was awake. The wardrobe doors hung open, uneven on their hinges. She peered between them at a handful of wire clothes hangers left behind on the cabinet's bar.

A faint waft of old smoke enveloped her as she pulled them out and threw them on the floor.

#

"What happened to Dad's things?" Felice demanded, pulling the sheets off Amira's bed. The coming dawn made the light blurred and grey. She wasn't sure where the hours had gone.

"What do you mean?" Amira asked, rising.

"His room. Where are his things?"

"They're gone. They've been gone. Everything's gone."

"When did you get rid of them? I wasn't done!"

Amira shook her head.

"When did I get rid of them? You cling to this, this magic," she said, and walked out of their room.

Felice followed her.

The sun had only begun to creep over the horizon. The halls were full of shadows, and Amira a moving shadow among them. Felice struggled to keep up with her pace.

Amira led her down the hall, where her father's bedroom stood bare, the wardrobe gaping open, the bed stripped down to its frame. Felice groaned, unbelieving, as her sister's shadow passed her, turning back to the room they had shared. She followed again, searching for bearings. Now the matching twin beds were gone, and the dressers. Felice's travel bag sat open and forlorn on the worn carpet. She gasped and turned away.

Felice lost sight of Amira, even as the rooms grew slowly brighter. She steadied herself with the banister as she descended the stairs. She didn't need Amira. She had to see his office again. She had so many good memories of him there. If she could be there again, she might be able to recall them, to know they were true.

When she entered, it was only an empty room. The cold snapped around her like teeth.

She sat down on the dirty hearth. There were no photographs in the fireplace. There were only ashes. There would only be ashes. She hung her head and sobbed.

Amira resolved from the waning shadows and stood over her sister in her grief. Felice rocked back and forth where she sat on the stones, her hair stuck to her face by tears and mucus.

"He's gone," she gasped out between sobs. "He's gone."

Amira opened a desk drawer and pulled out a dented pack of cigarettes. She lit one and held it out to Felice. After a moment of blank silence, Felice reached out and took it.

Amira's fingers were bitterly cold against her own.

Felice looked up. Amira smiled, her skin glittering, frost crackling over her lips.

"Yes," she said. "He's been gone for a long time. Longer than you'd think."

She lit another cigarette, exhaling a long plume of ice that shattered as it fell.

"And I'm still here."

An Endless Kind of Nothing

by Alexis DuBon

I awake in the back seat of a Tesla surrounded by white leather so soft, for a moment I think I am in a bed of marshmallows. The road is quiet as it races beneath the premium wheels and puffy luxury suspension. The driver hears me shuffling around behind him as I get my bearings, still half awake. He peers at me through the rear-view mirror.

"That must have been some rejuvenating treatment. Are you feeling good and relaxed?"

Have I been in a spa? Was I waking from some wellness induced trance? I suppose I do smell like cucumber. I feel rejuvenated. Renewed, I guess.

"I am very relaxed, thank you." I expect it is best to be polite, even though I'm not sure whether I had been in any spa. I can't say that—he'd think I was insane. Clearly, he had picked me up, right? So he knows.

I gaze out the window and watch as city dissolves into highway and eventually countryside until everything becomes craggy and mountainous. I don't have the courage to question where we're going. He seems to know me, and everything feels oddly rote, practiced. I hadn't fought or resisted getting into this car. Had I? I don't know what I was doing before I woke up in that back seat. But the driver is so calm and even. Clearly this had been arranged and I was forgetting something.

At every crest of the mountain, I anticipate our arrival, only to learn we have higher still to climb. As we drive, the landscape becomes buried deeper and deeper under thick snow, like a bed made in freshly laundered sheets, all tucked in and plush. I feel like I'm being sent away to exile, like those maidens in fairy tales, to live in a beautiful prison. Maybe I'm just going home. Nothing feels familiar though. We've been in the car for hours; if I ask him where we're going now… I missed my window. It's too late. I should just behave and see how this all plays out. Don't make a scene. Don't be a weirdo. The answer must be obvious, and it will make itself known sooner or later.

After still more time endlessly ascending, we arrive atop a wintery summit surrounded by the vast emptiness of uninhabited wilderness. We reach a plateau, and I am relieved to be on flat ground again. There, leaning against the trunk of a big old tree, is a young man waiting for us, and we pull over beside him.

I exit the car first, and upon seeing me, a look of absolute bewilderment strikes this man's face. He freezes, staring at me quizzically, as if some unexpected apparition had stepped out before him, then quickly turns his attention to the driver side of the car, where the driver is now standing. It all happens so suddenly, and I could see he hoped I hadn't noticed. But I did notice. I brush it off. I'm not going to start off here on the wrong foot. Wherever here is. I can't make a bad impression before I even know where I'm going. Just be polite. Patient. Everything will be revealed and it will all make sense.

The driver opens the trunk to reveal two suitcases, which I recognize as my own. Had I packed? If I brought luggage, this must have been a trip I planned. I begin to feel a bit more at ease, although I have no memory of planning any trip.

The young man introduces himself as Sylvan and loads my luggage and me onto an ATV he has parked nearby. And once again, we are climbing. Higher and higher, scaling the final slopes, winding around invisible meandering paths buried under banks of fallen snow, as we rise to meet the highest peak upon which a house is perched. We are here. I am on the point of a needle piercing the heavens, and this house stands immense and imposing, towering over the pristine woods that surround it.

My breath is thin at such an altitude, and the air is weightless. Snow covers the entire world, playing tricks and disorienting me. Looking back toward the driveway, I can't be sure whether I am staring into a vast expanse of blustering snow that goes on forever, or if all I can see is a thick haze before my face. Smothered in white, there is no depth. Nothing—but an endless kind of nothing, not the empty kind. However intimidated I am, I find myself equally enchanted as I look through eternity.

I face the house and attempt to count the windows. There are so many. There is a fire burning inside and light dances throughout, as if gifting them with sight. The faint shadow of a figure moves about through one of the windows on the top floor. Small and waifish, peering out the windows. This must be my host, I whisper to myself.

Sylvan guides me in, my luggage under his arm. There is a man sitting by the fire. He is maybe thirty years my senior, though it's hard to tell. His face is familiar, but I can't place it. I know I know him, but I don't know who he is. He has a calming presence despite his sharp, angular features and icy expression. And despite how large he is, practically a mountain himself, he has a gentleness that puts me at ease.

"Hello," he says, stretching out a thin hand. "I am Tumas Aubert. Welcome. I am so glad you have come." When he speaks, something in me clicks. I belong here. Everything feels new, but there's a clawing in the back of my skull telling me I should remember. It's as if his voice had cast a net of comfort over me.

"Hello." My voice quivers slightly and I realize this is the first time I've spoken since whatever small talk I had exchanged with the driver early on in our trip. The sound it makes is about as bold as rice paper, and dissolves into the air, unlike Mr. Aubert whose voice is so thick it clings to the space around me like sap against the trunk of a tree.

Everything in the house is very old, but very well maintained. Mr. Aubert informs me that he is a collector of beautiful things, that his joy is keeping the past alive. The house is a love letter to beauty long gone, bedecked in art nouveau fixtures and silk rugs. Family portraits hang on the wall, interspersed with paintings I would have expected to see hung in museums.

"You must be tired from your trip. Please, go upstairs to your room, take a bath, or a nap, and come down at your leisure to join me for dinner. Sylvan takes the room next to yours. If you need anything, feel free to ask either one of us."

A rush of safety and familiarity washes over me, and I open my mouth, wanting to glean some information about where I've been. But before any words have the chance to come out, Mr. Aubert gestures to the large Georgian staircase and sits himself back down on the couch. I hadn't even decided what I would have asked. "Where was I?" seems a silly question. I'm glad I was saved the embarrassment.

Somehow, I know exactly where to go. I walk without hesitation up the stairs, turn left, and open the second door on the right. I know this room. This is my room. Sylvan has unpacked my luggage. All of my things are right where I would have put them. I know just where to find everything.

There is a window seat and I look out at the vast expanse of woodland blanketed in pristine white. A gust of wind gives life to the fallen snow, whisking it off the ground where it had been slumbering, swirling it in the air for a moment before it dissolves into a niveous haze. Everything beyond the window is covered in white, and the snow that fills the air looks like eraser marks of a world that God has decided to take another go at. Every time the blankness subsides and settles back to the ground, a different landscape reveals itself. Always some iteration of tall and wizened pine trees, but never quite the same.

I feel at home here. The disquiet I felt on my journey seems so distant, light-years away. I settle into my new surroundings. I'm okay with this, this will be good for me. Lean into it. This will be a positive experience. I mean, this seems to be my life now; do I have a choice? It's better to be optimistic.

#

Mr. Aubert knows so much about the world. He is like a human encyclopedia. It is my third day here, and our third walk together through the woods. Already I can identify and decipher the different calls of the black-capped chickadee. Now, she is calling to her mate; she has found a bounty on a branch just above my head. Mr. Aubert speaks the language of the forest and I am beginning to learn.

His face softens when we are out in nature. I can tell how handsome he was as a younger man, and when he smiles, glimmers of warmth beam from his face. It is my favorite thing to do, to make him smile. It's like I've won something.

He lays his hand upon my shoulder and all the cells in my arm are pulled toward his touch, like I'm a living Wooly Willy. My head swims for a moment until I force my thoughts away from the sensation of gravity his hand has created.

Eventually, we turn back toward the house. It is time for dinner and my heart aches a little at the thought of leaving our private little wonderland for anything that resembles reality. I especially don't look forward to dinner. Not in that dining room.

On the wall of that room, there is a single oil painting; a portrait of a woman. It hangs over us, colossal and menacing. It is beautiful, but it makes me uncomfortable. I don't like the way she looks at me, all judgment and impatience. I don't like the way her eyes follow me and I don't like that I can tell she knows how I feel about my host. It's embarrassing.

"You don't like the artwork?"

Did I say it out loud without realizing? I put my fork down and sputter out an incomprehensible string of syllables.

"Is it because she looks so much like you? I gotta say, when I first saw you I was kind of weirded out," Sylvan interjects.

"What?" I hadn't really been able to look at her enough to realize, but it isn't so far from the truth. I suddenly have the urge to flee.

Mr. Aubert laughs. "That is my wife," he says. "She died many years ago."

"Oh," I say. And now I am compelled to inspect the painting, look at it with different eyes. Do I look like Mr. Aubert's dead wife? My heart is throwing a dubstep party for the rest of my body. "I'm so sorry. She was very beautiful." Still, I can't get myself to look too long.

"It feels at times like it happened many lifetimes ago, at other times, like it was yesterday."

"I love how you got it painted just like one of those old Victorian portraits. The clothes, the style, the strokes—the artist did a wonderful job replicating the work of that era."

"Thank you. She was enchanting." Mr. Aubert smiles, and the conversation is finished. I exhale for the first time in what feels like hours.

After dinner, I go up to my room. I stare at the ceiling and feel the hours pass. Sylvan is pacing his room again, pacing the hall. It is comforting to know I am not the only insomniac in this house. For the third night now, I drift away to the sound of his sleepless footsteps.

#

Time marches forward and the days grow shorter and shorter as winter swaddles us, enveloping us in snowdrift and silence. Some days, though, robust gales funnel themselves through hidden cracks in the foundation, whispering faintly as they penetrate the thick stone walls.

This is my home now; I shouldn't be bothered. I should be used to its idiosyncrasies. And I try. I have learned to ignore the wind and the noises it carries, but today it is wailing. It is so disruptive I am now on a mission to plug whatever crack is allowing its trespass. I tiptoe out of my room and into the hall, tracing the trails of its swoosh.

Odd, how I'm just now realizing how long this hallway is. It feels almost dreamlike, as if the house has suddenly stretched. Why have I never explored the rooms beyond my own? This is my house now. Why had I never realized just how long this hall went on for?

A narrow stone staircase closes the hallway and I follow the sound upwards to the third floor. My way is blocked by a heavy oak plank and, as I force it open, torrents of dust spill onto me. I find myself in a dark attic, abandoned for so long it seems certain that Mr. Aubert has never used it, and likely the previous tenants had forsaken it as well. The air is stiff and stagnant with neglect. The ceiling is low, but I am small enough to stand upright. Mr. Aubert would have had to duck quite a bit, and I could see why he would not want to venture up here.

I take slow, measured steps, a few at a time, fearing that somehow any noise I make would chase away the sound, and I would lose it, as silly a notion as that is. Part of me fears I will get trapped up here and no one will ever find me, in this bastille of forgotten memories. Moving forward, I see some old boxes, and among them, a large chest.

I have found the source. The chest must have been shoved against a crack in the external wall and used to stop the wind from entering, like a patch. I go to move it, just to check, and it is so light. Lighter than I would expect for something that would serve to reinforce a wall.

I listen for signs of that wailing wind, pressing my ear against the wall that was covered by the chest, but I hear nothing. The wind is still crying, but not from there. I stand still and close my eyes, focusing only on that drafty whisper. It is coming from the chest.

I brace myself in anticipation of what might be inside. Mice have been known to find their way into attics, and I steel myself against the terror of finding a colony of rodents huddling for warmth from this bitter cavern of a room like something out of Indiana Jones. Was it the sound of dozens of tiny claws scratching against my ceiling that I heard?

As I coax my body to come nearer to the chest, the weighted whispers rise, becoming a low howl. This is not the sound of a mouse scratching on wood. I proceed. Perhaps it really is a drafty house, carrying the sound of the wind, ventriloquizing itself and echoing through the emptiness of the air, playing tricks on me. Perhaps when I open the chest, it will be empty and I'll laugh at myself, alone up here like that one kid at a slumber party who's just a little too old for Ouija but plays anyway and ends up jumping higher than anyone else when the planchette twitches.

But I just want to know. I draw closer and it grows stronger, as if sensing my presence and robbing me of my breath to use for its own. I am standing directly in front of it. All I have left to do is lift the lid and uncover whatever lays inside, the big reveal. I am not laughing at myself anymore. I am nervous. I force myself to be brave and do it quickly, so as not to prolong the dread I can no longer deny.

I jump back in anticipation of what might reveal itself to me, and—it's empty. Just more dust. Shining my flashlight to confirm the welcome revelation, I run my fingers along the interior. Just dust. One last sweep reveals a single set of earrings. I pull them out and hold them in the light to inspect them. They are gorgeous. Once I blow on them a little to clean them up, I can see they are covered in tiny pavé sapphires and they glow like the last blue light that stretches over the snow before everything gets swallowed up by the black of night.

Up here all alone, they had been entirely forgotten. No one is missing them; to claim them for my own would harm no one. To return them to that abandoned dust-filled box would be the greater crime. So I place them gently in the breast pocket of my shirt, shut the trunk, and return downstairs, satisfied with my investigation and thrilled with my subsequent treasure.

Once I'm back in my room, I put them on immediately. They're gorgeous. Blue light dances against my cheeks, illuminating my face. I feel so pretty, and like a teenager, I have a stomach full of butterflies, the kind I remember getting before a first date. I can't wait for Mr. Aubert to see me with them.

#

When he sees me, with my hair carefully coiffed to showcase my score, and my makeup perfectly applied to accent my cheekbones, now lit from the blue glow of the sapphires, he is unable to conceal his reaction. His face, always so stoic and inscrutable, looks almost awed.

"You are a vision," he says, his eyes fixed on mine. "What is the occasion?"

"No occasion. It's just..." I suddenly feel insecure. It was all so natural at the time, like these earrings should have been mine. But to say it aloud, to breathe my crime into existence, suddenly makes it feel wrong. "I just wanted to look nice."

"You are enchanting." He smiles warmly.

"Do you like my earrings?" I blurt it out, not quite sure whether it's wiser to call attention to them or avoid the subject entirely. If he knew them, it would give me the opportunity to explain my discovery and show that I am not a thief. If not, I could avoid the conversation entirely. I don't want him to think I'm flaunting my bounty before him as if I had knowingly stolen them. Don't act like you have something to hide if you don't have anything to hide, right?

"I do. They are spectacularly unique." And with that, he goes to work on his vichyssoise.

The rest of the dinner is quiet. I feel exposed, and I cringe at the painting that has watched the whole awkward exchange. She must be laughing at me behind all that dried paint.

Each night that follows, I wear the earrings to dinner. It feels like putting them away would be an admission of guilt. It's a strange feeling, to feel beautiful and counterfeit all at once.

#

The season continues to deepen and we sink into winter, eaten up by snow. Mr. Aubert is thriving; he seems to grow stronger with the cold. I envy that, and wish I could keep up. I reflect on how old he had appeared the first day I met him, but now he is full of life. I wonder whether it's the feelings I've developed for him that shape my perception or if the winter really did alter him in some actual way. I flatter myself by thinking it's some effect I have on him, that he could feel the same way I do and it's making him feel young again. Maybe he just does better in the cold.

Winter does not have the same effect on me. I feel myself growing tired with the least strenuous activity, and preferring a seat by the fire to an adventure in the woods. I fight my fatigue and force myself to go with him more often than not, to enjoy the few meager hours of sunlight we have; besides, the thought of denying myself time with him hurts more than my aching body.

But as time passes and the snow falls thicker and more

frequently, we become engulfed in it, and I find myself brought to shame by how quickly I want to give up. Each journey out becomes more difficult than the last.

#

I force one foot to follow the other and we walk into the woods. I bat away the thought that this might be our last walk until the return of spring. The snow swirls around us, and thunder claps in the distance—an excuse to turn back.

Immediately upon returning to the house, I fall asleep by the fire where I stay until Mr. Aubert wakes me for dinner. We dine to the sound of a terrible storm outside. Hostile winds fire bullets of hail against our stone fortress. The snow, furious at having been disturbed, wails wildly. The house is ice cold, and no matter how I try, I can't find warmth. I am too cold to even pretend to eat, and Mr. Aubert guides me back to the fire and rubs my hands in his. They are stronger than I remember.

Driven by pure impulse, I grab him and bury myself in his arms, pressing my face into his chest. This is the first time we've held each other, and in his embrace, I no longer feel the chill of the storm. In his grasp, I exist outside of my physical body, where the cold can't touch me. I don't even realize when I succumb to the pull of sleep.

I open my eyes to the sound of Sylvan in the kitchen. The morning sun is caustic, like it's trying to bleach any evidence of last night from my mind. My senses slowly return to me, and I resent them. I hate the morning light for so violently pushing the night beyond my reach.

My body is stiff, and it hurts to move. My wrists crack from the pressure of shifting the weight of my aching body.

"Look at you!" My eyes focus, and now I could see Sylvan staring at me, a concerned look on his face which I try to ignore. "I didn't even notice you were growing a beard. You wear it so well." I feel awful and disappointed in myself. He has dinner with us almost every night. How did I not notice?

"Thank you. You slept well?"

"Maybe too well. I still feel it in my bones. They feel like they're made of chalk." I have no idea how long I've been on that couch, but I'm embarrassed to ask. It could only have been that night, I tell myself. Even though I feel like I would have noticed a few days of stubble growing into that shrubbery that's now sitting on Sylvan's jowls. Wouldn't I?

I hear Mr. Aubert on the stairs and my heart leaps, beating like a puppy's tail, as each step brings him nearer to me. Nothing seems to matter anymore; I just want to be near him again. In the light of the morning sun, he looks almost like a young man.

"Do you feel better?" His smile warms my blood. "Would you like to go for a walk in the woods? It's a beautiful day!"

We stroll through the woods for a while, but before long my body feels worn and depleted. I resist the urge to turn back and we move deeper through the trees.

"You look a bit drawn. Should we return to the house?" I want to accept the offer, but I refuse. His face is ruddy with a glow to it that is new to me.

I spot a hawk feasting on a small rodent, ripping at its corpse. Mr. Aubert has taught me well and I know it is a kestrel. Impressed with myself, I try to lift my finger to point it out to him, but my hand is so stiff, I can't move it. I finally yield to my discomfort and reluctantly suggest we head back.

His steps are light and effortless while mine drag. I am holding him back, but everything is beginning to feel impossible. The walk back feels miles further than the journey out, and I worry that something might actually be really wrong.

Again, I nap until dinner.

"Are you feeling well enough to eat, ma petite souris?" he asks.

I join him at the table, but my hands are so stiff I soon grow tired of fumbling with my fork and give up. I rub them together to help my circulation, hoping I could blame the cold for making them feel so arthritic. They are boney and pale, but hands have a tendency to shrink as the temperature falls. That's not abnormal.

I gaze up at the portrait of his dead wife, looking down at me, judging me. I realize she is the only other woman in the house, and right now I need a friend. But the scorn in her expression makes me feel even worse and I look away. The moment I do, it strikes me. These earrings. These are his wife's earrings. She was wearing them in that portrait. For all the time it had been hanging right over my head, I had never once noticed her ears.

I should never have snatched them and christened myself his imposter bride. I didn't know. I should never have worn them. I should never have touched them. They are hers. He is hers. How could I ever have entertained some fanciful alternative?

My hands ache, I feel foggy and light-headed, and pain hammers my bones, but I can't sit here. I have to get them off me. I run to my bedroom to rip them from my ears, but my hands aren't working. I turn to my mirror and for the first time since the storm, I really see my face.

I do not recognize the ghastly creature staring back at me. My skin is dry and white, my eyes are sunk deep into my skull, ringed by vortices of deep purple, my eyeballs look like they have a wash of skim milk spilled over them. My teeth have dulled to a filthy grey. I try to touch them, but all the wetness is gone from my mouth, and when my finger taps at the bone, it wiggles like a shell on the beach.

This is not me. I paw at my face and it crumbles at my touch. Frantically, I clean the glass with my sleeve, promising myself that dust is playing a trick on me. But no. The reflection in that mirror is my own; mine is the face of death. The beautiful, luminous earrings throw a blue light over my face, now enhancing the grey complexion of my monstrous face, my skin like shale that you pick up from the ground and crush between your fingers.

I throw myself onto the bed, burying myself in the covers, and there I stay until morning eventually comes. I want to pretend it was a trick of the night sky, casting shadows, painting darkness. I will look again in the daylight. This can't be right.

#

I open my eyes to the sound of Mr. Aubert knocking on my door. I try to call to him that he should enter, but instead of words, dust spills out of my mouth. I watch as it wafts into the air, like the snow had done in the wind.

Mr. Aubert opens the door and walks in. "You are growing weak and withdrawn again."

A warm tear falls down my cheek. Never had he looked so handsome. Never had I felt so frail. He touches my arm and it brittles to crumbs. Sheets of skin splinter off like a calving glacier, falling to the floor and disintegrating.

The morning light shines on him, illuminating him, and I notice, for the first time, that he is wearing a necklace. It glows blue against his chest, catching the sun in a way I recognize immediately. I shudder as I realize that it is the mate to the stolen earrings. He'd known all along.

He carries me down the stairs and sits me in a chair outside to enjoy the beautiful day. I had become so withered and he had become so strong, I feel like a feather in his arms. He tells me there are deer just ahead of us, bounding through the snow, but I can't see. There is a thick haze over the world, obscuring my vision. I ask him to bring me back inside; I can no longer move on my own.

The haze grows thicker until it turns to blackness and I can see nothing at all. All I can feel is the cold. I can no longer tell if my eyes are open or closed, and I hear his voice, faintly, from somewhere far away. "You agreed to this, my love," he says coolly. "You signed the contract when you took those earrings. Now you will be with me always. Is that not what you wanted?" He kisses me.

His soft, warm lips strike me somewhere deeper than I even knew existed. A calm falls over my body, soothing me as the physical world drifts away. The pain is gone, the cold is gone. I look into his eyes and realize I can see again. He brings me up the stairs and toward my bedroom, but he doesn't stop at my door. Instead, he continues climbing with me in his arms. He takes me to the attic, hunching so he doesn't hit his head, but I know he won't drop me. He sets me down in an unfamiliar room and leaves me, closing the door behind him. I hear the attic door close soon after and the sound of his footsteps fade.

The weakness and utter exhaustion have become so rooted they now define me, and I fall asleep in the darkness where I have been left. His kiss has cured me of the cold and pain, and restored my vision, though it is now clear my energy will never return.

I tell myself he's left me here to recover. He'll come back. One day he'll come for me. Until that day, I will remain asleep. What else is there to do? I can wait for him.

#

I can't say how long I sleep. Time is nothing to me now. A minute, a season, a decade, it is all meaningless. I sleep and I sleep until I hear a voice from far away. It wakes me. I feel as if I know it, but I can't place it, and I creep from my room with its thick, heavy door to the window to peek outside. I can stand there only a moment, it is so overwhelmingly bright in the sun, and I am so unaccustomed to the light. I rush away to my familiar darkness and hide.

Again, that voice. It gnaws at me. That familiar, yet unidentifiable voice. I'm now hearing it more and more. I slip out from my secret room to check the house, trying to locate it, but I can't stay long before the weakness overtakes me. It takes so much strength to leave my room. The door is so heavy and I am just a shadow of myself these days, but I have to find her. Who is this woman in my house?

I venture out, night after night, opening the bedroom doors. Where is Mr. Aubert? Where is this woman? Each night I get as far as Sylvan's room. I tiptoe around for a little, hoping he'll wake up and answer my questions. But eventually, I get a glimpse of his face and see that it's not Sylvan there anymore. It's another man I don't know. Someone new.

In my new room, I wait. Sometimes I cry. I don't know what's going on. I am scared and I am lonely and I am becoming impatient waiting for Mr. Aubert to come back to me. Who is this woman whose voice I keep hearing? Why isn't he coming for me?

I hear footsteps approaching. Has he heard me? He heard me crying, and he's coming back for me! The footsteps are coming closer. I can feel him outside my door. I shout for him.

The door opens to reveal the shape of a person I don't know. It is the woman. The light is shining from behind her, obscuring her face. I can't see who she is. She runs her hands over my body, clumsily and carelessly, fondling me like I'm the last cookie in the jar. She shines a light over me, and it's blinding. The torment continues until she notices my earrings. Without a thought, she pulls them from my ears, robbing me. My only possession, my last souvenir from a life I once lived; she tears them from me, tucking them away in the breast pocket of her shirt. Only then does she leave. She lets the door slam in my face and I am once again left in the darkness, listening to footsteps falling farther and farther away.

Henry

by Mo Moshaty

"Three whacks with the hand broom, Henry."

Mama said that was all because I carved my name—well, half my name—in Mr. Henderson's willow tree at the edge of town. I've seen boys carve worse than that. Bad Words. Real bad. But I was the one that got caught and I can barely feel it on my backside anymore. Mama wasn't mostly mad that I was carving you see, just mad 'cause a lot of those boys been missing lately. First was Andy Willers, he disappeared about a month ago.

I understand how the brain works a little. It gets mushy, Mama said, when you're too tired or didn't eat enough or just worked too hard on something. But I wasn't mushy. I know what I saw. I saw Andy Willers right there in my room, with half his head missing. Why? I don't rightly know. But I remember wetting myself and screaming. Mama let me stay home from school that day but scolded me for making up such horrible stories. I knew I hadn't, and I know what I saw, but I wasn't gonna argue.

I had taken to falling asleep with the lights on, which was working pretty well until a tap on my shoulder set me flying against the wall. There, three of them stood, side by side. Andy with his head outta sorts, Mike Fuller, with no nose and mouth, just a big hole, and Ferris Stunt with no arms.

I'm not mushy, I said over and over, and I closed my eyes shut tight and opened them again, but they were still there. I was alone. Trapped in my room with these dead boys. At least I think they're dead, but I can't be sure with them walking around so. Andy motions for me to come.

He smells real bad, but I still follow.

We're walking forever and I'm cold and damp. I smell real bad, too. Coming up over the edge of the hill, I notice we're at the back of Mr. Henderson's farm, that monster of a willow tree looming. The first scarecrow I see looks lumpy and leans to the side. Ferris Stunt, or what's left of him, heads towards the scarecrow. I sorta whisper shout for him. Andy places his ice-cold hand on my shoulder, and I jump.

He puts his finger to his lips. Mike Fuller takes a sharp left turn and stops to stare at me and Andy. The shock of his face sends my ill stomach lurching and I lose all my supper. Mike heads through the corn to the other scarecrow. Andy and I walk in silence. We come upon the last scarecrow and Andy stands for a bit before he points to a window in Mr. Henderson's house. The light is on in what looks like the kitchen.

Mr. Henderson is crying harder than I've ever seen anyone. Andy shoves me forward and points again towards the house. He too disappears into the corn.

Before I've got my wits, I stand outside Mr. Henderson's window and knock. He runs to the front of the house to let me in.

I stumble up the steps, and he hushes me, pulling me in. He drags me to the kitchen, looking out the windows every now and again.

"They came for you, didn't they?" he says.

"Yes, all three of 'em. Are they dead?"

"Yes." His face is sad but strong.

"You kill 'em?"

"No. No I did not. She did." Mr. Henderson points to the giant willow tree that seems to be staring right through us.

"Why?"

"I was going to cut her down. The moment I put the saw blade to her, she shrieked like nothing I've ever heard. And I felt it in my chest. Gave me a heart attack. So, I tried to be gracious to her. Plant flowers around her, read to her. And she was silent again. And then the boys came. And they cut into her flesh, her screams too high for them to hear her."

"So, she cut them."

"Yes."

"And the scarecrows to hide them?"

He nods, sobbing loudly. He stands quickly and grabs the butter knife off the table. I turn to run, and he grabs me.

"You have to finish your name, or the boys will keep coming after you. People will find out what she's done! And then, they'll come after me."

"What you've done." I'm not mushy, I'm NOT mushy. And trees don't kill little boys. Crazy old men do.

His hand is on my throat from behind. He shoves the butter knife in my hand.

"Please. Finish it." He shoves me.

I run to her and fight through the branches to her trunk. I see the etches of the boys, strangely glowing somehow, and off center to theirs is mine. My half- name. I kneel beside it and, through tears, I know what I'm supposed to do. I think of Andy and Mike and Ferris and I know it's gotta be so hard to be dead. They must be so lonely. Lonely enough to get me. Me.

I begin to carve solidly after the N. I'm ripping through. I hear it, small moans, then high shrieks. I turn back to Mr. Henderson, he's bent over like he's gonna run, teeth bared.

I cut harder, few more strokes, then I'm done. I drop the knife and stand back. H-E-N-D-E-R-S-O-N.

I run home, faster than I ever have before. I shake my mama. I tell her everything.

Several policemen and the coroner are on Henderson's farm wheeling out bodies covered in white sheets. A cherry picker is helping a few men cut down Mr. Henderson, hanging by several willow branches wrapped around his neck over fifty feet up. Some folks said there were branches runnin' all through him, like a wire tangle, and through his face like a mask.

We moved that summer to a town upstate. I love everything about the house, except for the willow tree on the edge of the yard.

A Scent of Cloves

by Helen Glynn Jones

She dreamed of shattered hearts and lost souls, of rotting fish cast upon a stony shore. Of dampness and darkness and broken things, porcelain dolls with their limbs askew, cracked faces half buried in soil. Woke each night to the same empty room, the same empty heart, bitterness in her throat. It was going to take time, it seemed.

"Morning. Shall I join you?"

Hannah looked up to see Mrs. Wilson, one of her neighbors, mug in hand.

"Of course." She gestured to one of the empty seats at the table. This had become routine since she'd arrived, the older woman joining her most mornings in the shared outdoor area. Mrs. Wilson—call me Sharon—sat down, crossing her arms beneath her generous bosom as she leaned back.

"Lovely morning, isn't it? A bit fresh, but you do get that at this time of year."

"Hmm. It is nice." Hannah yawned, covering her mouth with her hand. A breeze played along the terrace where they sat, curling through the iron fretwork, dancing across the long green lawns stretching down to silver-blue waves. It was idyllic, really. The perfect antidote to a broken life. Sunlight shone across her arm as she reached for her tea, picking out the reddened lines on the inside of her wrist. She pulled her sleeve down to cover them.

"Did you not sleep well, dear?" The question was sympathetic. Hannah tried not to be annoyed.

"Not so well." She cradled her mug, the tea inside still warm. She took a sip, trying to clear the faint acridness of spice lingering in her throat, strange aftermath of her dreams.

"Funny."

"It is?" Hannah paused mid-sip, wondering why her lack of sleep would be humorous.

"No, I mean it's odd." Mrs. Wilson nodded, tight grey curls bobbing. "The girl that was here before you, in the same flat. She suffered terribly with nightmares, never could sleep. Then she left, all sudden like. Didn't even take her things with her."

'Furnished country house apartment by the sea, short lease,' the ad had read, tucked away in the back of a magazine. It seemed like fate throwing her a lifeline. She'd packed her bags and left before she could change her mind. It had been several weeks now, and she was starting to settle in, as much as she was able. The nightmares that had plagued her since she arrived seemed like reaction, her mind working through the aftermath of break-up and breakdown, creating horrors in the night.

Hannah took another sip of tea, nodding but not really listening as Mrs. Wilson continued talking. A figure emerged from the distant surf, tall and lean in a black wetsuit, surfboard under his arm. Hannah's neighbor, from the only other apartment on her floor. He raised a hand to wave as he came up the long lawn. She smiled but didn't wave back.

Mrs. Wilson continued talking, leaning in close as though she thought perhaps Hannah hadn't heard her. "I did hear as someone's been trying to buy the place you're in, but the owner's refusing to sell. You hear anything, dear?"

"No." Hannah sipped her tea. It wasn't her concern. She would stay until her lease was up, then… Well, she'd figure it out.

"Yours is the last one, apparently."

"The last one?"

"Yes. That buyer, you know. Apparently, they own all the other apartments. But your owner's the only one holding out. Don't know why. The rental income's too good, I suppose."

"Well, it's not too bad." She didn't mind paying it, though. It had seemed a fair price to escape.

"Or maybe it's haunted."

"Haunted?" Hannah almost felt like laughing. It had been a long time since she'd laughed.

"Yes." The other woman lowered her voice, as though sharing a secret. "All those nightmares, you know? Maybe they were caused by… something else. There are stories here."

"Stories?" Hannah frowned.

"Well, of course. In an old place like this, there are always stories. This was a great house once."

"Did you know it then?"

Mrs. Wilson chuckled. "How old d'you think I am? No dear, this is just what I've heard round and about. The last lady of the house, she lost a child. Very sad."

"Lost it?" The breeze on the veranda grew cold, small icy fingers trailing along the back of Hannah's neck.

"Well, so I was told. No one knows what happened to the poor wee thing. They say her mother died of a broken heart."

A broken heart. She'd thought she might die of hers, once upon a time. Yet here she was. "Hmm." She took another sip of tea, swallowing the tears caught in her throat.

"Good morning." They both looked up. Hannah's neighbor stood there, his wetsuit replaced by dark clothing, a mug of tea in his hand. He was smiling, blue eyes creased against the sun.

"Hello." The knot of tension in Hannah's stomach loosened a little.

"May I?" He gestured to the other empty chair.

"Of course," she replied.

Mrs. Wilson smiled.

#

Shadows loomed, gibbering and moaning, cobwebs trailing like smoke across her skin. A bird, one trailing wing broken, flapped desperately, calling, calling…

Hannah woke with the bedcovers tangled around her legs, the bitter scent of cloves in her nostrils. Pale light glinted from the shoes and bags lined up along the mantelpiece of the old stone fireplace, jeweled symbols of the life she no longer had and didn't want. One of the bags had fallen to the ground, and she managed to uncurl herself enough to stand, walking over and picking it up, turning it in her hands as she fought to release the last tattered shreds of nightmare. She replaced the bag on the shelf before dropping back into bed and, this time, into a dreamless sleep.

#

The next day dawned cold, the sky filled with shapeless clouds that hung heavy, like pillows on a washing line. The ocean was a grey smudge at the end of the rain-soaked lawns. Hannah sat in the chair by her window, her knees pulled up to her chest, cradling her mug of tea. She stared out at the endless grey, feeling its echo inside herself. Perhaps it had been a mistake, coming here. A decision made in haste and the haze of grief. There had been other places to go, other people who might have been there for her as her life fell apart. But her phone lit up less frequently now, her inbox filled with unanswered messages, the tethers binding her to her old life loosening day by day.

She thought of Mrs. Wilson, then. The way the other woman's eyes had gleamed as she'd leaned in, telling her sad stories of dead children and broken hearts. If only she'd known. Hannah closed her eyes, trying not to think of the blood, the small vestiges of life, the last pieces of her future swept away. The thing that had broken her, set her adrift, like clouds tattered and taken by the wind. She'd not been able to see a way forward, a way out. Except for one.

It had been the old man downstairs who'd found her at her old apartment. Concerned at the water coming through his ceiling, he'd banged on her door, becoming increasingly frantic as his knocks went unanswered. She still wasn't sure whether to be glad she'd given him a spare key. The paramedics had pulled her from the bathtub, slippery and heavy as a seal cast to shore, bloodied and broken by the storm of her existence.

She'd survived, though. Survived it all. And now she was here. And if there were ghosts here, they were only the ones from her past. She sat until her tea grew cold, her fingers rubbing the empty space on her left hand, another missing piece. There was a knock at the door. She blinked, putting down the cold mug, sliding her feet into slippers and padding to her front door. She unlocked it but left the chain on as she opened it.

Her neighbor stood there, wearing a cream jumper over dark jeans, his dark hair tousled and damp. She ran her hand through her own hair, straightening up.

"I'm just off to the shops." He gestured, as though she might not know where the shops were. "Do you need anything?"

"I'm fine." She shook her head, managing to smile. Perhaps she was even telling the truth, at that moment. "Thanks, though."

When he smiled, his eyes crinkled at the corners, their blue color becoming even brighter. Like a patch of clear sky in the endless grey. As she closed the door, she realized she was still smiling.

He'd introduced himself not long after she'd arrived. Asked her how long she planned on staying. At the time, she'd barely been able to answer, frozen in her grief. She'd hoped he would leave her alone.

But slowly, she'd thawed.

Perhaps being friends with her neighbor was not such a bad thing, after all.

#

That night there were no broken dolls, no twisting, rotted flesh lining a silver shore. Instead, a hunched figure moved near her fireplace, running gnarled fingers along the carved stone, the paneled wall next to it replaced by a dark void. Voices howled and moaned, and a small shadow crept closer, one hand reaching out as it keened. The ocean breeze caught her curtains, belling them out like pale twisted lilies as a creature swooped down, its black wings unfurling, rearing up and back before disappearing as though it had been sucked up the chimney. She was suffocating, cloves bitter in her nostrils, a hand heavy on her neck. Cold air hit her, and Hannah recognized she was awake, her throat raw with screams. But the voices still shrieked and moaned. A child crying for its mother, a woman calling in the wind, the guttural groan of a man in pain. Terrified, she flung back the covers, running into the living room and curling herself into a ball on the chaise by the window, a blanket over her head, whimpering in the hot dark.

After a few minutes, she recognized the voices had changed. There was only one, calling her name, sounding more and more urgent and accompanied by banging. From somewhere, she found the courage to let the blanket slip to her shoulders. Her sitting room was bathed in silver and grey light, the familiar shapes of her things reassuring. The voice was still calling for her. She recognized it.

Hugging the blanket around her, she went to the door, her hands shaking so much she could hardly undo the chain and deadbolt. Finally, she got it open.

Her neighbor stood there, his dark hair tousled, his blue eyes creased with worry.

“Are you all right? I heard you scream, and—” His voice broke and she reached out, her hand hovering above his arm.

“I-I’m sorry. It was a bad dream.” She shivered, pulling the blanket closer around herself. Embarrassed, she started to cry.

“Come on,” he said, his hands on her shoulders as he turned her, steering her back into her flat. She was too dazed to resist. He took her to the sofa, pushing her gently so she sat, then switched on the nearby table lamp, the golden light soothing. "Shall I make tea?"

But she couldn't answer, couldn't stop crying, as though his kindness had unleashed an ocean of tears that seemed endless. She put her hands to her face and curled over, pain a deep hole inside.

His arms came around her, his hands smoothing her hair as she sobbed into his shoulder. He was murmuring something, a rumble under her cheek, but she couldn't hear him over the waves of sorrow. Eventually they abated, the tide of tears retreating, his arms a safe harbor against the storm.

"I can't stay here." She meant something else, but he seemed to take her at her word.

"Come to mine. We can have tea, and there's a spare bedroom where you can sleep."

"What? Oh, no…" She flushed, all at once conscious of how close he was, how little she was wearing. "I didn't mean—"

"It doesn't matter. It makes sense. Come with me. Even if you decide not to stay, we can at least have tea, talk a little."

It was like a dream. The golden light, his warmth against her, the release of emotion leaving her dizzy. She nodded, wiping her face, then rubbed at the mess she'd left on his top. He brushed her hand away, smiling.

"It doesn't matter. Come on." He stood up, offering his hand. She took it.

A short while later she was sitting on his sofa, her blanket still wrapped around her, her fear replaced by something else, something she hadn't felt in so long she didn't recognize it at first. Anticipation. The feeling that maybe, for the first time in a while, life was worth living. There was a clatter of cups from the next room, the reassuring sound of the kettle coming to the boil and she smiled, hugging the feeling to her, relishing the small flame within.

Her neighbor came back into the room, holding a tray with two mugs and a small plate of biscuits, which he set down on the low chrome and glass table nearby.

"Here." He sat next to her, close but not too close, and handed her a mug. "Are you feeling better?"

"I am." It wasn't a lie. "Thank you," she added. "How did you—"

He shrugged. "Hear you? I was out walking. I heard you scream as I was coming back." His blue eyes darkened and she took in a breath. "I'm glad you're all right."

"I am, thanks to you." She sipped her tea. It had a pleasant flavor, with a hint of something spicy. She drank more, unsure what to say next. "So, how long have you lived here?" It seemed a safe question.

"Oh, a few years now." He smiled. "Though it's only become interesting recently."

She smiled too, her head leaning back against the soft cushioned leather. She was feeling very relaxed. Close up, he smelled delicious, a hint of spice like the tea. "Really?"

"Really." He reached for his own tea, taking a drink. "Plus, it suits my work life at the moment."

"Oh?" She felt vaguely disappointed, but was too relaxed to really care. "What do you do?"

He paused, glancing at her. "Electronics, mostly. Special effects, voiceovers, TV, movies, that sort of thing. I also dabble in a bit of property. Just trying to work on a deal at the moment, actually, but the buyer isn't too keen."

"Oh. That's nice." She felt very sleepy now, drinking more of the wonderful tea. "Would I have seen any of your work?" Her voice was slurring, and she giggled. What was wrong with her?

"Yes." He smiled again, but this time his eyes seemed different. "Earlier tonight. And the night before. And the night before that."

"Wha—" Her eyelids were so very heavy.

"I've done some of my best work here, as a matter of fact. Hoping it will pay off soon."

Fear jolted through her and she tried to move, but her limbs refused to respond. He put his mug down, then stood and picked her up as though she were feather light, even though she felt made of lead.

"Please." She tried to cry out, but the word was a whisper of air. She felt as though she were sinking, back in the bathtub again. But this time, she desperately wanted to live.

He grunted, shifting her weight as he opened a door. The scent of cloves billowed out. He carried her into a room with a maze of wires disappearing into the walls and ceiling, lights blinking in an array of dark boxes set up on shelves against two of the walls. And next to the old stone fireplace, so like her own, a piece of panelling was swung back to reveal a passage, more wires disappearing into the void. Hannah glimpsed something pale inside the passage, which resolved into a woman's arm outflung, pale skin blotched with darkness. Next to it was a porcelain doll, its dress tattered and stained, a small hand still clutching it, the fingers pearly bone. Terror cut through her stupor, and she jerked faintly in his arms, but the drug he'd given her was too strong.

She thought of Mrs. Wilson, her talk of the mysterious buyer, of the young woman who'd left so suddenly, of the lost child long ago. Of an old house, filled with secrets, and the turn of events that had brought her here. Then of the ocean, silver light dancing on the waves. It was the last thought she had as he placed her in the small passage, the scent of cloves overpowering a darker, rotten smell.

The panel closed.

The Half Moon Casita

by Anna Fitzgerald Healy

A cloud of dust rose as I turned off Yucca Mesa Trail onto Security Drive. Security Drive didn't look terribly secure, with no houses, mailboxes, or telephone poles, just endless mounds of dirt. Then a left on Ducor Avenue, which seemed to be more of a dry creek than a road. My Audi skidded and lurched over rocky inclines wet with the memory of desert rain.

Our Airbnb glistened in the distance like a hipster mirage, a single speck of humanity in the Instagrammable unknown. The vacation rental was listed as the Half Moon Casita, with the tagline, "tiny house, big sky." I'd booked the bungalow for its teal exterior, peach interior, and unobstructed view of the not-so-Wild West. There was a Joshua tree beside the front door and a garden of blossoming cacti. The middle of nowhere was just as adorable as advertised.

As I parked and pulled open the gate, Ethan got out to document the scenery. I lugged our bags to the front door, sneezing as I unlocked the adobo bungalow. It smelled of mothballs and Irish Spring soap. Neither the rattan décor, vintage kitchen, or Hawaiian-themed wall art could explain the feeling of unease that clung to my skin, so I dropped our bags and rushed outside.

Ethan stood beside a Joshua tree in the blazing sunset. His expression of wow gave me this delicious feeling of maybe. Maybe we could work. Maybe I could fall for him. Maybe I wouldn't grow bitter and wrinkled and die alone. It was hard to believe that I was on a weekend getaway—a birthday weekend getaway—with someone as muscular, sensitive, and European as Ethan. On our first date, I'd saved him as British Dreamboat in my phone, and despite the occasional rocky road—but none as perilous as Ducor Avenue—

it was still smooth sailing.

"The Mojave Desert has exceeded my wildest expectations," Ethan said in his posh London accent. I wished that he would kiss me and pull me against his washboard abs as the desert sun fell to its knees—but instead, he took a selfie.

Dinner was at a Wild West set from the golden era of Hollywood. We pushed through swinging saloon doors into a crowd of ten-gallon hats and daisy dukes. Cow skulls and bottle-cap mosaics lined the walls. Our whiskey barrel table was topped with a broken wagon wheel. I'd thought that the cowboy kitsch would delight Ethan, but as he took in the cowboy bar, he pursed his lips and fell silent. He gazed out the window, as though for a means of escape.

I could never decipher the meaning behind these lulls in conversation. Did Ethan feel awkward because it was my birthday? Was this too much commitment for him? As the hush settled around us, I felt goosebumps rise on my arms. Shared silence has always unnerved me. While clowns, cockroaches, heights, and public speaking have never scared me, excessive quiet does. Sedatephobia was the word for that—a crippling fear of silence.

Other, slightly less all-consuming phobias: liverwurst, never being loved, and possession.

The sedatephobe in me always freaked out when Ethan got silent like that but I told myself it was just his British reserve. Quiet and mysterious was sexy, right? So instead, I talked at Ethan. When our waitress came, I spoke with her. When she left, I chatted with the guys at the next table. The more words I said, the more silent Ethan became, retreating into his catfish tacos.

"Can't we just enjoy a nice, quiet moment together?" he finally asked.

It was a relief when the waitress cleared our plates. As Ethan frowned at the bill, I asked if he would like to try another spot.

We drove down dark roads across undulating fields of cacti,

under an endless tundra of stars. In a city, it was easy to forget just how empty the world was, but in the desert, the void took center stage. The barren landscape reminded you of how much nothing could exist between two houses, or two people. Ethan turned in his seat to watch the dark landscape roll by, and I felt the distance between us lengthen. The silence was as endless and unbroken as the Mojave Desert.

Our next stop was the Joshua Tree Saloon. Ethan actually smiled as he surveyed the scene of flannel and karaoke, then he settled onto a barstool, hunched over his drink, and fell silent once more. I extended my wineglass across to clink it against his beer mug. He glanced up at me, then resumed scrolling through his phone. I sipped my wine and waited, but Ethan's lips were still. And, of course, he wasn't saying the two most important words of all: happy birthday.

Finally, he spoke: "Let's go to another bar. Let's take shots."

"We should probably call it a night. I won't be able to off-road if I'm drunk," I explained. As a dyslexic city boy, Ethan wasn't much of a driver, which meant that the chauffeur service was always up to me.

"Are you sure?" He sighed, then looked back down at his phone. "A pity."

#

We drove back to Ducor Avenue, gasping and laughing as the Audi almost—but didn't quite—got stuck in a ditch. "I have some wood in the car. Should we light a fire and count shooting stars?" I asked as I wrestled with the latch to the Half Moon Casita. "Or we could take long-exposure shots of the constellations." Words tumbled out of my mouth as the chilly November wind swept across the Mojave Desert, turning my breath into tiny nebulas. They drifted up into the sky as I huddled against the side of the building and struggled with the key.

A grunt from Ethan, who seemed uncompelled by either campfires or astronomy.

The door wheezed open, and the scent of Irish Spring wafted over us. As I sat down on the pink couch, silence settled over us. It was louder than the desert wind. Louder than the distant wail of a coyote. Ethan reached out to rest a hand on my thigh.

"Such a shame there's no telly," he said. As he leaned in to kiss me, I sighed with relief. Now that our lips were locked, it wasn't so awkward that no words were coming out of them.

Then—it was such a curious sensation—it was as if someone whispered: Never touch him again, into my ear.

I looked around. We were alone in the Half Moon Casita. Incredibly alone. Perhaps the most alone that I'd ever been with another human being. There wasn't another soul for miles. What had I just heard? Was I so desperate for conversation that I'd started conjuring up voices? Was this late-onset schizophrenia?

Please don't sleep with him.

Ethan's lips were on mine. His fingers tugged at my blouse, trying to unfasten it.

Never touch him again.

I tried to play it cool as I surveyed the room. Everything was nice and normal, so why was a prudish old maid inside of my head, slut-shaming me?

"Maybe we should go to the bedroom," I murmured. "This couch is—"

"So tiny. My thoughts exactly."

Never touch him again.

As we lay down in bed, I tried not to think about the nagging whisper inside of my brain. I relaxed into silence for the first time that day. Welcomed it, as it enveloped us.

#

The next day there were breakfast burritos and rock climbing and hammocks and so much beauty it was difficult to think about whispers in the dark. We sat on a cliff, overlooking an expanse of rocks and cacti. Joshua Tree, California, was located at the southern tip of the Mojave Desert. Where our hiking trail ended, the badlands began—135-miles of uninhabitable wasteland, stretching to the Mexican border. An eagle wafted past as we dangled our legs over the abyss. Ethan reached across the divide to take my hand.

Then it was back to the Joshua Tree Saloon for hungry tacos and exhausted beers. "Let's go back to Pappy and Harriet's. Let's take shots," Ethan said with his signature fake smile.

I laughed. "That road is a death trap. We should probably head back soon."

#

Back at the Half Moon Casita, I found Candy Land in a closet and turned it into a drinking game. We took shots of Café Patron as our game pieces journeyed across a confectionary obstacle course. When Ethan kissed me, his lips tasted like espresso-flavored tequila. He pulled me to my feet, led me to the bedroom and—

Never touch him again.

My eyes shot open. I was lying in bed with Ethan's arms wrapped around me, and the prude was back inside my head.

It isn't safe. Do not sleep with him.

I kissed rebelliously, with a conviction that I'd never felt for Ethan before. This voice didn't know who she was talking about. Sure, Ethan might look like he was training for the sequel to Gladiator, but he was also lazy and docile. Annoyingly, I couldn't imagine him hurting a fly. He would probably ask me to kill it for him.

Do. Not. Let. Him. Touch. You.

The silence receded as our skin spoke in a language that requires no words. Then Ethan turned on his side, and I rushed to the bathroom to change into a slip. When I opened the door, I found Ethan asleep with the lights on. I turned off the lamp and lay down beside him.

Please, never let him touch you again.

I longed for silence, but the warnings continued as my British lover gently snored. Hours passed in the Half Moon Casita as I listened to the words inside my head that were not my own.

Something is going to happen. Be very careful. You are in danger.

As if on cue, Ethan sat up. I felt the mattress shift beneath me as he rose. He stomped through the house, muttering and swearing. He flung open drawers then slammed them shut, his angry sighs echoing through the adobo bungalow.

Stay very quiet. Breathe in and out. Don't let him know that you're awake.

I wasn't sure if I was more scared by the mental instructions or Ethan's nocturnal temper tantrum, but I stayed put and did as I was told.

You are in danger.

I considered Ethan: the vision of British gentility, always mild-mannered and polite. He didn't enjoy talking about himself, and he hated being the center of attention. He was making more noise now than I had ever heard from him before.

Stay very quiet. Breathe in and out. Don't let him know that you're awake.

What did I know about Ethan? Like really, truly know about him? I knew he was from London. We'd hung out in England any number of times, but strangely, I'd never seen his apartment. When I came to visit, he always stayed at my hotel. Once I'd asked if we could spend the night at his place, but he blushed and coughed, as if I'd said something rude. I hadn't questioned it before, but now I had to wonder: what was he hiding?

I knew he was dyslexic. I knew he couldn't drive. I knew he was so averse to transportation that he even disliked ordering his own Uber. Ethan always preferred if I ordered it for us.

But what if that was a lie, too? What if he killed me now, took my Audi, and drove across the border to Mexico?

Our meeting had been completely random. I'd been rushing out of my art gallery when I ran into him on the sidewalk. There were no mutual friends. No background check on a dating app. I was essentially sleeping with a stranger. Which led me to wonder: was I really having a psychotic break, or was this irrational fear the first rational feeling I'd had in months?

Stay very quiet. Breathe in and out. Don't let him know that you're awake.

A crash as something fell in the living room. A muttered curse. Footsteps stomping toward me. Unexpected cold as my blankets were yanked off. I tried to look peaceful and unconscious as I trembled internally. I counted the seconds, mentally preparing to be ripped to shreds. I pictured my blood splattered across the walls of the vacation rental. Envisioned the cleaners' horror when they discovered my guts ground into their carpet. Imagined that headline in the local newspapers: "Tiny house, big carnage." I readied myself to receive the worst Airbnb rating in history.

Then Ethan sighed and settled down onto the mattress. There was a soft hiss of fabric as he arranged the blankets over himself. I stayed frozen for several minutes. Not moving. Barely breathing. Listening to the auguries inside of my head.

Then—screeching. Deep, guttural, soul-wrenching screams. The wails reverberated through the bungalow. Ethan was lying in bed with his eyes wide open, his face a mask of terror.

Surprise broke my paralysis. "Wake up!" I grabbed his shoulders, and Ethan screamed even harder. "Babe, you're dreaming."

The screaming stopped as suddenly as it had begun. Ethan collapsed onto the mattress and fell fast asleep. Then I lay back down, and so too did I.

#

I woke up at sunrise, feeling jittery and disoriented. I glanced over at Ethan, who was dosing peacefully under his mountain of blankets. Then I climbed out of bed and hopped into the shower. Ethan's wails echoed through my eardrums as I scrubbed my skin. When the hot water ran out, I wrapped myself in a towel and cautiously opened the door. Ethan was lying in the peach rattan bed, in the achingly hip vacation rental, scrolling through his phone. It was hard to imagine anywhere that chic being the setting of night terrors.

"So… you're a sleepwalker?" I asked. That seemed the only reasonable explanation: Ethan was a sleepwalker, and I was a schizophrenic. A match made in heaven.

"I wasn't sleepwalking." Ethan frowned. "I woke up at three o'clock, and the house was freezing. It was so chilly I could see my own breath. So I got up to look for blankets."

I laughed as I toweled off my hair. "How weird, I wasn't cold at all."

"I was surprised you were sleeping through it. You seemed so comfortable."

Ethan was swaddled in blankets, and he had stolen my sheets in the middle of the night. That much of his story checked out. But cold didn't explain why I'd heard him rattling around in the kitchen, or the silent commentary that accompanied it.

"Then that other thing happened." I hesitated. "You screamed."

Ethan blushed as pink as the bedroom walls. "It's rather awkward, but I dreamt that you were sitting up in bed, and your eyes were glowing."

"Glowing!" I gasped.

"It sounds mental, but you were muttering the same words over and over again. You were possessed. Like in the movies. I yelled your name and tried to snap you out of it, but your eyes glowed even brighter, and you began floating over the bed. Then I woke up, and you were shaking my shoulders."

"Me? Possessed?" I shuddered—my third biggest fear.

"I'm sorry. It's so embarrassing," Ethan said, then resumed scrolling through his phone.

"I had an odd experience, too," I said after a moment.

"Really? What happened?"

How to say: I-may-have-suffered-a-psychotic-break-and-my-subconscious-thinks-that-you're-trying-to-kill-me? "I dreamt that we were here, and someone was trying to hurt me in the house." I stumbled lamely on my words.

"Who was trying to hurt us?" Ethan asked.

I shook my head. "It gets all fuzzy. I don't remember."

As I locked the door to the Half Moon Casita, Ethan wore a wistful smile. "You know, I'm going to miss this place," he said. Then I closed the gate and drove back to the outside world. What had happened last night? Had something in my gut been telling me to end the relationship? Was the Half Moon Casita trying to warn me of impending doom? Had a ghost tried reenacting a murder? Was I schizophrenic? Was I possessed? Was Ethan possessed? What was possession? And could I ever really love someone who scared me so much?

In one moment, I had encountered my three greatest fears: silence, never being loved, and possession. I thanked God there hadn't been any liverwurst.

#

Four months later, we were in London, in a different (but equally cute) Airbnb. And this time, I was the one screaming.

"It's a dream," Ethan said, taking my hand. "Wake up. Everything is fine."

I swam back to consciousness. Ethan was lying beside me, concern painted across his aristocratic features. "I'm sorry, I had a nightmare." I gulped.

Ethan laughed. "I can see that. What happened?"

I was too disoriented to come up with a convincing lie, so instead I told the truth. "I dreamt that you were watching me sleep, and you kept winking and giggling. Then you started to advance, and I don't know why, but I was convinced you were trying to hurt me. I begged you to stop." But I didn't mention the voice from the Half Moon Casita. I didn't confess the unease that had clung to me ever since. I could still hear the chorus in the back of my head: Stay very quiet. Breathe in and out. Don't let him know that you're awake.

Ethan brushed a stray curl away from my cheek. "I promise never to giggle," he said, then gazed deeply into my eyes and pouted.

#

Six months later, we were in my bungalow in the Hollywood Hills. I lived in the carriage house of an estate from the Victorian era that had once housed the horses of such silent film stars as Clara Bow and Bela Lugosi. The house was cute but dilapidated, gradually decaying into the scenery. I was sitting on the rug and Ethan was lying on the sofa, swiping aimlessly on his phone. I could tell from the way he occasionally batted his eyelashes at me that he wanted me to initiate sex. But the silence that hung between us was hardly an aphrodisiac.

"I'm going to bed," I said abruptly. As I climbed upstairs, I saw a vague flicker of hurt in his eyes. Was Ethan upset I hadn't been seduced by his disinterest? Was he offended that I hadn't offered him an invitation to join me on a silver platter?

As I pulled on pajamas and drifted off to sleep, I suddenly realized I was living in a horror story. But not the fun kind—there were no zombies, witches, or sexy vampires here. This was a spine-tingling tale of apathy. A blood-curdling story of mediocrity. A bone-chilling yarn of poorly matched lovers. The silence between Ethan and I was more terrifying than any possession film. It was as if I were lying in the bed of an achingly hip vacation rental, pretending that everything was okay, while screaming internally at the top of my lungs.

I awoke to a whimper at the foot of my bed and squinted into shadows. Something was in my room. Was it a wild animal? Had a raccoon somehow broken in? It was one of those dark nights without even a fragment of moon shining through the windows, so I had no idea what was skulking through my bedroom.

Stay very quiet. Breathe in and out. Don't let him know that you're awake. The voice from the desert had followed me home.

The snivel came again, but closer this time. I turned on my lamp to discover Ethan clutching a blanket at the foot of my bed. He was shivering uncontrollably, looking extremely pissed off.

"Your house is s-s-soooo c-c-colllldddd," he stuttered through chattering teeth. As he spoke, I could see his breath drifting out of his mouth, to hang suspended in the dimly lit room. This was surprising, as the heat was on and we were in Southern California.

"Wh-what is wrong with your house?" Ethan stammered. "Wh-wh-what is wr-wr-wrong with all the p-p-places that we stay together? Wh-why do I always wake up in the mm-mmm-middle of the night feeling as if I'm going to fr-fr-freeze to death?"

I suppressed a smile. "You should get your circulation checked out, bro."

"Nn-nn-noooo," Ethan moaned. "It isn't something that is wrong w-w-w-ith me, it is something wrong with you." As Ethan stuttered, I glimpsed movement in the dark hallway behind him. Something lurked in the shadows.

Ethan didn't hear the footsteps approach us, but I did. He didn't see the shiver of movement behind him, but I did. Ethan was frozen with fear, yet he didn't sense the quiver of air creeping up beside him. I strained my eyes. It was dim, but it was there. Something dusty and imprecise hovered about a foot behind Ethan. I could barely make out the blurry shape in the weak glow of my bedside lamp.

And suddenly I realized: we weren't alone. We had never been alone. There was a not-so-passive observer, watching our every move. An overlooked bystander that chilled Ethan at night and whispered sweet nothings into my ear. In the daylight we didn't notice it, but at night that lingering, eerie something took center stage. All the night terrors had had one intent—to drive a wedge between us. To save me from another day of tedious silence. Whatever presence I'd felt in the Half Moon Casita was still here, and it was trying to end our relationship.

And—I knew it was a rather rude and unladylike thing to do—but I laughed.

Ethan grew even paler, which I hadn't thought possible. "You really are p-p-possessed, you disrespectful b-b-bitch," he said through chattering teeth. Swearing was so out of character for him, it made me laugh even harder. Ethan was horrified by my rudeness. More alarmed by my bad manners than he was by the supernatural chill freezing him from the inside out.

"If the house is freaking you out, then why don't you leave?" I asked as I wiped tears from my eyes. Ethan's eyes widened and his fists clenched. Was he going to hit me?

"Don't worry, I'll order you an Uber," I said, then grabbed my phone and hopped out of bed. As I rushed past Ethan, I felt something tingly and warm briefly brush across my skin.

The Uber was right around the corner. It was as if it had been waiting for us the entire time. I sat on my staircase and watched Ethan slam the door, then listened to his receding, sulky footsteps. I felt like I could still see that shy, shimmery something, out of the corner of my eye. I continued to sit there as the blushing sun rose, and silence enveloped us.

The thing I'd never understood about silence was how subjective it was. While the wrong company could be worse than no company at all, and the ensuing silence made your skin crawl, the right kind of companionship could produce the opposite effect. When the other person really got you and had your back, silence wasn't so scary anymore. Sometimes it could actually be rather pleasant.

I smiled into the shadows of my not-so-empty house and relaxed into the not-so-silent silence. And I stayed very quiet and breathed in and out, relieved to know I was finally awake.

Scabrous

by Victoria Nations

The shed stood at the back of the yard and stared at the house. It had been built by the first owner, the one who cleared all but the copse of trees that hemmed it in. Their branches hung low, dribbling Spanish moss across its face like messy hair falling into filmy window eyes. The aluminum roof bowed from a fallen branch, giving it hunched shoulders above its cataract glare. Whether shame or furtiveness made it duck its head, when the sun crossed its face, and its smeared windows seemed to light with different emotions, fear was not among them.

#

A new family toured the house, and the shed thrummed with each of their steps, shaking awake until it was giddy with anticipation. The first owner had toured the place with the same dazed joy. He'd marveled at the deep yard, large enough to build a workshop set far from the house. He'd set each plank despite the stifling heat, wishing for hands that were too busy to commit sin, for a mind too distracted to follow the dark trail of his thoughts. First two walls, then three, but when he finally closed himself in, gruesome appetites rose in his throat and choked him.

The family stood on the back lanai, getting closer. The parents asked the realtor for details on lawn care, while the daughter stood at the edge, her eyes on the shed. She had been dubious of this move, holding her emotions back from her parents. But seeing the dark wooden building tucked under trees like a witch's cottage broke her mask, and excitement seeped out. The family locked eyes, close to a decision.

#

Hazy sunlight filled the inside of the shed, empty and still for many years, coating everything in a butter yellow glow. The work bench even looked clean in that light. The splotched concrete floor showed dust tracks of roaches and mice, and there were remnants of snakeskin coiled in the corner, but there were no footprints despite the five little girls that dwelled there.

The girls huddled together, away from the work bench the first owner had called an altar. An animated discussion passed through the circle, with open palms and hands planted on hips, their voices kept low so they wouldn't bounce off the wooden walls. The girl in running shorts shook her head, hands rising to her ears as she argued with the girl in a floral jumper. The girl in an off-shoulder T-shirt looked ready to cry, and another in a cotton dress put her arm around her in a practiced gesture. The girl in threadbare shorts and a sleeveless top watched the back and forth without speaking, looking between the windows and the debate of adding another to their play group.

#

The first owner had sanctified the shed. Scabrous lichen covered the outside, curled and thick at the edges like his crusted skin where they'd scratched and bit him. The splotched concrete hid a tooth he'd pried out with needle-nose pliers. Mildew crawled up the window frames in the same tracks as his blood when he'd sliced his fingers and painted the walls. Rot was taking it from inside and out, just as the grisly memories overtook him. When the police had finally come, they were both tumbling down. But the first owner was gone, and the shed built with his body and blood still stood, a squat toad brooding in the backyard.

#

The daughter stepped off the lanai and walked towards the shed. People moved behind the grimy windows; flashes of bright clothes like little girls would wear. They turned and saw her walking towards them, she was sure of it. Pale faces with dark eyes, topped with tousled hair and maybe a colorful scrunchie. She raised her hand to wave and walked faster to the neighborhood girls, girls she might play with if they bought the house, girls who might be future friends. Their heads ducked as a long, breathy sigh blew by. The breeze keened in the branches overhead.

The girls had heard that sigh before, though it had been a long time. The sound started like grasses rustling, tentative and breathless, as if someone was holding their excitement in and had let free, the release nearly a groan. One had heard it at the edge of the field behind the house, another from a hedge on the next street over. It had become panting after the man had grabbed them, faster and more guttural as he squeezed them until they couldn't catch their own breath.

#

Voices grew closer in the backyard. The shed shifted, setting its footing, its roof crunching as it arched and squatted deeper, as if ready to leap. The floral dress girl held up her hands, gesturing at the creaking walls. Pops and groans tolled around them, sounds like bones clacking together and sinews stretched until they twanged. The blue jeaned girl dropped her head, mouthing "no, no." The girls startled as air sucked in through the cracked frame, a fetid breeze swirling dust off the floor and lifting their hair not at all. Four sets of eyes stared at the swelling ceiling. The last set stared at the door, willing it to stay closed, willing this family to leave.

The shed settled itself, a sharp maw ready to spring shut and swallow.

#

The realtor opened the door to the empty shed, and the parents exclaimed at the storage space. Tools, the lawnmower, their old bins of toys would all fit in there. It just needed some cleaning. The daughter looked around for the girls in bright colors she'd seen moving behind the windows, but everything was grim shades of gray and brown, so dark they were nearly black.

Arbor Hills

by Deana Lisenby

Richard stared at the intricate droplets that swirled and dribbled along the windowpanes. Their formations looked like a spider's web of drooping wet lines. Each flash of lightning enhanced the web's trickling design. The only thing missing was an arachnid, lurking, awaiting its prey.

The walls around Richard shifted and creaked, and the bulb in his lamp flickered. The storm was strengthening, and the shabby old building fought to withstand the harsh winds. He wondered how much more Arbor Hills could take.

He sighed and rose from his rickety desk. It was getting late, and tomorrow held a busy schedule. He began stacking his paperwork into a neat pile but froze as a chill came over him. A painful cry, somewhere beyond the window, competed against the sounds of pattering rain. Richard snapped his gaze toward the brutal howl, but the stormy darkness was too dense to see beyond the glass.

Movement from the corner of the windowpane.

Richard's heart pounded as he focused on the spot, each of his breaths becoming shallow.

Blurred edges of a withered face stared at him from the filmy glass.

No, not from the glass—reflected from behind him.

Richard knocked his chair back and turned to face the room.

Nothing. No one. He was alone, just as he'd been all evening.

His hands shook as he looked toward the window once more. The face was gone.

Richard opened and closed his eyes in forceful blinks. He was exhausted—that was the only logical explanation. But a current of unease still rippled across his nerves. With a shaky breath, he righted his fallen chair and readjusted his stack of papers. When everything was in its place, Richard shuffled away from his study nook toward his bedroom, but a sharp rap on the apartment door halted his steps.

"Who's there?"

A soft click sounded from across the room. The doorknob twisted, and the wooden door rattled with movement. He gripped the nearby door frame as his heartrate accelerated.

"Knock, knock," a voice called. "Dr. Reed? It's Angie." A petite woman poked her head through a crack in the doorway. The corridor behind her was filled with a gloomy dimness.

"Angie." He sighed, exasperation coating his voice. "You startled me." He took a step toward the young nurse. "What's going on?"

"Sorry, Dr. Reed. I was just passing by and heard some commotion. I wanted to make sure everything was okay. It's pretty late."

A reassuring smile crossed her lips, and Richard's breathing steadied. Angie was the best nurse he knew, and he appreciated the extra concerns she held only for him.

"All is well, Angie," he said. "I'm just heading to bed now. I've got a full schedule tomorrow."

"Of course, Dr. Reed," she replied. "Sorry to disturb you, then. Have a good night." After another smile, she turned and left the apartment.

A beat passed before Richard realized his front door had been unlocked.

Strange. He could have sworn he locked it, but how else could Angie have opened the door? He decided not to dwell on the abnormality of it. It had been a long day, after all. Instead, he locked the door to his apartment, all thoughts drifting toward his comforting bed.

After completing his residency in medical gerontology, Dr.

Richard Reed secured a coveted position at Arbor Hills Skilled Nursing and Memory Care, complete with room and board in designated staff quarters. His days were long and often grueling, but he relished his elusive position, and he took pride knowing the work he did elevated the quality of life for the residents of Arbor Hills.

Richard clung to this thought as he picked at the soggy oatmeal delivered with his morning breakfast tray. The pale sludge was tasteless without an ample addition of sugar, but even then, it was a struggle to eat. He wondered if the Arbor Hills residents were privy to finer cuisine compared to what was offered to the staff. Then again, did most of these residents even know what they were eating?

He glanced at his watch. With a groan, he rose to his feet and assembled his half-eaten breakfast dishes on his tray. Richard picked up his briefcase and, holding the tray in his other hand, pulled open the door to his apartment. He placed the tray on the small ledge in the hallway, locked his door, and began his walk down the narrow corridor.

Fluorescent lights illuminated the windowless interior as Richard passed the closed doors of empty staff apartments. He lived toward the end of the hallway, and initially he'd loved the privacy that afforded him, but lately he felt alone, isolated.

"Help me! Help me!"

Richard turned toward the muffled call, swinging his briefcase out to steady his sudden movement. What was going on with his balance lately? Maybe he wasn't getting enough rest.

The feeble voice hollered again from behind the nearest closed door. Richard stepped toward it and jiggled the handle. Odd. It wasn't locked. He pushed open the door to reveal a dark room, the only visible light creeping through a bleary window.

"Help me," a woman moaned, and it took Richard a moment to locate the poor voice. A Victorian couch sat next to the window, cushions in disarray, and a frail body slumped at its base behind an oval coffee table.

"Ma'am," he said. "Are you okay?" Richard hurried toward the woman, careful not to step on her shoeless toes as he reached her side. He stifled a gag as he knelt beside her and averted his gaze from the cracked, yellow toenails staring up at him.

"Get away!" she spat. "I don't want you. I need the nurse!"

"My name is Dr. Reed. I'm here to help you."

"No! Nurse! Nurse!" The woman's eyes were wide and frantic.

"Please," he replied, "Why don't you tell me what happened? Are you in pain?"

"No! No!" she cried. The woman closed her eyes and shook her head. "Help me!"

"Did you slip off of the cushion?" Richard asked, gesturing at the disheveled couch.

"He's here!"

"Who's here?" A jolt of adrenaline surged through him as he recalled last night's blurred face in the windowpane. Had this woman seen it too?

No, that was preposterous. He couldn't let his thoughts get carried away. Exhaustion was the culprit for his strange anomalies, nothing more, nothing less.

"Please," Richard said again, "tell me what happened, and I promise I'll be able to help you."

Light flooded the room as a nurse he didn't recognize entered the apartment, followed by Angie and two nursing aides.

"What's going on?" the first nurse asked, her eyes sweeping the room. "Dr. Reed, what are you doing in here?"

Richard bristled at her tone, but he didn't retaliate. This wasn't the time or place.

"I heard someone calling for help, so I came to see what was wrong. She must have slipped from her seat." He nodded toward the woman on the floor.

"Lies!" she shouted. "Lies!"

"Dr. Reed," Angie said. "Why don't you come with me and explain what's going on." She gripped his elbow, guiding him to his feet.

Richard tightened his fingers around the handle of his briefcase and cast another glance at the woman on the floor.

"I really think I need to stay," he said. "It looks to be a serious situation."

"Yes, sir," Angie replied. "But I know you have a booked schedule today. I don't want it on my conscience if you fall behind."

Richard grunted in response as the two of them entered the corridor, leaving the chaos behind. As much as he hated to admit it, Angie was right.

"Besides," she continued, "if anything escalates, you'll be the first to know."

Richard scoffed. "Are you sure about that? I've never even seen that woman before. Why haven't I been notified of her arrival?"

"She's new here, Dr. Reed. The plan was to introduce you after she got settled." They stopped at the medical station, and Angie pulled out the chair at his usual spot behind the counter. "You know how the logistics of new move-ins work. It takes some time to get situated."

"Yes," he replied. "That's true, but what is a new resident doing in the staff accommodations?" Richard sat down. His regular cup of coffee was already waiting for him on the countertop.

"Oh, no sir. The rooms at this end of the hallway have been converted to house residents. You know, because of the higher census. I thought someone told you that. Sorry for the miscommunication, Dr. Reed."

He frowned at her statement, unsure of what to say. The entire situation was completely bizarre. Luckily, he didn't have to remain in awkward silence for long. Angie soon stepped away, leaving

Richard to settle into his workstation.

He spent his morning devoted to monotonous paperwork. Though tedious, it was vital to keep his patients' medical records up to date. He worked in methodical silence, honing his attention to his work rather than the bustle of Arbor Hills. Nursing staff came and went from the medical station. Housekeepers and dining staff passed by with large rolling carts. Clusters of residents—most using walkers or wheelchairs—scuffled to and fro, doing their best to pass the time between breakfast and lunch.

A clatter sounded at the front of the medical station. Richard gripped his chair and twisted to the noise, startled to see an old hag hunched at the main counter. He forced himself to blink, to refocus his vision, but the image didn't clear. Rather, the weathered face craned to look at him.

"What do you want?" the hag croaked. She traced a deep wrinkle from her mouth to her cheekbone with a brittle, yellowing claw. The lines on her face were dark and unmoving, like calcified crevices in a forgotten gorge.

Who was this woman? Surely there hadn't been another new move-in without him knowing. He scanned his memories of recent admissions and discharges. Nothing new or different flagged his attention.

"Well?" she said.

Richard peered back at her, subtle recognition inching into place. This was the woman on the floor, the woman calling for help this morning. He opened his mouth to speak, but words evaded him. The woman smirked and shook her head.

"It's time for lunch, Dr. Reed."

Angie was back, approaching from a door on his left.

He glanced down at his watch. Where had his morning gone?

"Will you take your meal privately today?" Angie asked, "or are you planning to visit with the residents?"

Richard lifted his gaze, first to Angie, then toward the old hag.

His breath caught in his chest. The woman was gone.

"Dr. Reed?"

"The woman—" he began, unable to do anything more than gesture toward where she'd stood. He cleared his throat and shook his head, trying his best to see beyond the haze closing in around him.

"What woman?"

"She was just here. Where did she go?"

"Hmm," Angie said. "I didn't see her. She must have left before I came back. Sorry, Dr. Reed."

His heart thrummed with relentless speed, and his knees threatened to shake. He hoped Angie didn't notice. Keeping a firm grip on the chair, he made his way around it with careful, deliberate steps before sinking into the seat.

"I'll take my lunch here today," he said. "Thank you, Angie."

The day remained overcast and gray as the hours passed, and by late afternoon, a new storm brewed in the distance, bringing with it an anticipated front of cooler temperatures. Richard was in the midst of patient rounds when the first crack of thunder sounded, sending vibrations through the bones of Arbor Hills. He made his way toward the residents' central common area, preparing to search for his next patient, but traces of a hushed conversation halted his steps before rounding the corner.

Four women hovered around a square table with a jigsaw puzzle in its center. Two sat in wheelchairs, one motorized and one normal. Both had similar hairstyles of white, curly helmets. The third woman sat on the seat of her walker holding a water bottle between shaky hands. The fourth woman, the frailest of the group, stood overlooking the table. She seemed to be the only one paying any attention to the puzzle.

"What do you mean you haven't heard anything?" asked the

woman in the motorized chair. "Don't you pay attention to what goes on around here? How dense are you, Betty?"

"Now Judy," said the woman working the puzzle. "There's no need to be rude." She lifted her gaze from the expansive jigsaw. "Betty isn't the only one. I haven't heard anything either."

"Doris and I aren't your neighbors," said Betty, the woman in the plain wheelchair. "We aren't around the same things as you and Ramona."

Judy scowled, but her feisty demeanor seemed to settle. Richard inched closer to the conversation, careful to remain out of sight. He didn't want to startle the ladies into silence.

"Very well," Judy said. "But you still need to keep an ear out. That voice is haunting our entire wing."

"I've seen him too." The woman sitting on the walker gestured with her water bottle. "Roaming the halls. I've even seen him in my room."

Richard's stomach clenched at their words—a haunting voice, a man roaming the halls. His thoughts drifted back to the blurred face in the corner of his window. It sounded like these women had encounters similar to his. A shiver ran through him at this possibility. Maybe exhaustion wasn't the culprit, after all.

A loud thunderclap ricocheted through Arbor Hills, sending the hallway lights into a blinking frenzy. Richard's vision swam at the sudden strobe effect, and he slapped his hand against the wall to offset his rising vertigo.

"What the hell is wrong with this place?" Judy exclaimed from her spot near the table. "Everything is falling apart around here."

"It's just the storm," Doris replied, seemingly unfazed by the horrific light show.

Richard pressed his eyelids together and inhaled while counting to five. He exhaled to the same rhythm before opening his eyes. The lights gave a final, feeble attempt to remain on, but it was in vain.

With a sharp buzz, the power failed, leaving Arbor Hills in complete darkness.

"Well, isn't that great," Judy grumbled. "Now we can't see a damned thing."

"The emergency power system ought to be kicking in," Doris said. "We'll have more light soon."

"It should be on now," Judy countered, a string of exasperated mumbles following her statement.

Richard found himself silently agreeing with the old woman. Arbor Hills was a healthcare facility. It was designed to maintain power through the most severe outages, so this delay was concerning. He needed to find the other staff members and offer his assistance. Finally feeling stable, he stepped away from his place against the wall.

"Unless this wasn't caused by the storm."

Richard paused, his attention shifting back to the four women.

"What was that, Ramona?" Judy asked.

"The reason the back-up system isn't on," Ramona said. "Maybe it wasn't the storm. Maybe it was him."

"Come on now, don't be absurd." Doris's disbelieving voice echoed down the hallway. For such a frail woman, her mind was clearly intact.

"I agree," Betty said. "That's just crazy talk."

"Maybe. Maybe not," Ramona said. "With everything I've experienced though, I think it's a real possibility."

"How could another resident cut off the power?" Betty asked.

"Well now," Judy cut in, "we never said he's a resident."

"What do you mean?"

"This place is haunted, Betty. He's a ghost."

"Or a phantom, or maybe a lost spirit," Ramona said.

"Hogwash," Doris scoffed, her silhouette shifting behind the table. "Arbor Hills isn't haunted. You two sound like a couple of conspiracy loons."

"Believe what you want then," Judy crooned. "I'm with Ramona on this one. I think it was him."

The hairs on the back of Richard's neck pricked upward as he stood in the darkness.

Him—the nameless ghost haunting the grounds of Arbor Hills.

Doris was right. The entire idea was ridiculous, but he felt a small, internal tug claiming otherwise.

As afternoon shifted into evening, full power still eluded Arbor Hills. The back-up lights did their job, but the glow emitted by the dim bulbs cast eerie shadows along the walls. With his daytime schedule fulfilled, Richard weaved through the dull hallways, making his way toward the wing relegated to staff housing. His shoulders sagged as he lugged his briefcase, the weight of the strange day looming over him. He envisioned a relaxing evening for himself—his body and mind clearly needed it.

Richard twisted the doorknob to his apartment and pushed open the door. The hinges emitted a low, creaking groan. Chills prickled his skin at the sound, and he shivered, straining to shake the uncanny sensation tightening in his chest.

His door—had it been unlocked?

Fatigue settled over Richard as he shuffled toward his desk. The finicky door was just another item to add to his to-do list. Sighing, he heaved his briefcase on top of his desk and pulled the chain on his lamp to test the electricity. Nothing. He huffed and sank into his chair, the gloom of the evening threatening to overpower him. At least his dinner would arrive soon.

Low emergency lights shone from the apartment kitchen and bathroom, illuminating the rest of the rooms enough so Richard could see to move around. He faced his briefcase. The metal clasps unfastened with a soft click, and he lifted the lid and removed the top stack of papers.

It took his mind a few moments to comprehend what his eyes were seeing. Richard looked at his paperwork -no, at what should have been his paperwork—in utter disbelief. An assortment of pages filled with incoherent scribbles mixed with a selection of printed crosswords and sudoku puzzles returned his stare.

He scattered the papers over his desk, searching for anything he'd spent the day working on. When nothing familiar caught his eye, he opened the lid to his briefcase once more and rifled through the remaining contents.

"Son of a bitch."

His heart raced. The edges of his vision blurred. All of his paperwork—patient assessments, notes, records—all of it had been replaced by random blank pages and puzzles. Richard slammed a fist against the desk and shot to his feet. He only saw red as he stormed toward the front door, determined to confront the nursing staff about what had to be a ridiculous attempt at a prank.

Richard's hand touched the doorknob when an uncomfortable chill crept down his spine. A strange, muffled noise, the sound of a pitiful moan, filled the air. He halted all movement and strained to listen to the increasing volume. His mind raced back to the conversation of the four women, to the discussion of a ghost roaming the halls of Arbor Hills. His pounding heart faltered as he considered the possibility.

Focusing on each intentional breath, Richard turned to examine his apartment. The moaning voice quieted, leaving him in complete silence. He inched toward his desk as a surge of reigniting power thrummed to life. The bulbs in his overhead lights and lamps blinked in a furious manner, and a sudden gust of air sent the scattered papers on his desk fluttering. Richard swiped at the falling pages, preventing a few from leaving the desk.

"What the hell," he cried, unable to stop himself. Instead of printed puzzles or pages of doodles and scribbles, he held the paperwork he'd expected to find upon opening his briefcase.

Richard's head spun, the dizziness intensified by the indecisive lights, and he gripped his desk for support. How was this possible? How did his papers magically morph into something else? He began counting his breaths, just as he did earlier in the hallway. Luckily, after a few breathing cycles, the flickering lights stabilized and remained illuminated.

Maybe it was him.

Ramona's words burrowed deeper into his brain. She said she'd seen him in the corridors, in her room. Her tone was convincing, too, like she truly believed she'd seen a ghost.

Dread curdled in Richard's gut. He needed to find her. He needed to speak with Ramona about this. Perhaps her experiences were similar to his.

The moaning sounded again, this time muffled and distant, but Richard did his best to ignore it. He released his grip on his desk and straightened his spine. His knees threatened to buckle as he strode to his front door, but he remained steady. Richard twisted the knob and pulled the door open, determined to learn the truth of the recent oddities once and for all.

Even with the electricity running normally, the long hallway seemed darker than it did with the power out. Richard followed the square tiles through the dim gloom and rounded the corner of his hallway, entering the section that now apparently housed the newest residents. He scanned the nameplates on each door, searching for Ramona's room. His stomach lurched when he finally saw it.

Richard stopped in front of the room he'd entered that morning—the room where he'd heard someone calling for help. The door was cracked open, but no lights illuminated the apartment interior.

He sucked in a breath and knocked on the door.

Silence.

He rapped harder, adamant about making his presence known.

Nothing.

Richard cursed under his breath and looked at the remaining doors in the hallway. All were securely closed.

He focused his attention on the door to Ramona's apartment. His extreme knocking had pushed it open even farther. Richard glanced behind him once more. No one lingered in the hallway, no soul to witness his next move. Without another chance to reconsider, he stepped inside Ramona's dark apartment.

Richard's hand brushed the interior wall, feeling for a light switch as he trekked deeper into the shadowy room. His knees buckled with each step. His nerves wavered with every heartbeat. Unable to locate a switch, Richard squinted through the darkness, willing shapes of furniture into view.

A wheezing breath exhaled behind him. Richard froze, listening for any other sounds of movement, any additional gasping breaths.

Silence.

Pressing his left hand against the wall, Richard turned in a slow half circle to face the doorway. He saw no one, but an eerie presence lingered in the room. Richard wasn't alone. Someone—or something—was in there with him.

He quieted his breathing as a temporary paralysis consumed his body. The soles of his feet glued themselves in place. His posture went rigid, his spine ramrod straight. A creeping tingle crawled across Richard's skin. He was being watched. He could feel a predator's eyes tracking every fearful breath.

The clatter of a rolling walker broke the spell.

Richard snapped his attention to the doorway as Ramona entered the apartment and flicked a discretely positioned switch. A golden overhead light surged to life as Ramona's gaze landed on Richard.

"You again," she spat. Disgust rippled across her face. Her hand flew to the emergency alert button hanging around her neck. "If you don't leave me alone, I'm pressing the button."

"Ramona, please. I need to talk to you." Richard swiped his clammy palms against his shirt. "My name is Richard Reed. I'm a doctor."

"You don't look like a doctor."

Richard flinched at her harsh words, but the old woman didn't seem to notice or care.

"Ramona, please," Richard said, on the verge of begging. "I overheard what you said earlier. About the ghost, or spirit, wondering around Arbor Hills." Ramona's eyes narrowed. Richard continued, "I think I might have seen him too. Last night. And then again today, strange things have been happening."

Ramona's gaze remained stony, but the tightness loosened around her jaw.

"Follow me," she said, and pushed her walker past Richard, her steps surprisingly quick.

He followed her into a small living area, the room with the Victorian couch. He glanced at the windows as Ramona pulled the cord on a nearby lamp. Flimsy excuses for curtains drooped over the glass. A large, ornate mirror hung on the wall behind the worn couch. Paintings of landscapes filled the remaining space on the otherwise unimpressive wall.

"I don't know what he wants," Ramona said, her voice low. "He moans at night and wanders the halls, always disappearing before morning."

Richard shuddered at her statement as his uneasiness returned.

"Is he—" His voice faltered. "Do you think he's dangerous?"

Ramona eyed him with an amused stare.

"That, Doctor, I cannot say."

Richard's chest tightened as that familiar creeping sensation filled the room. He felt Ramona's eyes on him, but he felt something more, something sinister as well.

"Do you think..." Richard paused, both wanting and not wanting to know the truth. "Is he, is he here with us now?"

Ramona's posture shifted, transforming into the disheveled, kyphotic hag. Her toothy grin returned, and she lifted a sharp, yellow claw and pointed at the large mirror fixed over the couch.

Richard's heart pounded as he looked where she was pointing. He only saw a reflection of the room.

"I don't understand," Richard said, but a menacing cackle erupted from Ramona, cutting off his train of thought. Richard stared, dumbfounded, as her cracked lips spread wide, filling the room with maniacal, ear-splitting laughter.

A heartbeat passed before his confusion shifted into horror.

A tiny, black bug crawled across the crevices in Ramona's face and disappeared behind her gaping teeth.

"Ramona," Richard gasped, unable to pull his eyes away, unsure of what to say or do, but he didn't have a chance.

Ramona's terrible laughter continued, her eyes wild, as a torrent of those tiny bugs swarmed from her mouth. They crawled over her skin, down her neck, into her clothes. Richard took a step back, away from the horror before him, when a sharp tingle rippled over his body.

He glanced down and screamed. Creeping black bugs crawled over the sleeves of his shirt, down the legs of his pants. Richard swatted at the tiny, moving spots and shook his arms and legs, desperate to rid himself of the swarming insects. He spun away from Ramona's unending cries of laughter and collided with the oval coffee table sitting in front of her Victorian couch.

Richard grunted with pain and steadied himself, somehow avoiding a major fall. The remaining bugs fell to the floor as he righted his posture, his vision snagging on the ornate mirror overlooking the room.

Pure terror seized his body.

A face, a terrible, withered face stared at Richard from the mirror's filmy glass—the same face he'd seen in the reflection of his windowpane during last night's storm.

A shaking hand rose in the mirror and pointed at Richard, a howling moan escaping the black hole of the face's open mouth. Richard turned on his heels and bolted away from the haunted man, away from Ramona, delirious with cackling laughter. A sickening crunch followed each of his steps, but Richard didn't dare look at the carpet of insects as he barreled toward Ramona's door. He was almost there, the dim corridor calling to him like a beacon.

Richard reached the open doorway, and just as he stepped a foot across the threshold, a suffocating grip tightened around his throat. Richard gagged and swiped at his neck, but nothing physical restrained him. His vision blurred as he twisted and fought the invisible noose, each moment becoming more difficult to breathe.

A terrible moan filled the space around him, and in that moment, Richard knew. The man from the mirror, the ghost of Arbor Hills, had finally gotten him, and there wasn't anything else Richard could do to escape. His body slumped against the doorframe as the pressure on his throat rose. Then, complete blackness.

A rhythmic beeping drew Richard from a deep slumber. He cracked his eyes open and was greeted by the sterile atmosphere of a small hospital room. The stiff sheets groaned as he shifted positions, but a shooting pain in his hip halted any additional movement. Richard moaned and blinked hard, encouraging his vision to focus on his surroundings.

"Oh good," a gentle voice said. "You're awake. How are you feeling?"

Richard squinted toward the voice, but everything remained blurry.

"I can't see," he rasped.

"Oh, sorry about that, Dr. Reed. Here are your glasses."

Glasses? He didn't wear glasses. Richard opened his mouth to say this when a soft hand placed a pair of glasses in his palm. His body acted of its own accord and unfolded the frames and settled them onto his face. The room around him suddenly came into focus.

Richard blinked in confusion and shifted his gaze to the woman changing the fluid bag on a nearby IV pole.

"Angie?" His voice cracked with desperation.

"Yes, Dr. Reed." She patted his shoulder. "It's me."

Hot tears stung his eyes as relief swelled in his chest. Angie was there, beside him, making sure everything was okay. She really was the best nurse he knew.

He cleared his throat. "What happened to me?" Fragments of memories floated at the edge of his mind, and he grasped for them with no avail.

"You took quite a spill the other night," she replied in a casual tone. "You broke your left hip when you fell. You've already had surgery to repair it."

"Surgery?"

"Yes sir. You've been pretty out of it for a while, but don't worry. Your family has been here each day to check on you."

Richard frowned at this statement. What was she talking about?

"I need to change the line now," Angie said, reaching for Richard's left hand. He lifted it in response, but his breath seized as he glimpsed his bare arm.

Thin, papery skin sagged from his forearm, replacing the defined muscles once present. The back of his hand and fingers were marked with bloodspots, and deep lines traced along the edges of bone. Richard lifted his opposite hand and stared, only to be greeted with a similar sight. He brought his hand to his neck, his face. More loose skin. He rubbed the top of his head, expecting thick locks of hair, but loose, thin wisps met his touch instead.

This couldn't be right. His body was wrong. It wasn't his.

A loud knock sounded from the doorway followed by a female

voice saying, "Knock, knock. Dad? May I come in?"

Dad? That wasn't right, either. Surely this person had the wrong room.

"Of course," Angie replied without consulting Richard. "He's finally awake." She turned to face him. "I'll let you two have some privacy."

"But—"

"I'll be back to check on you soon, Dr. Reed."

He opened his mouth, but Angie was already leaving the room, maneuvering around a smiling woman carrying a small vase of roses.

"Hi Dad," the woman said. She placed the roses on the bedside table and planted a gentle kiss atop Richard's head.

"Hi Stephanie," he replied, the words automatic on his lips. He blinked in surprise, but the woman didn't seem to notice.

"How are you feeling today?" she asked.

How was he feeling—such a casual question. Richard shook his head, unsure of how to answer. He felt many things, none of which were comforting.

"I'm…I'm a little disturbed, to be honest."

Stephanie frowned at his statement.

"What do you mean, Dad?"

Richard looked into Stephanie's eyes, peering into beautiful depths of hazel. Warmth filled his core at the sight of those eyes, and sweet memories of her childhood and adolescence flashed through his mind.

Stephanie was his oldest child, his daughter.

His grown daughter.

"Steph, do you have a mirror handy?"

"Why do you need a mirror?"

"Please," Richard replied with a sad smile. "I only need it for a moment."

Stephanie rifled through the purse she clutched in her lap and extracted a silver compact mirror. She flipped open the lid and passed it to her father.

Richard lifted the mirror, angling it to see his reflection.

A face; a worn, withered face stared back at him.

It wasn't the face he always remembered. It wasn't how he pictured himself, but it was still his face all the same.

A deep pit opened in Richard's chest as he understood the reason he was now hospitalized. He wasn't a doctor working at Arbor Hills.

He was a memory care resident.

He'd been diagnosed with dementia prior to his move to Arbor Hills. He wasn't being haunted; he'd never encountered a ghost. The face in the window, the face in the mirror, it was his own.

He was the man roaming the halls.

Richard blinked, sending a stream of tears down his cheeks.

"Dad, you're crying. What's wrong?"

He looked at his daughter, her face filled with concern.

"I think the dementia is getting worse, Steph." Richard paused, unsure of how to continue. "The reason this happened, the reason I'm here..."

Her expression softened at his words, and she wrapped her warm hands around his.

"I know what happened, Dad," she said, her voice barely more than a whisper.

Richard nodded at his daughter; grateful he didn't need to explain further. He closed the mirror and handed it back to her before settling his head deeper into his pillows.

"Everything is going to be okay," Stephanie said. "You don't have anything to worry about."

A small smile appeared on Richard's lips to appease his daughter, but internally, emotions swarmed. He wanted to believe her. He didn't want to worry, but anxiety was inevitable. After all, he was the ghost of Arbor Hills, haunting the east wing night after night.

And as much as he hated the idea, he knew it would happen again.

His memories would keep fading, and he'd continue wandering the halls, a lost, lonely spirit searching for peaceful relief.

Old Lady Name

by Jolie Toomajan

It happened because I opened a text that said, "I am going to marry the ghost that lives here!" and I went with it. I nestled into atheism long before my 40s, but I was open to being wrong. Even eager. Let me be comforted after death by everything I have ever known, every goldfish ever slipped down the drain during a water change; the small army of spider plants I murdered; the ancestors I am surely disappointing. I've never been against devotion. It's that I have no evidence.

"Alexa, play message," I said. I preferred the calibrated tone of Alexa's voice to my own. She sounded like a woman with a corner office—confident and extremely navy blue.

"Message from Agnes. 'I see shadows,'" said Alexa.

I shouted at Alexa to reply, "Sounds shady."

"Lucy. I'm serious. Some days I hear a man's laugh. I found a lot of money in my purse that I know I don't have. One tree blows away from the others."

The truth was, I went with it. I could have refused to participate at the videos or the Ouija board or the bizarre phone calls or, or, or, or, or. But I craved something uncomplicated. Agnes and I had been friends-more-like-sisters for twenty years, but after graduation I ran for another college town forty hours in the opposite direction, where I could be an unbothered, anonymous fish in the smallest of ponds, and we settled into a strange friendship of extreme intimacy and very little familiarity. I wanted to talk about something other than estrangement, how I never learned her true details; the ones with raw and salted edges that sent her careening from her home. How I had taken the first opportunity out of the business and, therefore, my family, everyone glad to see the back of me. How both our mothers said, “Maybe it would be best for everyone if you left.”

There are a lot of sins, and it turns out inaction is one of them.

#

Agnes embarked on the thrilling adventure of homeownership after the extirpation of a long-term, live-in boyfriend. Ellis’s easy smile always showed sharp teeth; he was the kind of man who would make friends with a squirrel. I liked him, but Agnes assured me the problem wasn’t Ellis. It was the sameness of it all, that this was what life would look like, more or less, until she died. Every morning Ellis would disappear into a featureless bathroom, and she would drink her Folgers standing in some apartment kitchen staring out a window surrounded by wood trim painted white. The same beige apartment carpet, the same eggshell walls, the same painted white doors and fake brass doorknobs with small, pickable keyholes. The same vertical blinds that fall out of the plastic clips. The corners would never be clean.

“It’s a terrible thing,” she said, her voice pitching, “to definitively know how the rest of your life is going to look.”

That was enough for Agnes. Two months later she called, and, without saying hello, said, “Old Lady Name, I bought a house, closing in six weeks.”

This was our private language, that of an Agnes and a Lucy. Originally hyphenated, over the years Old Lady Name lost her tail and became an entity all her own, a shared identity, a skin that stretched over us both. We composed a short, blasphemous, call-and-response prayer—Who is Old Lady Name? She of the impromptu road trip! Our lady of midnight highway karaoke! You’ve got her blessing? To get up and run at any time! We joked about picking up a third and starting a coven of women who would have to age into themselves; desperate for a Gertrude, we would have settled for an Olive, but never found so much as a Rose.

"Hi! Congrats! But with what?"

"I got a mortgage. Sub-prime, but they don't call it that anymore. Get this, they call it the 'Another Chance Mortgage'. I am sure the realtor bought the expensive champagne because he thinks he will sell the same house two times in six months."

"Does it even work like that?" I realized I didn't know. During my house's construction, I became intoxicated with making choices, so I accidentally built a series of experiences instead of a place to live. A small theater, a large parlor with a built-in aquarium, a sweeping curved staircase I asked for only after I pictured myself clicking down it. I hand-selected every knob and doorstop (the harder to find and more difficult to install, the better) and ordered an entire level re-painted because I said maroon, not burgundy. Instead of a home, I built an ornate set—glossy, staged, constantly maintained. Then I never thought about it again. Even my bills were mailed to someone else. It was like having a fairy godmother.

"I actually have no idea, and who cares. I got a house, and it's perfect! There's a tile tub. A tile tub, Lucy!"

"Why didn't you let me give you a down payment?" I asked.

"Let's do that on the second of never," she said. "I love you! I can't wait for you to see." And she hung up.

#

Agnes said she bought the house because it was a sunny emerald green without the slightest hint of sickness. The roofing and trim were offset in maroon, and two layers of indoor wood flooring stacked, glued, sealed, and sunk level with the ground—spilled from the front door. A meandering front path stretched to the driveway, where hairy tufts of grass sprouted between old-fashioned brown bricks. The house should have, by all rights, been ugly, but it wasn't. A realtor would have said the house had personality, and it did.

My phone pinged into the night from Agnes—videos of her talking about cold spots, moving shadows, weird sounds, all shot from a low angle and looking up her nose. Then an EMF meter with a twitching needle and a ball rolling slowly across a stone floor.

I tapped out, "So we need to get you a carbon monoxide detector and a level," and deleted it.

I tapped out, "I'm not sure if this is healthy," and deleted it.

I tapped out, "Are you feeling okay," and deleted it.

I tapped out, "Spooky!" followed by the ghost emoji and sent it.

She then dropped a shared folder full of photographs of her arms. The first photos showed scratches as delicate as single strands of hair, then cranberry-colored bruises, then blueberry ones, and finally deep gouges running the length of her forearm. The folder was named "Love Bites."

I tapped out, "I'm not kinkshaming," and deleted it.

I tapped out, "Jesus fucking Christ, Agnes," and deleted it.

I tapped out, "Who did that to you?" and sent it.

Agnes answered, "Ghost." She also attached the emoji.

"There's no such thing as ghosts, Old Lady Name."

"Now there is."

"Did you do that to yourself?"

Silence.

"This was fun, Ag, but we both know there are no such things as ghosts."

Silence. Two days of silence, ignoring my texts. I Googled her name every six hours, picked up the phone fourteen times to call her local police for a wellness check, and hung it up every time. That would be a point of no return, a severing, so after six texts and four voicemails apologizing and promising to treat the ghost as a serious possibility, Agnes relented and answered me again.

#

Agnes bought a wood burning kit and a chainsaw to make a Ouija board. She rooted out a large walnut tree concealed in the woods behind her property and promptly defiled it, carving oblong disks from its side with the chainsaw. I received a photo of a pile of cracking slices scattered underneath a battered tree overspread in swaths of raw wood. The photo caption said, "Living wood works the best." The brutality of the scene dried my mouth.

Once the Ouija was finished, more texts and calls poured in. Agnes' urgent reveling in the ghosts' details reminded me of the first time she ran from Ellis, when I came home and found her in my pool, flipping herself face down and then face up in the water. The same excited voice flush with freedom. Everything was delicious, divine, sublime, everything had been quelled, and the roller coaster was creaking towards the summit of a new and astonishing hill.

The ghost's name was Adam and, in 2015, his wife launched her body against the car while he was changing the oil and stamped him into the gravel. His recent deadness startled me. I expected Adam, like all ghosts, to be powdered, bespectacled, and vaguely Edwardian. Adam would have had a Wi-Fi password, a North Face jacket, and an opinion on Obama; this somehow made him more alien.

Poor, unwitting Adam in salmon orange shorts and a blue dotted shirt, carefully set up his oil, jack, and pan. Poor, unwitting Adam dusted the clinging cobwebs off his creeper before wheeling himself under the car. A hissing wife in a yellow sundress stalked barefoot across the grass, at the last moment throwing her entire hissing body against the side of a sensible, midsize SUV. The sensible, midsize SUV rocked once and seemed to settle before poor, unwitting Adam saw the jack slip sideways. Poor, unwitting Adam had to know that his book just slammed shut, not even granted the mercy of ignorance. And the hissing wife? She ended up dead for her trouble, but poor, unwitting Adam would never tell Agnes how she died. The hissing wife was nameless.

"So, you'll be his second dead wife and not his first?" I said.

"That's fucked up! I'm not dead."

"Not right now, but mixed-survival marriages don't have a great success rate. It's the societal pressure, and you almost never see a positive representation in the media."

"You're not taking me seriously. Let me go."

"I'm sorry. You're right. Why did she kill him?"

"He doesn't know," Agnes said.

"How is that possible? He haunts the house."

"You're not being very sensitive. It must be hard being dead. Mentally taxing. Adam and I both love the house; we want to stay here." The silence between us was fat with distrust, and I balked.

"Let me come meet him." I pictured a rock rolling over a cave entrance, snapping out the sun.

#

I had met Agnes at a party, sophomore year of college, sitting too close on an itchy gray couch wedged onto a narrow porch. I chewed the end of a clove cigarette, and, not really knowing how to make a friend, brushed her lightly on the shoulder and tilted the pack towards her. She took one and held up her lighter, a brass replica of a naked woman with no head and stumps for arms and legs. Agnes snapped one bicep and fire shot from a wide hole in the woman's breast. As I leaned towards her, I noticed she wore a necklace that said "Abortion!" in slanting gold script, indistinguishable from any other nameplate unless you happened to read it. I gestured towards it with the tip of my nose and gave her my brightest smile. "Hiding-in-plain-sight is one of my favorite things, too," I said.

The two boys next to us looked like someone else had leaned them against the wall and left them there, but my comment caused them to scan her necklace, and one launched. He was powerful in his exposition. He sermonized. He pitched ideas. We were this close to someone yelling Sapere aude! It was also about fairness, about equity. A pregnant girl could take him for everything he has, or what if he wanted to be a father himself? Frankly, it was insulting to say to a man, "Hey, you're not carrying this child, so you don't have a say." In what possible way could a man having veto power over a pregnancy possibly be bad? He was equally involved in the creation, right? He was being excluded based on his gender, and, according to feminism, that was bad, right? He and his friend agreed with one another for an uncomfortably long time, though he occasionally paused to wobble the lip of his beer at us. When he was done, he turned expectantly towards Agnes.

Agnes said, "I hear some people feel that way."

I loved her instantly.

#

I tripped out of a rental car and yelled, "Old Lady Name!" Agnes stood just off the porch floor, waving at me with one arm and cradling a fat stone cherub with the other. An insect whine, cicada-like, hung in the air. When I tried to focus on the sound, it stopped.

"Old Lady Name!" Agnes placed the cherub near a stone bird bath painted bright blue. She looked just like herself. The same Agnes who lolled on a sun chair flanked by a pressed white cushion on the balcony outside my bedroom, the ashes of her cigarette rolling over the edge. The same Agnes who said, I'm telling you, Old Lady Name would wear a gold turban and smell like Chanel and alimony payments. She says things like 'Excuse me. It's pronounced Ola-dee Nah-may.' The same Agnes who dropped the drink, laughing at her own joke. A bit of blush wouldn't have killed her, but it was Agnes in a pilling yellow sweater and brown corduroy pants, Agnes kicking a pair of green Chuck Taylors off her feet, Agnes tying her unconditioned hair practically at the back of her neck. Agnes having a nervous breakdown, convinced she's marrying a ghost.

"Am I in the middle of nowhere?" I asked. Each home here was scooped from the woods, which were otherwise left undisturbed.

"No, the Google Maps guy even came through a couple of days ago," Agnes answered.

"The porch is beautiful," I lied. Agnes loved the porch, and when I first saw the photos, I lied and said that putting indoor flooring outside was innovative and artistic. In person, it was unmooring. The dirt swept over every edge exposed to the yard before fading into the glossy wood, making it difficult to tell where the yard ended and the house began.

As I turned to get my bags, I noticed that my rear tire rested on the upper curve of a heart drawn in chalk in the driveway. Dusty and pink, recently refreshed, the faded outline of previous hearts peeked tantalizingly past the edges like a stocking top. I strode possessively towards Agnes, pulling her into a hug.

"But I'm only here for the tub," I said.

#

The front door opened directly into the living room, and I recognized the stone floor from the video with the rolling ball. Freshly installed slate tiles contrasted with wood paneling old enough to have a scent and new, stainless-steel appliances held down a buckling linoleum floor. The newer objects looked completely out of place and time, like they absolutely had to go next, and Agnes would be better served pitching the water-filtering, ice-making monstrosity into the yard and getting herself a Coppertone Amana.

Agnes tugged me through a mudroom, her bedroom, and the extra room. While she hoisted my bag to the top of a filing cabinet, I peeked back into the hallway. Her apartments with Ellis maintained a level of controlled chaos that never quite reached critical mass—the laundry crumpled clean in hampers, dishes rinsed and sitting in the washer waiting to be run, watered plants and dirty windows. This house was carefully and lovingly cleaned. Not a single fingerprint deposited on any of the appliances, every bed sharply made, even the garbage cans were empty. Finally, she pulled me into the bathroom.

A peachy nude mosaic tile covered every surface, sparing only the cabinet faces, the mirror, the bowl of the sink, and the ceiling. A metal bar holding a white privacy curtain ran across the entire length of the room. Agnes swept the curtain back, an angular tub sunk into the floor jacuzzi style confronted me, the same tile crawling over its edge and lining the inside. On the other side of the tub, a floor to ceiling glass wall faced the woods. The buzzing noise vibrated the surrounding air.

"Well? Vintage or outdated?" she asked.

"Absolutely vintage," I called over my shoulder. "You don't slip? I'm going to die in this thing, so good thing it's pretty."

"Pretty, but inconvenient," Agnes said.

"Hey, that used to be my life goal."

"That never stopped being your life goal."

"Shut up, I brought weed." I snorted at her, giggling. As I turned from the tub, the curtain rod liberated itself from the wall, falling so close to me I heard strands of hair breaking with disheartening snaps. I hurled myself at Agnes, who had not changed expressions, and the echoing crack of the bar hit the floor much later than I expected. I gripped Agnes' sweater and turned. The rod rolled after me, catching itself on the corner of the vanity. Two tiles cracked away from the wall, and the counter dropped powdery ceramic flecks. Brownish circles of glue stuck to the wall where the rod used to be.

"That glue looks a thousand years old. We should hit the Lowe's," I said.

"I think that's Adam saying hi," said Agnes brightly. "Here I am cleaning up after him again. Who would have thought I'd make a proper wife?"

#

The first night, Agnes dropped the Ouija board unceremoniously on the kitchen table, set up five mismatched brass candle holders with half-melted taper candles already shoved inside, and turned out the light. A thick darkness waited outside the dome of the candles. Sitting booth style next to me, Agnes dropped the pointer and ring finger of each hand on the planchette, an unfinished and crude wooden triangle with a hole stabbed through it, splinters still peeling away.

"Honey, are you home?" she asked into the air. "Honey? You here?" Yellowed by the light, Agnes leaned forward, angling her breasts towards the Ouija board. I sagged in my seat.

"You try," Agnes said.

"Adam?" I asked tentatively. The planchette stayed perfectly still.

"Maybe you need to ask him a question."

"I don't want to ask him a question." This seemed less like fun, more like enabling. I let go of the planchette and Agnes yanked my hand to the board by my wrist.

"Make a good impression," Agnes grumbled through lightly clenched teeth.

I grew beady and bloated with frustration, like a swelling toad. Blistering in my seat, I finally decided to take Agnes seriously.

“What did you do to get that woman to drop a car on your head?”

Agnes stood up fast. Her chair slapped against the floor as she banged both hands on the table, knocking down two candles that went out as they went down.

“Fucking disrespectful!” Agnes shouted. She wetly blew out the rest and left me alone and silent in the dark.

#

A heavy silence hung over the house the rest of the night, but the next day it was like Adam never happened. I pushed coffee through the French press as Agnes slid into the room wearing slippers shaped like crowned swans, smiled, and hip bumped me. During the daytime, we fell easily into the clean patterns of our friendship. Every day, I crushed tomatoes with a wooden spoon to make Menemen for breakfast. Every day, Agnes produced a pack of clove cigarettes hidden above the refrigerator and a partially melted plastic ashtray. We pulled on boots and wandered through the thin woods nearest the house to collect smooth rocks to be saved in a jar. We somehow returned. We ate greasy slices of salami with our fingers.

Agnes refused to leave the grounds, so for dinners I stuffed peppers and grape leaves, smeared lamb and tomato paste across flour tortillas, pressed kabob with onions, tied up a chicken, soaked bulgur for Eech. When she requested horror movie marathons, I handpicked The Craft, The Hunger, Scream, The Descent, Hush. Nothing with a ghost. Just before bed each evening, Agnes and I sat on towels at the ledge of the tub, submerged to the knees in steaming water, transferring a joint between us, our laughter terrifying the rabbits shoving themselves through the grass outside.

I thought the days were as good as normal.

#

The nights were somewhat different. The hum of crickets turned into a sour whine that crawled through my body, leaving behind a shivering, aggravated disgust, and though Agnes warned me about fox screams, nothing prepared me for how much it sounded like a woman, punctuated and terrified. Starting on the second night, the heat clanged on from baseboard radiators and assaulted me with fetor. Peppery, sharp and burned, thick enough to dry my throat, the only way to escape was to sleep with the blanket rolled twice and deposited over my face.

Then the chattering would begin—Agnes hum-speaking in a low voice, not quite singing, on and on, into the hours, with none of the confused chanting quality of speaking in tongues, none of the mosquito-hum of crying. An unbroken mumble, the timbre of conversation but indecipherable.

The first night I heard it, I pushed the blanket from my face, and called "Ag?" into the hallway.

The chattering stopped, and after a few lumbering seconds, she called back, "Luce?" her voice scratched with the obvious rasp of sleep.

I leaned back into the bed. "Nothing, sorry. I'm not used to the woods."

"Don't wake me up again," Agnes said.

Moments later, the chattering came back, Agnes' voice thrumming, prodding at the darkness in the room, pushing it closer to me. I never heard it end, only ignored by my exhaustion, and when I finally went under, the same nightmare waited every night. Ellis sliding over the edge of a cliff, me holding a rope tied to nothing, somehow still being dragged to the edge. The dream ended as soon as I began to scrabble, and every night when it woke me up, I heard Agnes still chattering in her room.

#

Several nights later, the chattering changed. Instead of a mumble, it turned into a continuous, single-note hum. In the dark of the house, I inched my way to the filing cabinet Agnes kept hidden in a back room. The bottom drawers erupted with yarn and crochet needles, but the top held unorganized stacks of paper. Looking for anything that might tell me about Agnes' mental state, I burrowed into Christmas cards, college transcripts, books of stickers, half-empty journals, and then rifled immodestly, throwing bills to the ground immediately, considered the tax documentation before it joined their fate.

At the other end of the house, the kitchen light snapped on, and I whirled around. Agnes leaned in the doorframe, swinging the planchette around one finger. I nudged the drawer closed.

"What are you doing, Old Lady Name?" The anger had slipped into her voice so easily, I realized it had been living just underneath her tongue the whole visit. "Leave us alone, we're happy."

"There's no 'us' in this house, Agnes. Not one that isn't me and you."

"You never even said congratulations."

"Listen to yourself. Are you okay?"

"I'm getting married."

"To whom?"

"Adam and I talk at night and he doesn't like you."

"Ag, if this were me, you would never let this go on. Is it a joke? Let's see what Lucy does if I start talking about imaginary men?"

"He's not imaginary!" Agnes screamed.

"You're screaming at me now?" I screamed back. "Agnes. Who changes the oil in a car by sticking their head directly under a tire?" She turned and ran for the bathroom, and I followed her. The formerly aggressive rod leaned casually against the wall with the curtain tangled below it. I slammed my hand on the counter and chips from the broken corner clacked to the floor. Agnes slapped my wrist away and stepped between me and the counter, blurring the features of her face.

"He's real," she said.

"Okay, great. In fact, let me agree. Adam is real and appears only to you. Great. Congratulations. What if it's a demon? A djinn? Fucking fairies? What if it isn't a ghost?"

"I know what my gut is telling me. He's real. He loves me."

"My gut tells me you're one of those 18.98-hertz people and some pipe in this house rattles at the exact frequency that makes you see husbands."

Agnes hurled the planchette at my chest. It hit square, and my arms snapped up involuntarily to catch it. I ended up holding it against my heart.

"He's not imaginary. I'm not hallucinating,"

"Yeah? Prove both things to me."

"That's the difference between me and you, Lucy. You may not like my marriage, but Shadily Rich Dilettante isn't a career path, and I leave you the fuck alone about it."

"Until you lose your job because you can't wake up on time and Ellis can't know. Until you need someone to let you make shitty decisions undisturbed for a few weeks. Then I am the unimpeachable fucking Lucy." I threw the planchette into the bathroom mirror, where it slid impotently into the sink, shattering nothing.

"And that's why I wouldn't ask you for a down payment."

"What is that supposed to mean?"

"It means you probably shouldn't stay here anymore. Adam doesn't like you."

I pushed past her and clawed the countertop. The textured hunks of tile gripped me back like a second hand, and I spit past the tub onto the window, turned, and hawked what was left at the wall. "And that is what I think of your fucking husband."

"Lucy Hakobyan, get the fuck out of our house!"

"Great, save yourself!"

#

I waited a week at a hotel for her to call. We had fought before, hissing battles illegible to anyone but us. Real fights are as intimate as sex, something unique in the microcosm of a relationship, a nightmare built for two. Arguments in the movies have a tinny quality because the relationship is broken down to make room for the audience, the interloper. I felt the same way about our last fight, like it was done for the benefit of a witness, like it wasn't even ours.

When Agnes didn't text me, I went back to the house and found her car in the driveway, the door unlocked, but no Agnes. The police told me that grown women can go wherever they want without telling me and, one coughed, maybe she didn't want to see me specifically. For days, I sat in front of the house, calling her cell phone and listening to it ring into eternity, never reaching voicemail. A few times I swore it rang inside the house, but the sound disappeared as soon as I stepped on the porch. I thought about going inside and staying there, but every time it crossed my mind, my jaw shook uncontrollably. I took the hint and left, making sure to leave the door unlocked in case I changed my mind.

When I changed my mind less than eight hours later, the door was locked, and Agnes' car covered in a membrane of spider webs and dead leaves. The window above the bayberry bushes showed the inside lock turned, and the chain set on the door. The glass bathroom wall displayed the blank expanse of the privacy curtain drawn across the re-hung rod. The whine started from the woods again, doubled. Howling and joyful. I went home.

The first night back, I became suddenly aware of the machinations of my own home, how it had the closed and limited echo of a museum, how the temperature changed with a hushed click, like a door being carefully closed. I tried to think of ways to find Agnes, but every road led back to the house, and I could not bring myself back. My only course of action, finally, was to resolve I would never disconnect that phone number, the last number for me Agnes would have.

I check the city records once a year, and the house has never been sold or foreclosed on, which meant that someone was-is-paying on it dutifully and so there it remains, sealed up and Agnes-less. Or maybe Agnes-full. Google Maps never updated their photograph, either, so I can always plug in the address and be confronted with a photo of the house, Agnes' car squatting in the driveway, and Agnes leaning on the handle of her chainsaw, the blade sunk into the earth, waving at nobody with the brightest smile of recognition on her face.

Speak Ill of the Dead

by Briana McGuckin

No one need stamp handle with care on a coffin; to be gentle with the dead is an expectation writ across every grieving face. At once a plea and an admonition, it says to the hospice nurses, the investigators, the folks in the funeral homes and in the churches: "Please don't hurt him. Don't you dare."

But what the rest of us don't realize is that, for the employees concerned, dealing with this crushing, wringing, life-defying death thing is as common as baristas filling coffee orders. And you know how that goes: they misspell names, forget the syrup, use the wrong kind of milk. It's not that they're bad people; it's that they do this every day, for everybody, and you're not nearly as important as you think you are.

So yes, if you were worried, somebody who cares a lot less than you do about your deceased friend or loved one probably screwed up along the line in some little way that you'd find downright disrespectful.

But, whoever it was that screwed up, it was not Dr. Merrily Coughlin.

Merrily prided herself on being gentle, because the dead folks she had reason to meet had had it rough. She determined cause of death when cause of death was unclear. This usually meant either foul play or some freak accident, not somebody slipping away in their sleep. She moved slowly, lifted carefully, touched respectfully—and even then, only when absolutely necessary.

She was used to her colleagues tapping their feet around her. Today, it was Investigator Deedee Simms. The sound echoed off the floor tile in the morgue.

"He waited three years," Merrily murmured. She was bent low

over the body, clipping what hair she could find from a fragile scalp. “You can wait another five minutes.”

But time in the morgue was a precious commodity of late: lots of exhumations scheduled, cold cases getting warmed up again thanks to an advancement in assessing bacteria. The big news was that when two people intertwined, for good or for ill, so did the microbes in their hair. A match between two mops’ microcosms could mean justice for murder victims.

Merrily set her scissors down on a metal tray and tweezed strands of hair onto a slide. She let out a tense breath.

“Okay,” Simms said. “If you’ll be heading back to the lab, I can get this guy back where he belongs.”

“I have samples from all the suspects right here,” she replied, walking her slide back to a microscope in the corner opposite Simms. “I’ll have an answer in just a moment.”

Simms uncrossed her arms, pushing off from the door on which she’d been leaning. “But you don’t need the body here for that.”

“If we’ve got Tommy’s killer,” Merrily said, “I want Tommy to hear it.” The slide clicked home in the microscope, punctuating her sentence.

“Don’t see a lot of doctors going in for that afterlife stuff,” Simms said.

“I don’t go in for it.” Merrily adjusted the focus of the lens, frowning. “But hey, I could be wrong.”

“Now that’s something I’ve never heard a doctor—”

“We have a match.” Merrily drew herself up. “It’s McDonald.”

She strode for the door, to make her report. On the way by she touched Tommy’s cold hand, as if to reassure him. Simms stepped aside to let Merrily pass.

#

Alone in the room with Tommy, Simms said, "You got a good one on your side, friend."

Tommy, of course, said nothing.

#

That night found Merrily Coughlin on the couch, being not at all gentle with a bag of popcorn. Poor Tommy hadn't warranted a very big news story, but the ticker this evening said it all: "Leading suspect Rufus McDonald charged in murder of teenage Thomas Morrows."

Merrily got up for a victory drink. There wasn't any champagne in the house, but she could make do with cider. She got herself a proper flute, poured, and slid the Granny's Orchard jug back into the fridge.

"Here's to you, Tommy," she said. She drained her glass in one and turned around to find she hadn't quite shut the refrigerator door, and now it yawned wide. This was always happening. The seal was old.

She took a step toward it, but before her eyes it swung closed again. "Windy tonight," Merrily said, though when the wind shut things, it was usually with a slam, not a nudge. She made for the open window.

Then that shut, too.

Merrily stared. It was an old house. The windows had always been a little loose; sometimes they fell on their own, though thankfully never on her sunbathing cat. But it hadn't slammed. It had been brought down gently, as she would have done it.

She put her toasting flute in the sink, then crossed back toward the living room, glancing back once to look at the window.

Then she settled on the couch. Now that she had seen the verdict for Tommy, she had no more need for the news. She got enough of the grim stuff at work. She was scrolling through the channel guide when she heard running water.

"Shit," she muttered, already sprinting for the stairs. Just last week a valve had come loose on the toilet, spraying the second-floor bathroom with so much water that the hallway flooded. It had rained in the living room that day.

But even from the top step, Merrily knew this wasn't a re-run of last time. The rush wasn't getting louder. In fact, it was fainter there. She turned around, taking the stairs two at a time.

The sound was coming from the kitchen.

But then, as she was almost to the door, it stopped.

Merrily looked all around as she came around the corner. Nothing glistened on the floor. She ran her hands along the cabinets in front of the sink, but they weren't dripping. The counters had nothing on them but some breadcrumbs.

The sink was empty.

Merrily's gaze skipped to the dish drain. Sure enough, there was the champagne flute. She picked it up and found that it alone was wet—on the outside.

And there was something else wrong, though at first she couldn't place it. It was just a tickle in the back of her throat, a thought like the twitch before a sneeze. On impulse, she brought the glass to her nose. It didn't smell like cider, but soap.

"Did someone just… do my dishes?"

Merrily knew there were people who got off on just being in other people's houses. They didn't take anything, or hurt anyone, they just wanted to see what they could get away with. But if she were breaking and entering for kicks, other people's chores wouldn't have been on her to-do list. If that wasn't absurd enough, it had only been the glass. In the already small pool of burgling neat-freaks, how many were that particular?

When she reentered the living room, Merrily had traded the

champagne flute for a chef's knife but there was no danger awaiting her. In fact, somehow the TV had landed itself on Willie Wonka & the Chocolate Factory.

Merrily's favorite.

#

Merrily could account for every second of that night, but she couldn't make sense of them. After a white-knuckled search of the house, she had been forced to conclude she was alone. But she hadn't been, so she'd sat awake on the couch, clutching the knife and staring at the kitchen doorway.

When her alarm went off in her bedroom, she rose like a zombie to shower.

She dressed and went down to the kitchen. Fortunately, her coffee was not already made for her. Her good Samaritan was gone. Scooping grounds for herself, and waiting for the machine to brew, Merrily thought it wouldn't be a bad idea to get an alarm system—after a good nap this afternoon. Taking a sick day never crossed her mind. She had another autopsy to do.

Later, in her lab coat, she bent over a body newly dead, found half-buried on a beach: male, about twenty, green eyes. His hair looked brown, but when Merrily combed it with her fingers, she disturbed fistfuls of sand. She sifted the strands, finally striking gold. "Blond," she said, for her recorder.

She cut the rope of his shark-tooth necklace and bagged it. There was a tiny red ring where it had been, which she noted aloud. She cut his shirt, easy as wrapping paper, in one smooth slide. She clipped left, then right, to open the tunnels of his sleeves, and lifted him between the shoulder blades so she could slide the fabric out from underneath. A load of sand hissed to the floor as she did it.

"No markings on his chest," she observed. "High muscle-tone.

Probably a surfer."

Merrily bent again, this time to cut into ratty, cut-off jeans. But the scissors slipped her grip, as if someone had snatched them out of her hands. But there was no one. Brow furrowed, she bent to retrieve them.

She did not expect them to launch themselves at her.

She leaned backward to avoid them, over-balanced, and fell. Behind her, the struck doors of a chrome cabinet echoed like a gong.

Merrily twisted her body, and saw the scissors lying, innocently inanimate, on the tile by the cabinet. It felt important to crawl, to hold her breath as she advanced. In truth, she did not want to touch them; it was only the vague idea that they could do more damage if left unattended that made her reach for them.

As her fingers grazed the red handles, the scissors flew in a high arc, and stuck point-down into John Doe's body with an indecent, jam-jar squish.

"Hey!" Merrily shouted. Fury drew her to her feet. She rushed to defend the now-defiled deceased—as if her passion would make the unknown foe fightable. But as she reached John Doe, the autopsy table rolled away, crashing into the opposite wall and causing an avalanche of sand.

But instead of dropping straight down, the sand blew across the floor. Words formed:

YOU BITCH

Merrily's mouth fell open. Her stomach dropped away, then her whole body, like sandbags off a hot-air balloon, floating off into a dream world. Maybe she was at home. Maybe she had fallen asleep on the couch.

The sand blew again, swirling and resettling into a new message:

I THOUGHT YOU WERE DIFFERENT

Merrily barely had time enough to read. The autopsy table took flight again and crashed into her. Now it was her turn to slam into a cabinet, and the doors rattled with the force of impact.

"What the hell?" Merrily demanded. She pushed the table away, panting, and felt her ribs for breaks.

John Doe had crumpled to the floor. Merrily could see the sand over the corners of the table.

YOU WERE KIND TO ME

The room felt calmer now—no. It felt morose. It was like the air pressure had dropped, or a cloud had passed over the sun. Merrily thought of the rain in her living room.

"Did you wash my champagne flute?" she asked. "And put on Willy Wonka?"

The sand seemed to twitch but did not rearrange. Merrily might have imagined it. Then, with a slow, tender shyness, whatever spirit was speaking made one adjustment—as if with a single finger:

YOU WERE KIND TO ME

Merrily crouched down, eyes wide and her injury forgotten. "Who are you?" she wondered.

The words in the sand didn't budge at first. When it finally got moving again, it slithered instead of flew.

YOU SOLVED MY MURDER

And then, as if these words were not right, this was dashed away and replaced with:

YOU CARED

Merrily said: “Tommy Morrows?”
But the sand was shifting again.

OR I THOUGHT YOU CARED

She could feel it — the pressure coming back. “Of course I care,” she said, testing her weight on her knees.

ABOUT STRIPPING SOME SURFER

Then, like pushing everything off a table, these words slid right and were replaced by:

TAKING ADVANTAGE

“I wasn’t stripping him,” Merrily said, as gentle as she was in all of her work. She was getting to her shaking feet, and she needed time to walk them to the door. Or the phone. “This is just my job, Tommy.”

She glanced down. All the sand had piled together to form a one-word response, emphatic as bold type:

OH

Merrily was blasted off her feet, rolling across the floor in a wicked squall of sand that pricked her skin everywhere it landed.

Whimpering, she opened one eye. The floor before her read:

I SEE

Merrily swallowed, panic rising in her throat so that it shoved words out before they were properly organized. "No, Tommy—you matter. I…"

But he wasn't listening. As she spoke the autopsy table rose into the air, straight up, toward the ceiling.

"Coughlin?" Simms, her voice muffled by the door. "What's all the noise?"

The autopsy table could go no higher. It hung still and silent, waiting. Merrily dared not call out. Instead, she whispered, "Tommy, please…"

A jangle of keys, outside, then the door swung inward.

Merrily could only bear to tear her eyes away from the table for a moment, to see Simms and the shine of metal keys poking out between her fisted fingers. When Merrily's eyes swung back up to the ceiling, Simms's followed.

"Oh, this again?" Simms said, and the loudness of her voice was such a shock to Merrily that she trembled. But Simms had eyes only for the autopsy table, which she addressed as if it were a bear that had wandered into her backyard: "Back off, fucker. Back right off."

"Deedee…" Merrily whined, watching wide-eyed as her colleague came closer to the danger. "You don't understand, he's—"

"Nope, he doesn't understand." She kept coming, and with strong hands moved Merrily behind her. She stood in her place, and, crossing her arms she said, "You want to take liberties with other people's bodies, friend? You want me to get yours back out of the drawer?"

Nothing moved. Not the sand, not the table—or did it waver, in the air?

"Coughlin here is nice, she wouldn't harm a hair on your head. But I would. Give me a reason. Go ahead. Just give me a reason, see what I do."

Nothing.

And then, slowly, the table came back toward the floor. It touched down on the tile so lightly the wheels didn't squeak.

"You want women to be kind to you," Simms said, "you gotta make the world a safe place for kindness. You got that?"

Silence. Then sand, slithering, like a toe in dirt. Merrily looked.

YES, MA'AM

"Good," Simms said. "Now get out."

Merrily felt it when he left. Like the pressure dropping in the air, again. This time it stayed low. The storm had passed. Simms's shoulders lowered.

"You didn't tell me," Merrily said.

Simms looked around. "Huh?"

"You said 'again.' 'Oh, this again.' You've dealt with him before."

"Oh," Simms said, lowly. "Not him, specifically. But ghosts like him, yes. I think every woman in forensics does, sooner or later."

Merrily swallowed. She was still shaking. She couldn't seem to stop.

"You need to take some time off," Simms observed.

"Oh, no, I'm fine." Merrily clasped her hands, to hold them steady. "It's so busy here, I couldn't possibly—"

"You can," Simms said. "And you will."

She considered.

It was a busy time in forensics. Someone else would have to do all her autopsies, inspect wounds, get to the bottom of uncertain deaths. And somewhere along the way, someone—an investigator, maybe Deedee Simms—would screw up in some small way that Merrily would have found downright disrespectful. She bit her lip.

But maybe that's as it should be, she thought. Maybe ghosts need a bump on the head now and again, to remind them that they're not as important as they think they are. Just like people.

After all, just because they're dead doesn't make them angels.

Lagniappe

During a staff meeting one gloriously stormy night, the idea of having a section titled “Lagniappe” near the end of some of the works published by Brigids Gate Press was discussed. The staff unanimously voted in favor of the idea.

Lagniappe (pronounced LAN-yap) is an old New Orleans tradition where merchants give a little something extra along with every purchase. It’s a way of expressing thanks and appreciation to customers.

The Lagniappe section might contain a short story, a small handful of poems, or a non-fiction piece. It might also feature a short novella. It may or may not be connected with the theme of the work.

#

The extra offering for this anthology is “The Sweetlings”, a splendidly creepy little tale by S.H. Cooper. It involves...dolls. ‘Nuff said!

The Sweetlings

by S.H. Cooper

There is an allure to emptiness.

I had always been drawn to it. The silence, the separation. It sang to me.

It was why I'd chosen to make my home in a rundown apartment building abandoned by its previous owner mid-renovation. The current landlord didn't care to complete the work and most prospective tenants couldn't look past the unfinished floors looming above the smattering of livable units, so my neighbors were few, far between, and, like me, solitary.

It was also why I found myself wandering the old flea market grounds on a gray Saturday morning.

Since The Mall—a giant, centrally located warehouse where booths were cheap and the climate controlled—had opened, the outdoor market had fallen out of favor. Most of the faded stalls, previously piled high with things people hoped would pass as antique, were shuttered. The few that remained did so out of stubborn pride. Their owners had been coming to the market grounds for decades and weren't about to let a little thing like "progress" stop them from offering their assortments of odds and ends, even if it was only to a skeleton crowd.

I respected them for it, I supposed. The desire to hold fast to what was theirs.

It was chilly that morning, and I'd wrapped up tight against the autumn wind, already sharp with winter's promise. I stopped briefly at a handmade jewelry stall, considered a beaded bracelet under the half-lidded gaze of its leftover hippie creator, then moved on, my hands dug deep into my pockets.

I was familiar with almost all the folks who were left. We never spoke, merely existed beside each other, sharing disconnected moments before drifting apart again.

I liked it that way.

"What a pretty girl."

A voice like tissue paper interrupted my meandering, and I turned toward it, one brow raised.

An elderly woman draped in layers of shawls with a heavy quilt spread across her lap was staring unabashedly from behind a folding table.

Upon the table sat a collection of dolls.

Varying in size and style, seated in neat little rows, they were all wearing neat little dresses, their hair—some brown, some blonde, some black—all brushed into neat little styles. Eyes of glass and button gazed flatly toward me.

I'd never seen this woman or her collection before. Curiosity drew me toward her.

"Excuse me?"

"You're a pretty girl," she repeated.

Proximity proved an enemy to her wares, and I started to see the cracks spiderwebbing through porcelain, the clumsy stitchwork scarring cloth faces. Age had thinned their neat little dresses and yellowed their ruffled edges.

"A pretty girl needs a pretty baby."

My smile only went as far as my lips; polite, but insincere. "No thanks. Not for me."

"Oh, we all say that, don't we?" She chuckled, turning her tissue voice to sandpaper. A strange light twinkled in her hooded eyes. "You'll change your mind."

"Sorry, they're not my thing."

This seemed to amuse her even more. "It's not up to us, is it?"

Not sure how to respond, I just shrugged and prepared to be on my way.

"Off you go, then," she said, sitting back. "But just you wait. You'll change your mind."

I dismissed her strange sales tactic and carried on across the market grounds to complete my rounds before returning to my car. I didn't intentionally give the old woman a wide berth on my return journey, but still, I took the longer path around the outside of the grounds instead of my usual route cutting through the middle.

I was enjoying the crisp weather, I told myself, then thought no more of it as I drove home.

The stonewall sign reading Lorelei Fields, in fancier script than the apartment building deserved, welcomed me as I turned into the parking lot. Initially paved with the hope of parking nearly a hundred cars, it now served as a cracked and creviced host to just over a dozen. I had my choice of spots, but always ended up back in the same one beneath the shade of an untended tree.

My apartment was on the fifth of fourteen floors, the highest one could get before they hit the construction zone. I shared that floor with only one other person, a college aged guy who stank of weed and never managed to string more than a few coherent words together. Thankfully, he was on the opposite end of the floor and our run-ins were rare.

I took the rickety elevator up from the lobby, a more dangerous venture every time, and did my best to ignore the groaning of tired gears and cables from overhead as they carried me upward.

Dinner that night was a lazy call to the nearest pizza place for a small pie and a side of cheesy bread. By the time it arrived an hour after I'd hung up, my stomach was growling.

"Hey, Antonio," I said, and it occurred to me, not for the first time, that I should probably be a bit embarrassed about being on a first name basis with the delivery guy.

"Got your usual," he replied, unfastening the insulated bag containing the food.

Over the tearing Velcro, an unusual sound caught my attention.

I cocked my head slightly, gaze turning toward it. It carried on faintly, coming from somewhere down the dimly lit corridor.

"Misty?"

"Oh, sorry." I flashed a short-lived smile and placed a trio of fives in his outstretched hand. "Just not used to hearing that up here."

Antonio's forehead wrinkled with his bemusement. "Hearing what?"

"The baby," I said, and when he just continued to frown, I added, "That crying. You don't hear it?"

"Nope," he said, following it with a good-natured chuckle. "One of the perks of getting older; don't have to hear every little thing your neighbors get up to. You want any change?"

"No, keep it. Have a good night."

"You too. See you next weekend."

I let him go with an absent nod, my eyes moving down the hallway again, its walls stained with a brown tinge by the cheap light fixtures.

The baby's mewling cry continued.

I'd never heard any kids, much less infants, in my building, but maybe the stoner dude had some company. I was relieved it didn't carry once I closed my door. I didn't want to share my evening with the sound of an unhappy child.

I ate in peace while watching a terrible horror movie I found on some freebie app. By the time it ended, my eyelids had started to droop and my thoughts had become wrapped in a sleepy haze, so I stashed my leftovers in the fridge and went to the bathroom to get ready for bed.

Night had settled deeply over my room once I shut the lights out. So far from town, there was no steady thrum of traffic to act as white noise, only the wind passing through the poorly sealed window, the occasional call of some nocturnal bird perched upon an enshadowed branch.

And the crying.

The high-pitched, steady squall, just loud enough to disturb my attempts at sleep, like an itch on the back of my brain from which I had no relief. I tossed and turned, attempting to bury my face against and then beneath my pillow, but still it persisted.

Why wasn't anyone shutting that kid up?

If it was bothering me from all the way over wherever it was, surely it had to be driving the people immediately around it nuts. Maybe it was, and the adults were doing their best to calm it, but the baby was having none of it. I could picture it, purpled face wet with tears and snot, writhing against its parents' attempts to soothe it. I tried to tell myself to have some compassion for people struggling in a situation that was bad for all parties involved.

As the wailing continued, however, my ability to empathize shrank until all that was left was irritation.

Already preparing a speech about common courtesy, I threw back my covers and marched, clad only in my tank top and legging pajamas, out of my apartment and down the hall toward the stoner's apartment. As I stomped my way past closed doors concealing vacant units, drawing ever closer to what I presumed was the offending party, I was struck by a slow realization.

The crying wasn't getting louder.

If the baby really was in his apartment, then its tantrum should have been almost unbearable.

My pace slowed, and I tilted my head slightly, trying to get a better sense of where the crying was coming from if not from across the building. But just as it hadn't gotten any louder, it also hadn't gotten any softer, leaving me standing in the middle of the empty hall, bathed in the sickly yellow fluorescent, ears strained for a noise with no discernable source.

I turned and scurried back to my apartment, locking myself

behind the perceived safety of the door, and shook my head as if to dislodge the sound.

What was going on?

Sleep came hard that night, and each brief snippet I managed to slip into was haunted by the distant echo of a child's cry.

I had to drag myself out of bed the next morning. I moved mechanically through the usual routine, my thoughts thin and fogged. I couldn't tell if it was only my imagination, but had the crying somehow gotten louder? Closer? I clutched my head between my hands and took a deep breath with the flimsy reassurance that the baby was on another floor below instead of on mine, like I'd previously assumed. I just had to get out of the building. I pulled on whatever clothes I found first, grabbed my keys, and left.

I got on the elevator, and still I heard the crying.

I shoved my way through the front door, and still I heard the crying.

I climbed into my car and cranked up the radio, and still I heard the crying.

It never grew or softened in volume, never changed pitch, just the same distant wailing, burrowing into my ears, digging, digging, digging.

It was an earworm, I decided. Like lyrics that got stuck and could take days to bury again. I must've just heard a baby at some point and, for some reason I didn't know, it was being played on loop. I just had to find some way to get rid of it, that was all. Replace it with a song or a quote, something far less maddening than a baby's tantrum.

I went through my day, trying to focus all my attention on whatever song was playing or the nearest conversation. All were tainted by the crying undercurrent. The more I fixated on the other sound, the more it seemed to blend and blur with the relentless baby's voice. A stop at a fast-food place for breakfast, a quick walk through a thrift store, grocery shopping.

It followed me everywhere.

I convinced myself I just needed to give it time, that it would fade on its own.

I maintained that hope for two sleepless days. By then, I was functioning on some primitive level of basic caveman survival skills and caffeine. The crying was my only constant. It ruptured any attempt at thinking, tiny fingernails scraping across my skull. I wasn't able to concentrate and became disinterested in everything, until I was reduced to lying on my couch, staring up at the ceiling, listening to the distant cries.

My apartment, my very body, had become a prison, trapping me with this far off, miserable infant, and I had no idea why or how.

I had never been around babies, never cared to be, so why was this the sound that raked at my consciousness?

Because a pretty girl needs a pretty baby, the tissue paper voice cooed.

I shot upright, clutching my chest. That's when it had all started, hadn't it? That woman and her dolls. Every horror film I'd ever seen, every book I'd ever read, came flooding back with tropes of old witch women casting their curses. Had I offended her with my refusal?

Despite it being a weekday, during which the flea market wasn't operating, I grabbed my sweatshirt and ran for my car. However unwise it was to get behind the wheel in my current state paled in comparison to my desperation.

As I drove toward the market, for the first time since I'd started hearing them, the cries grew louder.

The dirt parking lot was empty and the grounds, as I'd suspected they'd be, deserted. The crying was a cacophony now, so loud I could feel it in my teeth. I staggered through the lines of stalls, bloodshot eyes sweeping back and forth. Up one row, down another, until I was shouting, "Hello? Where are you?" into the bleak autumn air.

Her sandpaper laugh, coming from an aisle somewhere nearby, told me I was moving in the right direction.

I flung myself around the next corner, chest heaving, hair flying wild, and almost collapsed.

There she was, same as before, a crone in her endless layers, seated behind her dolls.

As soon as they came into view, the crying ceased.

The woman grinned at me, a gummy expression, as I crossed to her and slammed my hands on her table.

"What did you do to me?" I demanded.

"Nothing," she said, tittering. "Have you changed your mind?"

"No!" My voice rose into a shout. "I don't want your damn dolls. I just want you to make it stop!"

"Oh, that's not up to me, my dear," she replied. "Just like it's not up to you."

"What do you--"

"They've chosen you, just like they chose me."

As she spoke, I became aware that all the dolls' heads had turned toward me. I screamed and stumbled back, one arm raised defensively.

"I'm afraid I can no longer be their mother. You see, I've given them everything and can no longer care for them. My little ones, my sweetlings," she crooned. "And now they've chosen you."

My mouth gaped open dumbly, unable to form a response to this insanity.

"You'll learn to love them in time," she continued. "You have no choice." Her smile began to widen, eyes burning with a feverish light. "They're yours now, to love and to feed, just as I did. Once they've made you their mother, there's nothing you can do but care for them. Running won't help. You should know that by now." Her words transformed into a throaty cackle. "And I am free!"

She sprang upright from her chair, throwing back her mountain of shawls, letting her blanket fall away. Beneath was not a body of flesh and blood, but only gleaming bone, atop which sat her cackling head. She swayed unsteadily on skeletal legs, crazed gaze boring into me.

"They're so hungry, the sweetlings," she said, her words deteriorating as they left her twitching lips. "Always hungry."

She crumbled to the ground in a pile of bone and shawls. Her head, free of its body, rolled sideways and came to lie, still and silent, against the foot of her table.

My screams tore through the barren grounds, and only grew louder when, as one, the dolls bore broken, jagged teeth at me in matching smiles.

About the Authors

Lindsay King-Miller is the author of *Ask a Queer Chick: A Guide to Sex, Love, and Life for Girls who Dig Girls* (Plume, 2016). Her fiction has appeared in *The Fiends in the Furrows* (Nosetouch, 2018), *Tiny Nightmares* (Catapult, 2020), *Planet Scumm, Grimdark Magazine,* and numerous other publications. She lives in Denver, CO.

Jen Mierisch's dream job is to write Twilight Zone episodes, but until then, she's a website administrator by day and a writer of odd stories by night. Jen's work can be found in Sanitarium, Dark Moments, Horla, and numerous anthologies. Jen can be found haunting her local library near Chicago, USA. Read more at www.jenmierisch.com.

Miriam H. Harrison writes among the boreal forests and abandoned mines of Northern Ontario, Canada. Her poetry and fiction vary between the eerie, the dreary, and the cheery. She is a member of both the Horror Writers Association and the Science Fiction and Fantasy Poetry Association, and updates about her work can be found on her website: miriamhharrison.

Kasimma is from Igboland. She is an alumna of Chimamanda Adichie's Creative Writing Workshop, Chigozie Obioma's Masterclass, IWP workshop, and SSDA Flow workshop. She's been a writer-in-residence in artists' residencies across Africa, Asia, and Europe. Her works have appeared or are forthcoming on The Puritan, Kikwetu Journal, The Book Smuggler's Den, Jellyfish Review, Afreecan Read, Orbis Journal, cacti fur, Sledgehammer, Trampset.

Find out more about her on her website: www.kasimma.com. Say hello to her on twitter: @kasimmam.

A resident of Toronto, Canada, author **Mary Rajotte** has a penchant for penning nightmarish tales of folk horror and paranormal suspense, exploring mythology and superstition. Her work has been published in Shroud Magazine, and in anthologies from the Library of Horror Press, the Great Lakes Horror Company, Fabled Collective and Burial Day Books.
Website: maryrajotte.com
Twitter: twitter.com/MaryRajotte
Patreon: patreon.com/maryrajotte

From deep within the Welsh countryside, **Catherine McCarthy** spins dark yarns that deliver a sting in the tail. She is the author of the collections Door and other twisted tales, Mists and Megaliths, and also the novella, Immortelle (published by Off Limits Press July 2021). Her work has been published in various places online and in anthologies, including The British Fantasy Society Horizons, Flame Tree Press, Kandisha Press and Curiosities. When she is not writing she may be found hiking the Welsh coast path or huddled among ancient gravestones reading Machen or Poe.
Links: https://www.catherine-mccarthy-author.com/
Twitter: https://twitter.com/serialsemantic

Patricia Miller is a US Navy veteran born and raised in Cincinnati, Ohio, USA, a mostly retired IT Type with a BS from Miami University, Oxford, Ohio and an MS in Library and Information Science from the University of Tennessee. She started reading at 3 1/2 after becoming obsessed with Batman. She is hooked on QI, British murder villages and professional cycling.

Jessica Lévai has loved stories and storytellers her whole life. After a double major in history and mathematics, a PhD in Egyptology, and eight years of the adjunct shuffle, she devoted herself to writing full-time. You can find her work on Strange Horizons, Cossmass Infinities, and Tor.com. Her first novella, *The Night Library of Sternendach*, is a vampire romance in Pushkin sonnets. She dreams of one day collaborating on a graphic novel, and meeting Stephen Colbert. Check out her website, JessicaLevai.com, for links and more.

Emily J. Cohen lives in Rhode Island with her husband and tiny dog. She received an M.F.A. in Creative Writing from Lesley University and her work has appeared in Jitterpress Magazine and Outlooks Springs.

Kathleen Palm began writing seventeen years ago, making her way from fantasy to horror while her husband and two kids watched in terror. She lurks within her old, sadly-not-haunted farm house surrounded by her fuzzy minions and stacks of books. She can be found reading a creepy tale, watching scary movies in the dark, dancing with the faeries, chatting with friends on Twitter @KathleenPalm, and spreading light through her love of the dark. Her work can be found in the anthologies Gothic Blue Book VI: A Krampus Carol and Blackberry Blood.

Evelyn Maguire (she/her) is an MFA candidate at the University of Massachusetts Amherst. She loves horror movies and anything with olives.

Cindy O'Quinn is an Appalachian writer who grew up in the mountains of West Virginia. In 2016, Cindy and her family moved to the northern woods of Maine, where she continues to write horror

stories and speculative poetry. Her work has been published or is forthcoming in Shotgun Honey Presents Vol 4: RECOIL, The Shirley Jackson Award Winning Anthology: The Twisted Book of Shadows, Shelved: Appalachian Resilience During Covid 19 Anthology, Attack From The '80S Anthology, The Bad Book Anthology, Chiral Mad 5, HWA Poetry Showcase Vol V, Space & Time Magazine, Weirdbook Magazine, Nothing's Sacred Vol 4 & 5, Sanitarium Magazine, & others. Cindy is a two-time Bram Stoker Award Final Nominee. Her poetry has been nominated for both the Rhysling & Dwarf Star Awards. Member of HWA, NESW, NEHW, SFPA, Horror Writers of Maine, and Weird Poets Society. You can follow Cindy for updates on:
Facebook @CindyOQuinnWriter, Instagram cindy.oquinn, and Twitter @COQuinnWrites.

April Yates is a writer of dark and queer fiction, living in Derbyshire England with her wife and two fluffy demons masquerading as dogs. She should be writing, but is easily distracted by the squirrels in her garden. Her debut novella, ASHTHORNE, a queer, historical horror-romance will be published by Ghost Orchid Press in 2022. Her short stories appear or are forthcoming in anthologies by Ghost Orchid Press, Black Hare Press, and Black Ink Fiction. She also suffers from a micro-fiction addiction, leaving them scattered across the web and in various anthologies. Find her on Twitter @April_Yates_ or aprilyates.com

Erica Ruppert, HWA. lives in northern New Jersey with her husband and too many cats. She writes weird horror and dark fantasy, and her work has appeared in magazines including *Unnerving*, *Lamplight*, and *Nightmare*, on podcasts including *PodCastle*, and in multiple anthologies. When she is not writing, she runs, bakes, and gardens with more enthusiasm than skill. Her novella, *Sisters in Arms* was released by Trepidatio Publishing in July 2021.

Alexis DuBon is a work of fiction. Any resemblance to actual persons, living or dead, is purely coincidental. You can find her in the Hundred Word Horror anthology series by Ghost Orchid Press, Field Notes From a Nightmare by Dread Stone Press, A Woman Built By Man by Cemetery Gates Media, on the Horror Oasis YouTube channel, The Wicked Library podcast, and on twitter at @shakedubonbon.

Mo Moshaty is a genre screenwriter and journalist with Nyx Horror Collective and co-producer of the 13 Minutes of Horror Film Festival featured on The Shudder Channel. With a concentration on psychological and possession horror in her writing, her background as a Trauma Specialist provides a sturdy foundation. Mo is the creator of the course, "Writing Trauma Respectfully for Screen" and was a Guest Lecturer for Prairie View A&M University's Film and TV Program. As a core member of Nyx, she has recently partnered with Stowe Story Labs to provide a fellowship for women writers over 40 working in genre.

Helen Glynn Jones is a prize-winning author of six novels. Born in the UK, Helen has also lived in both Australia and Canada. A few years ago, she returned to her native England where, when she's not writing stories, she likes to hunt for vintage treasures, explore stone circles and watch the sky change color. She now lives in Hertfordshire with her husband, daughter, and wonderfully chaotic cockapoo.

Anna Fitzgerald Healy works in fine art. Her writing has been featured in the Hoxie Gorge Review, the Santa Monica Review, and the Centifictionist. She has a BA from Emerson College. Anna lives in a decrepit castle in the Hollywood Hills, where she is working on her first novel. For cliché beach-picnic content, follow her on Instagram: @annaluvstheinternet.

Victoria Nations writes horror and gothic stories about creatures with emotional baggage. Her work appears in IN SOMNIO: A Collection of Modern Gothic Horror, Gothic Blue Book, Volume 6, A Krampus Carol, and Burial Day Books' short fiction. She lives in Florida, USA with her wife and son, who indulge her love of monsters. Visit her online at www.LeavesandCobwebs.com and on Twitter and IG at @Leaves_Cobwebs.

Deana Lisenby lives in Texas with her husband, children, and two dogs who think they're humans. When she isn't writing, she enjoys learning new things such as baking from scratch or crocheting blankets. Most recently, she has signed up for a web development course, and she is telling you about it now as a twisted form of accountability, or perhaps, motivation. Deana loves black coffee, red wine, and dark chocolate.

Jolie Toomajan is a PhD candidate, writer, editor, and all-around creep. Her dissertation in progress is focused on the women who wrote for *Weird Tales* and her work has appeared in *Grim, LampLight*, *Upon a Thrice Time*, and *Black Static*. Despite all of this, her plan for the zombie apocalypse is to pour a bottle of hot sauce over her head.

Briana Una McGuckin lives in a charmingly strange old house in Connecticut. Her debut novel, On Good Authority (Gothic Romance/Romantic Suspense), is forthcoming in Fall 2022. Her short fiction appears in the Bram Stoker-nominated horror anthology Not All Monsters, modern Gothic horror anthology In Somnio, and elsewhere. Briana has spastic diplegic cerebral palsy, an M.F.A. in Creative Writing from Western Connecticut State University, and an M.L.S. from Long Island University. She also has a perhaps concerningly large collection of perfume oils, and a fascination with all things Victorian. For more information visit www.brianaunamcguckin.com.

S.H. Cooper is a Florida based, multi-genre author with a focus on horror and fantasy. Her titles include Inheriting Her Ghosts, The Festering Ones, and The Knight's Daughter, in addition to short story collections and the horror comedy podcast, Calling Darkness. You can find out more about her
through her website, www. authorshcooper.com, and follow
her on Twitter at @mspippinacious.

About the Illustrator

Elizabeth Leggett is a Hugo award-winning illustrator whose work focuses on soulful, human moments-in-time that combine ambiguous interpretation and curiosity with realism.

Much to her mother's dismay, she viewed her mother's white washed walls as perfectly good canvasses so she believes it is safe to say that she has been an artist her whole life! Her first published work was in the Halifax County Arts Council poetry and illustration collection. If she remembers correctly, she was not yet in double digits yet, but she might be wrong about that. Her first paying gig was painting other students' tennis shoes in high school.

In 2012, she ended a long fallow period by creating a full seventy-eight card tarot in a single year. From there, she transitioned into freelance illustration. Her clients represent a broad range of outlets, from multiple Hugo award winning Lightspeed Magazine to multiple Lambda Literary winner, Lethe Press. She was honored to be chosen to art direct both Women Destroy Fantasy and Queers Destroy Science Fiction, both under the Lightspeed banner.

Elizabeth, her husband, and their typically atypical cats, live in New Mexico. She suggests if you ever visit the state, look up. The skies are absolutely spectacular!

About the Editor

Alex Woodroe is a Romanian writer and editor of dark speculative fiction. She's a member of the SFWA and HWA, and a staff writer for the videogame Decarnation. Her Weird SF "Midnight Sun" will be featured in Dark Matter Magazine, and her Folk Horror 'Abandon' in Horror Library Volume 7. She's passionate about infusing her country and culture into her work, and loves talking shop at @AlexWoodroe.

Content Warnings

What the Dead Whisper to the Living by Mary Rajotte: suicide.

The Lake in Winter by Emily J. Cohen: attempted suicide.

Henry by Mo Moshaty: child murder (off page).

A Scent of Cloves by Helen Glynn Jones: attempted suicide.

Scabrous by Victoria Nations: child death, ritualistic cutting.

We hope you enjoyed this anthology. Please visit our website, brigidsgatepress.com, for news and future releases!

Made in the USA
Coppell, TX
15 December 2022